"Show me the body and then we'll go for help. Where is it?" Truth to tell, I didn't believe there was a body.

She looked around wildly. The fog had not lightened.

"Follow your footprints," I suggested.

"Okay, but don't leave me. I was lost in the fog, all alone up there. I heard a crow cawing. It flapped in my face. Then I...I stepped on her hand."

"Her?"

"It's a woman."

I was cold in my sweat-soaked running suit and almost as freaked out, by then, as Bonnie. The fog was demoralizing. The setting came straight out of Poe.

We climbed a fat, grass-choked dune, stumbled down the other side, and rounded a single coast pine. A woman lay sprawled in a small hollow beyond the tree. Someone had bashed in the left side of her head.

---- ★ ----

"Sharp characterization—particularly of the marvelously wry Lark..."

—*Publishers Weekly*

SHEILA SIMONSON

MUDLARK

WORLDWIDE.

TORONTO • NEW YORK • LONDON
AMSTERDAM • PARIS • SYDNEY • HAMBURG
STOCKHOLM • ATHENS • TOKYO • MILAN
MADRID • WARSAW • BUDAPEST • AUCKLAND

This novel is for my parents,
Charles and Norma Haggerty, with all my love.

MUDLARK

A Worldwide Mystery/June 1995

First published by St. Martin's Press, Incorporated.

ISBN 0-373-26170-5

A Note on Geography

The Shoalwater Peninsula is my gift to the state of Washington. In *Larkspur,* I inserted a fictional county on the northern California border. Nobody objected, so I have felt free, in this book, to edit Washington, too.

Residents of the Long Beach Peninsula will recognize some features of their own corner of the state. However, I made the long needle of land stubbier, with a little hook of expensive real estate at the northern end, where the peninsula terminates in the Leadbetter Point wildlife sanctuary. I subtracted all six towns and replaced them with two purely imaginary ones—Kayport and Shoalwater. The demography of my fictional peninsula, including ethnic composition, is deliberately different from that of the Long Beach area. The Nekana are an imaginary tribe. Shoalwater Bay is the old name of Willapa Bay.

None of the people or communities in this book is real, though the issues facing the Shoalwater towns bear a resemblance to problems common to all beach communities from the Canadian border to Brookings, Oregon, on the California border.

ONE

IT WAS STILL EARLY when I came back from my run on Shoalwater Beach. The sun had not yet burned off the mist. Jay had already left for work and Freddy wasn't up. I showered, dressed in jeans and a long-sleeved T-shirt, and dawdled around the kitchen. I was wondering whether I ought to start in on the living-room wallpaper and reward myself with breakfast afterward, or fortify myself with breakfast first, when the doorbell jangled.

I kept my eyes averted from the U-Haul cartons still stacked in the dining room and opened the front door. "Hello."

A woman I had never seen before stood on the porch. She was short, with blond-streaked hair and wide gray eyes behind businesslike black-rimmed glasses. I thought she was about my age—thirtysomething. She didn't smile at me.

She waved a vague arm seaward. "I live over there."

"In the summer cottage? Come on in. I'm Lark Dodge." I stood aside to let her enter. She had moved in the previous week. I had meant to call on her.

She hesitated, mouth trembling. Then she lifted the bag she was holding in her left hand. "Do you know anything about this?"

I stared at the squidgy thing. It was made of heavy brown plush with a dim pattern and smeared with what looked like grease. "What is it?"

"A carpetbag. It's full of dead seagulls."

"Ugh." I recoiled. I had noticed a faint fishy odor, but faint fishy odors are common around beaches. So are dead seagulls.

"You don't know about it." She expelled a sigh that fluffed her bangs. "I apologize for being so abrupt but I'm scared."

"Scared?"

There was a note with it. It was rather..." She cleared her throat. "I thought it was pretty hostile. I'm alone over there, and I don't know anybody except the real estate agent."

"Jim Knight?"

"Yes. Nice man."

Knight had sold us our house, too, and taken us home to dinner to meet his wife, who turned out to be a high school biology teacher. I liked the Knights. They were coming over for a Labor Day barbecue the following week.

I shoved the door wider. "Leave the bag on the porch and come in. I can give you coffee."

"Please." Tears filled her eyes. "I'm sorry. I'm not usually so gauche."

I ushered her past the shambles of the living room into my state-of-the-art kitchen.

"May I wash my hands? That bag was filthy."

I showed her the soap dispenser at the sink and she scrubbed away while I poured two mugs of coffee.

"Cream and sugar?"

"I take it black." She dried her hands on my dish towel.

We sat in the breakfast nook with its view of the pines behind the house and its sunny southern exposure. I had done the room in pale yellow with off-white tiles and soft yellow curtains—appropriate for rainy weather but very bright in the unaccustomed sunlight. Everything except my faithful Boston fern looked a bit too new.

The woman glanced around. "This is nice. A fixer-upper?"

"The house? Yes. We came up from California in June and it was cheaper to buy than to rent."

"California? Oh!" She began to cry.

I stared, then went into the kitchen for Kleenex. When she had stopped sobbing and was mopping her face and glasses, I said carefully, "California?"

"I...it...the note said 'California Carpetbagger Go Home.'"

I sat down again. "Not nice."

"No." She sniffed and replaced her glasses. "I'm from the L.A. area—Santa Monica. I'm used to living alone but not way out in the country like this. I keep hearing noises in the night...."

"And imagining rapists and ax murderers—I know the feeling." I've never met a woman who doesn't know the feeling.

She took a gulp of coffee. "So I was edgy anyway and then this morning, when I let the cat out, I found the damned bag on my porch."

"Nasty. Did you buy the cottage or just rent it?"

"Bought it. I paid cash—$35,000. Can you believe it?"

I nodded. Having lived through the California real estate boom, I understood her astonishment at Washington prices. We had purchased the bungalow—four bedrooms up, one down, two bathrooms, kitchen, dining room, a huge living room, and an ocean view, for $85,000. I said. "You got a bargain—it's a nice little place."

"A steal. Thirty-five thousand dollars wouldn't buy a doghouse in L.A." She was staring out the window at a crow cawing in the pines. "I'm an only child. When my folks retired to Arizona they deeded their house in Santa Monica to me. It's small—two bedrooms. I grew up there. I sold it this spring for $200,000. I bought this place after one viewing, just made out a check. Maybe I should've shopped around, but it seemed ideal. Naturally, I handed over extortionate taxes on the rest before I came north."

"Naturally."

"Right. But I have almost half of the $200,000 left. I can live on that until I finish The Novel." She said the words with capitals.

"You're a writer?"

She gave a smile that was half grimace and wrinkled her nose. "Trying to be. I was an English major but I've been working as a secretary for ten years. I was in a rut at the office, a relationship didn't pan out, and I've always wanted to write, so when these newlyweds made me an offer for the house I grabbed the money and ran."

"I don't blame you, but why here?"

"A friend spent a month up here a couple of years ago. He said it was quiet and unspoiled—and he couldn't believe the real estate prices." She swallowed coffee. "I was so happy, so excited. And now this."

"It's probably just some teenager acting up. We haven't had any trouble with our neighbors. Everybody we've met has been pleasant." I pointed in the direction of the mobile home south of our house. "The Cramers live there. He's a retired civil servant—something to do with the Washington State Fisheries Department. His wife's in a wheelchair. Lottie had a stroke last year and Matt takes care of her. She's shy—the stroke affected her speech—but she appreciates visitors. She likes to sit there and look out at the ocean."

"Poor thing."

"Yes. Matt's a talker, though, so watch out. A big developer has bought the land beyond your house. Matt's afraid the resort they're going to build will block his wife's view. He was circulating a petition when we first moved in, trying to get the county to stop construction." I paused. "Do you know, you haven't told me your name."

"Bonnie." She blushed. "Bonnie Bell—sounds like a romance writer."

"Is that what you write?"

"No. Gosh, I'd die of embarrassment. I *was* an English major." She grinned. "Though I have been known to read a romance now and then."

"I like science fiction," I volunteered. "And fantasy, but not horror. I used to run a bookstore." I missed Larkspur Books. I had sold the store in May.

"Wow! That's wonderful." Bonnie was warming up. "I love book people. You can tell me all the facts of life on the business side. I'm probably hopelessly uncommercial."

"What are you writing?"

"Just your basic mother/daughter conflict." The gray eyes gleamed. "Plus your basic growing-up-in-California saga."

"Serious or comic?"

She pondered. "Seriously comic, I guess. Confessions of a Mall Rat. That sort of thing. I'm having fun with the writing."

"If you enjoy it, your readers are more likely to."

"You are so kind."

We exchanged grins.

A thumping on the stairs suggested either an ax murderer or Freddy was descending. "My brother-in-law," I murmured as he entered the kitchen. "Good morning, Freddy. We have company." I performed introductions, adding "Bonnie just moved into that house across the street."

He blinked. He was wearing rumpled sweats and his red hair stood on end. "Coffee?"

"It's made."

"Nnng. Thanks." He poured a cup and wandered off vaguely. I smiled at Bonnie. "Freddy's not a self-starter."

"He looks about thirteen."

"He's twenty-one." I hesitated. "Twenty years younger than my husband."

"No lie. Half brother?"

"Yes. Freddy just flunked himself out of Stanford. That's a sore point."

She considered. "Flunked himself?"

I sighed. "He's very bright so he had to work at it. Don't feel too sorry for him. His father died a year and a half ago and left Freddy pretty well fixed. He won't have to pump gas. The dirty Trans Am in the drive is his. Freddy's been a computer addict since junior high with all the social disabilities that implies, and he fell in love for the first time this spring. It addled his brain.

Bonnie laughed. "Poor kid."

"I make him steam wallpaper off. Takes his mind off Darla."

"Darla is the girlfriend?"

"Darla Sweet. Sweet by name and peppery by nature. Darla lives in Kayport. She thinks Freddy's just a friend. *She* graduated with honors and is going to law school next month. Maybe Freddy will follow her to Portland."

"You hope."

I cocked my head. "Shower's running. He should be human in half an hour."

Bonnie had gone back to brooding. "Who else lives around here?"

"A lot of retired people on the crest." The crest was a ridge of sandstone that ran the length of the peninsula like a spine. "The mobile homes on the flat between the crest and the dunes are a mixed bag—summer homes for families from Portland and Seattle, and some year-round residents. Fishermen and farmworkers. More retirees."

"Loggers?"

"Not here. They tend to live in Kayport." Kayport was the metropolis—about six thousand loggers, fishermen, and retired couples living on pensions. Shoalwater C.C., where Jay was working, lay outside Kayport, a drive of about fifteen miles. The town also contained the hospital, the high school, and the public library. The village of Shoalwater, at the north end of the long finger of land that formed the Shoalwater Peninsula, was really just a post office, a grade school, two taverns, and a couple of grocery-and-dry goods stores. There were ephemeral restaurants, boutiques, and souvenir shops. To the east lay Shoalwater Bay, to the west the Pacific Ocean. We lived three miles beyond the village, on the Pacific side of things.

"Who has the house north of me?" Bonnie was asking.

"I'm not sure. Jim Knight called it the old McKay place."

"As in the shipwreck?" The remains of the *Mollie McKay*, a small coastal freighter, provided the only permanent obstruction on the long featureless beach.

"There's probably a connection," I said. "A man lives there alone. We haven't met him yet, though I've seen him pottering in his garden. He keeps to himself."

"Sinister." Bonnie's face darkened. She was only half kidding.

I offered to heat up her coffee, poured a refill, and finished off the pot in my cup. "I'd better brew more. Freddy's blood flows slowly before noon."

She watched me fiddle with the big fifteen-cup coffeemaker, the kind that turns itself off if you haven't poured a cup in two hours and leaves you with quarts of cold coffee. "What does your husband do?"

The coffeepot burped. "Jay runs a training program at Monte Junior College. Did you drive up on Interstate 5? Monte's just north of Mt. Shasta."

She nodded. "Pretty country. Practically in Oregon."

"Yes. Jay's on sabbatical this year writing a book." He was writing a book on physical evidence in the era of DNA fingerprinting.

Bonnie laughed. "The place is lousy with writers."

I said, "It's a textbook. Jay's working part time at the college in Kayport, setting up a similar training program for them. That's where he is right now."

"And you're taking a vacation from the retail trade."

Actually I was spending the year trying to get pregnant, but that seemed a somewhat libidinous revelation to make to a stranger, so I just smiled and sipped my coffee.

I was a little indignant that I hadn't conceived immediately. My body was cooperative, as a rule, but I—or rather we—had been trying now for three months without result. I had even read a book on infertility.

By way of changing the subject, I asked what Bonnie had done with the note.

"Huh? Oh, the note about carpetbaggers. Dropped it on the porch, I guess. Should I go get it?"

"You probably ought to save it. Handle it by the edges and put it in an envelope." Cop's wife speaking. Preserve the evidence.

She grinned. "You've been reading Agatha Christie."

I hadn't. I rarely read mysteries, and when I do my taste runs to K.C. Constantine and Eric Wright. I let her assumption ride, though, and we discussed whether she ought to report the incident.

She decided to toss the gulls in the garbage, put the bag in her garden shed, and save the note, if it hadn't blown away, but not to bother the police. Although Shoalwater was an incorporated town, it was so small the mayor contracted with the sheriff's office for police protection. We were outside the city limits, anyway. The deputy in charge covered a lot of territory.

I invited Bonnie to dinner and she said she'd take a rain check. That provoked the usual comments about the Pacific Northwest climate, though the sun was shining bravely at that moment and the temperature was probably eighty degrees. Bonnie left and I dragged out the rented steamer.

Freddy and I spent the day removing ghastly red-flocked wallpaper, vintage 1965, from the living room. We got it all off by the time Jay came home. Early, around four-thirty, looking pleased with himself. He allowed that we'd done well by the wallpaper, which lay in nasty pink curls all over the wretched pink shag carpet.

"At least the living room no longer looks like a San Francisco bordello." I wiped my face on the sleeve of my shirt.

Freddy gathered up an armload of wallpaper. He was red from exertion and the stifling 82-degree heat. He'd been with us for two months. Long enough to acclimatize. "Lark wants to remove the rug," he said gloomily.

I laughed. "Not today, cowboy. Thanks for wielding the steamer."

Freddy beamed. "I'll take it back for you, Lark." He was rather like a plump Irish setter—he responded well to praise.

"I got it at the U-Haul place in Kayport."

"No problem. I have to shower first, though. I'm taking Darla out to dinner."

Jay took off his jacket and helped me dispose of the wallpaper while Freddy showered. As we drooped over the burning barrel I told Jay about Bonnie Bell and her beastly bag. It sounded like a Nancy Drew story.

He agreed that the trick was unpleasant but didn't seem to think it was serious enough to warrant investigation. That relieved my conscience. Jay sounded preoccupied, so I asked him how the day had gone. He had got his way with the college administration and was going to set up two tracks of courses—a certificate for people just starting out in police work and an associate's degree for professionals who were serious about careers in law enforcement.

Like most state governments, Washington's was strapped for funds, though, thanks to Boeing and common sense, it was not as near bankruptcy as California. Jay had persuaded the college authorities that many of the courses the degree students would need were already in the curriculum—sociology and history and report writing, that sort of thing. The dean of instruction wouldn't have to hire new professors.

"I told the dean I'd teach the civil rights course myself," he admitted.

"Hot dog."

He grinned. "I'll have your mother give a guest lecture."

My mother is a poet of note and a civil rights activist. I thought she could probably handle a classful of cops.

We spent the evening in amiable anticipation of another attempt at parenthood. Freddy returned around two a.m., squirreling gravel in the drive.

Jay roused briefly. "Lark?"

"Mnnn?"

"Are you sure you want a kid?"

The front door slammed and we lapsed into unconsciousness.

Jay was already gone when I staggered downstairs at seven-thirty. A pot of fresh coffee awaited along with a big pink rose he had clearly swiped from Matt Cramer's yard. The rose reposed in a juice glass. I drank coffee and looked at the late-blooming flower. Outside the air was gray with mist.

I was dressing to go out for a run on the beach when the doorbell rang. I stumbled back downstairs with my shoelaces dragging. It was Bonnie and she looked guilty.

"I saw a light."

"I'm up," I said. "Come in." I hoped she wasn't going to want to talk a lot at that hour.

"It's a bit foggy but I wondered if you like to walk on the beach."

I explained that I ran. She shuddered. I offered a cup of coffee and we agreed to go down to the beach together. I would run and she could walk around looking for sand dollars and interesting driftwood. I suppose she didn't want to go out alone in the mist. I didn't blame her but I still felt cross as we made our way through the dunes in front of her cottage to the beach.

I ran north past the wreck of the *Molly McKay*. At that point I turned my ankle on a bit of driftwood. The damage wasn't serious, but the fog was thickening, so I turned and trotted back. I had meant to run a good five miles.

In the dim light the ribs of the vessel—it had sunk in 1901—looked like ghostly fingers grasping at something just beyond reach. The fog was heavier, almost spooky. I wondered if Bonnie had gone in. The beach itself lacks benchmarks, no rock outcroppings or streams or cliff faces, just bare sand, and I was beginning to feel disoriented. If I missed the access road I could wind up miles to the south without knowing it. I veered left onto softer ground and stopped running.

I crossed the ruts of the access road and noted a light in the old McKay place. No sign of Bonnie on the beach—no sign of anyone. It was suddenly very cold and the fog beaded on my eyelashes. I climbed to the edge of the dunes, plodding now in the soft sand. My ankle hurt a little. I concentrated on the surface under my feet. Dune grass grew in tough, ankle-twisting clumps and pieces of driftwood tossed high by winter storms made the going awkward. I didn't want to miss our path so I kept my eyes on the ground. I had gone perhaps fifty yards when a scream tore the air. Wings flapped by me—a crow.

I whirled, peering, but saw nothing. Sound does odd things in a fog. The scream had seemed to come from all directions at once. My pulse thrummed in my ears as I tried to listen.

"Help!" This time the voice came ahead of me and slightly above me. "Oh, please, somebody, help!"

I started into a stumbling trot. "Where are you?"

"Lark?" It was Bonnie and she sounded closer.

"I'm coming." I skirted a small clump of pines. "I don't see you."

"Over here." I could hear her weeping, hiccupping.

"Where?" I stopped again and stared around me. The fog was so thick I could barely see beyond my groping hands.

I had taken a tentative step forward when she loomed suddenly from behind another clump of shrouded beach pine. She careened into me and I steadied her. "For God sake, what's the matter?"

"A body." She panted. "There's a body over there. In the dunes. Oh, God, I'm going to be sick."

I turned her away from me in the nick of time and she threw up the coffee I'd served her half an hour before. When she stopped retching I gave her a little shake. "Show me."

"I . . . no, I won't go back."

"Cut it out, Bonnie. If it's dead it won't hurt you."

She blinked at me and gave a shudder I felt the length of my arm. "I'm being stupid, aren't I?"

I ignored that. "Show me the body and then we'll go for help. Where is it?" Truth to tell, I didn't believe there was a body.

She looked wildly around. The fog had not lightened.

"Follow your footprints," I suggested.

She heaved another shuddering breath. "Okay, but don't leave me. I was lost in the fog, all alone up there. I heard a crow cawing. It flapped in my face. Then I . . . I stepped on her hand. Jesus." She was tugging me along, bent over her own trail as if she were in pain.

"Her?"

"It's a woman."

I was cold in my sweat-soaked running suit and almost as freaked out, by then, as Bonnie. The fog was demoralizing. The setting came straight out of Poe.

We climbed a fat, grass-choked dune, stumbled down the other side, and rounded a single coast pine. Bonnie was right. A woman lay sprawled in a small hollow beyond the tree. Someone had bashed in the left side of her head.

TWO

THE BLOW OR BLOWS to the woman's head had done evil things to her left eye. The right stared upward. Dried blood crusted the wound and some had splattered on what looked like a silk patchwork jacket, but there was none I could see on the ground around her. She had fallen almost gracefully. I had a weird impression of elegance—matching silk trousers and beige leather sneakers, slim gold watch, rings, designer scarf. I didn't see a handbag but the woman had obviously not been raped or robbed, just killed.

Though I was almost sure she was dead, I forced myself to kneel by her and hunt for a pulse. I didn't look at her face very closely. Her skin was cold and yielded to my touch. I detected no sign of a heartbeat. The thought of attempting CPR was nauseating, and I also began to worry about disturbing the scene of the crime. There obviously had been a crime and the crime looked like murder. All the same I had to check for signs of life. There were none I could detect.

I looked up at Bonnie. She stood by the pine and she was staring off into the fog, anywhere but at the corpse. She was rubbing her arms in her bright, red sweatshirt.

I levered myself up. "We'd better find a phone."

"She's dead?" Bonnie had also had doubts.

I swallowed. If I tried CPR . . . "I think so," I muttered. "Head injuries can be deceptive. Can you tell where we are?"

"We must be near that McKay place." She waved her hand landward. "What if the killer is still somewhere around?"

I was pretty sure the woman had been lying there for a while. Hours perhaps. The silk fabric was soaked and so was the smooth blond hair, but I was no expert on the condition of corpses—nor was I without imagination. We needed a phone.

"Let's go." I still couldn't see much, but I thought the McKay place lay back toward the access road and farther inland, over the crest of the dunes, so I took a couple of steps in that direction. Then I stopped. We needed a marker of some kind. "Give me your scarf."

Bonnie was wearing a pretty red-flowered scarf around her neck. She yanked it off and handed it over without question. The same thought had probably occurred to her.

I am six feet tall. I tied the scarf to the tip of the squat pine tree. "Let's go."

We trudged more or less northeast. A breeze had begun to swirl the mist and I thought the fog was easing, but I could see no more than four or five yards in any direction. The dunes were without distinguishing feature, bland humps of dun-colored sand and gray green grass. The walking was strenuous. I could hear Bonnie's labored breathing. She didn't say anything. Neither did I.

After what seemed like half an hour but was probably much less, I saw the wooden fence that rimmed the McKay property and I picked up my pace. I was not running exactly, the ground was too treacherous, but I pulled away from Bonnie.

A gate in the façade of pale, unpainted boards led to the dunes but I couldn't unlatch it. By that time both of us were yelling for help. When no one responded, I led the way around to the north side of the enclosed yard. I knew it opened on a short graveled drive with a big garden on the left and the house on the right. I ran up the drive with Bonnie at my heels and began to pound on the weathered front door.

At first I thought the house was empty, though the blue Toyota pickup with its metal camper sat in the drive. I was beginning to wonder if we'd have to break in when the door yanked open. A dark-haired man in jeans, an old gray sweatshirt, and bare feet scowled at us.

"What the hell?" The expression on my face must have registered. The frown eased and he said, less belligerently, "What's the matter?"

I gulped for air. "There's a dead woman over there in the dunes. I think she was murdered. Will you call 911?"

He stared, frowning, then opened the door wide. "Come in." He was already poking out the numbers on a gray desk phone when Bonnie and I entered the house. The phone lay on an end table beside a tired-looking Morris chair. The table held a lamp and a stack of paperbacks. An oval rug lay on the linoleum floor and a couch, circa 1950, sagged against one wall. There were a couple of floor lamps. Books, mostly library books with slips of paper sticking out of them, littered a dark sideboard of the sort that usually stores linen and silverware. The sideboard needed to be refinished. Above it hung a beautifully framed two-color print of Killerwhale. I thought it might be Kwakuitl work.

The man glanced at us as we came in but the dispatcher must have answered, for he said, "This is Tom Lindquist at the old McKay place. Two women are here saying there's a body in the dunes." He looked at me. "How far?"

"About two hundred yards, uh, southwest. More south than west."

He spoke into the receiver. "Couple of hundred yards south of the approach. He'd better come on the beach. It's foggy up here. Okay. Thanks, Betty." Nothing like a small town. He listened. "Sure. Right away." He hung up and turned to us.

"I'll get some shoes on. Then I want you to show me the body. We're supposed to wait with it until the sheriff's car comes. Are you okay?"

Bonnie said, "I need a bathroom."

He gestured through an archway. "It's in there, off the kitchen. Have some coffee." Then he jogged to a stairway that led up from the small, cramped living room.

Bonnie and I looked at each other. "My need is greater," she said with dignity, and bolted through the archway into what turned out to be a large country kitchen. It was the real thing, not some tarted-up *House Beautiful* fake, and much more cheerful than the dreary living room. It was cluttered but not disgusting. The bathroom door—it was indeed off the kitchen, right next to the refrigerator—slammed. I went to the aging electric range and found the coffeepot. My teeth were chattering.

The old McKay place was a fixer-upper that had not been fixed up. I rummaged in a cupboard with apple green doors. They had little square panes like an ad from a 1920s *National Geographic*. I found a mug and poured a cup as Bonnie emerged. The toilet was still flushing. I left my cup on the counter and used the facilities. Oddly enough, the bathroom was very clean. The fixtures, including a claw-footed tub, were of the same era as the kitchen cupboards.

Bonnie was drinking my coffee when I emerged. I was about to protest but at that moment our host came through the arch. He was shod in sneakers and had one arm in a windbreaker.

"Come on." He struggled into the jacket, pulled the kitchen door open, and stepped out onto a side porch. "I was upstairs working when you knocked." He led us around the back of the house and across a small, neat yard to the back gate. "I assumed a bunch of kids were playing games. Sometimes they think the place is deserted."

"Must be a nuisance."

"Only for a few weeks in the summer." He stood aside to let us pass. "Lead the way."

The fog had not eased. I floundered in what I hoped was the right direction. None of us spoke. Bonnie spotted her scarf before I did and we began to jog. It had occurred to me that the children from those mobile homes on the flat should not be allowed to stumble on the corpse. What was shocking and frightening to an adult would be downright traumatic for a little kid. I halted about five feet from the body and turned to the others. "There it is."

Lindquist was staring. He was a dark man—dark-haired and dark-eyed with a tan complexion. His face turned gray. "My God, it's my wife."

I gabbled some kind of shocked apology and Bonnie was also making horrified noises.

Lindquist shut his eyes briefly. When he opened them he said in calmer tones, "My ex-wife. Sorry for the melodrama. I was...surprised." He drew a ragged breath. "I think I'm going to cover her face."

I opened my mouth to warn him that he shouldn't disturb the body but he just took off his jacket, knelt by the woman, and covered the head with its staring eye. He touched the right hand gently, then stood up again.

"I'm sorry," I said.

He shook his head. "It's okay. I wonder what the hell Cleo was doing up here."

The police were going to wonder exactly the same thing. I cleared my throat. "It's hard to tell but I think she's been dead for a while."

"Yeah," he said absently. "The birds have been at her."

I gulped. Perhaps the damage to the left eye had not been caused by the death blows. I was fiercely glad I had not attempted CPR. I am not necrophilic.

"I scared a crow off when I...found her." Bonnie's voice broke.

His eyes narrowed. "Are you all right? You've had a shock, too. I'm sorry. I don't know your name."

"Bonnie Bell." She pointed due south. "I live in that summer cottage."

"The Williams place? I heard they were selling it." He turned to me. "I think you're probably Mrs. Dodge."

"Lark," I said. "You must've lived here awhile."

"I grew up here," he said flatly. He looked around. "I suppose one of us ought to walk down toward the ocean. The dispatcher said the car was just south of Shoalwater. He'll drive up the beach—it's faster."

"At twenty-five miles an hour?" That was the speed limit on the beach.

He didn't smile. "I think he'll move it a little."

I sighed. "I'll go. What do I do, wave my arms?"

"Whatever." He met my eyes. "If you're afraid, I'll go, but someone has to stay with the...with Cleo."

"I don't mind." I did rather, but I was sure Bonnie would *not* want to walk alone across the featureless dunes to the beach.

Lindquist pointed me in the right direction and I went fast. I perched on a driftwood log a few feet back from the packed sand that was safe to drive on. The fog was patchy by then with odd swirling patterns that magnified and distorted the gulls probing the waterline. I watched a skitter of sanderlings, tiny sandpipers, hopping one-footed at the edge of the surf. Each of them was mirrored on the wet surface. Far off, I thought I saw a man walking a dog, but I was not at all sure.

At last the sheriff's car, with its lights whirling, raced up from the south. I jumped up and waved wildly. The driver skewed the car round when he saw me and got out. He was wearing the brown county uniform. He was fair and his face was as open and ingenuous as a ten-year-old's. He had round pink cheeks.

He introduced himself—Dale Nelson—and I told him I could lead him to the body.

"Up by the old McKay place, Betty said."

"That's right."

"Hop in, then, I don't want to leave the car here. Tide's coming in. Besides, there's a lot of kids around here."

"Where's your partner?"

"What partner?" he said wryly. "We're shorthanded." His voice sounded less innocent than his face.

I got in and we jounced over to the access road and up to Lindquist's graveled drive. Nelson parked behind the pickup, I got out, and he locked the car.

"You find the body?"

"My neighbor, Bonnie Bell, found it and, er, got my attention. I did check to make sure she . . . the woman was dead. We asked Mr. Lindquist to call in. All three of us went back to the body."

"Know who it is?"

I hesitated, then said neutrally, "I'd never seen the woman before but Mr. Lindquist said she was his former wife."

Nelson stopped dead. "You don't say? Cleo Hagen?" He whistled through his teeth. "I'll be damned. Cleo Cabot Hagen. I think I'd better call in, Ms. . . ."

"Mrs. Lark Dodge. I live down the road."

"Okay, back in a minute." He returned to the cop car and I could hear the radio crackle. I waited. He must have had himself put through to the head of the CID, at least, maybe even the sheriff.

I was thinking about the dead woman's name, trying to remember where I'd heard it. One difficulty of moving to a new community is that you have to deal with a lot of unfamiliar names in a hurry. I sorted through the names of people I knew until I thought of Annie McKay, the editor of the Kayport *Gazette*. A small light flashed. Cleo Cabot Hagen had been the target of one of McKay's many editorials on the deterioration of the local ecosystem.

The dead woman was associated with the group building the resort complex half a mile south of Bonnie's cottage. The resort would include a lodge with spa, shops, restaurants, and the usual condominiums. There was a golf course in the works and, surrounding it, a number of single cottages. Although no buildings had yet been erected, bulldozers had kept busy all summer rearranging the sandy soil, and helicopters had flown in and out bearing engineers, architects, and company executives.

The dead woman's name recurred in news releases about the resort. I had gathered that Cleo Hagen was the local liaison and probably fairly important in the organization. Annie McKay had printed news stories about the elaborate project. The editorial in which she attacked Cleo Hagen had also bitterly condemned the county commissioners for permitting a development of that size in an ecologically sensitive area. The planned population density, McKay claimed, would disrupt wildlife habitats and threaten both the razor clam and Dungeness crab harvest along our stretch of beach.

I thought Annie McKay's editorial was strong and well reasoned. My neighbor, Matt Cramer, cut it out and gave me a photocopy, though we had subscribed to the *Gazette* as soon as we moved to Shoalwater. I think Matt blanketed the area with copies. In the editorial, Cleo Hagen was characterized as the representative of rapacious California real estate interests. Apparently she had been associated with other large resorts.

California. That word again. I remembered Bonnie's bag of seagulls and the words of the note, which Bonnie had not found: "California Carpetbagger Go Home." Bonnie was not a great threat to the ecology of the Shoalwater Peninsula. I wondered if anyone had sent Cleo Hagen a similar warning. It was a troubling thought.

By the time Deputy Nelson had finished his conversation the fog was definitely beginning to burn off. Also my running suit had dried out. I was conscious of needing a shower, and I was sweating again by the time Nelson and I reached Bonnie and Lindquist.

Nelson shook hands with the other man and I introduced Bonnie. Nelson took her name, address, and phone number, and mine as well. Then he turned to Lindquist.

"What do you know about this, Tom?"

"Not a damned thing."

"I heard you was married to her."

"We were divorced six years ago."

"And you haven't seen her since?"

Lindquist shoved a wing of blue black hair from his forehead. "I saw her off and on in San Francisco before I came north."

"Let's see, that was when, four, five years ago?"

"Five."

Nelson waited.

After a pause Lindquist said, "I saw her at the bluegrass festival in April. And once, at a distance, at the Blue Oyster." The Blue Oyster was a pricy restaurant on the Shoalwater Bay side of the peninsula. "And she called on me at the house yesterday."

Nelson whistled. "Just dropped by for old times' sake?"

For some reason the question eased Lindquist's air of tense wariness. The muscles at the hinge of his jaw relaxed. "Don't be a horse's ass, Dale. She came to proposition me."

Nelson's eyebrows rose. Like his hair, they were blond.

Lindquist said amiably, "She made me an offer for the house. I told her I'd think about it."

"That was the proposition?"

"That was it. We had a cup of coffee. I congratulated her on her marriage. She congratulated me on the book. She drove off around six-thirty, said she was going to dinner at the Blue Oyster."

Book. Bonnie's eyes had widened. I remembered the stacks of library books on the old sideboard. She was right. The place was lousy with writers. At least Tom Lindquist wasn't a poet.

Or maybe he was. Hastily I reviewed the poets I knew of who were roughly Lindquist's age—roughly my husband's age, I guessed. Lindquist was one of those men who could be anywhere from thirty to fifty-five. He was clean-shaven, had a lean, wiry build, and moved with no sign of stiffness, but something about his eyes suggested he was not thirty. I couldn't remember a poet named Lindquist.

Abruptly it came to me. *Starvation Hill.* A novel, a very good novel, in my opinion. It took the Western Book Award the year it came out, but the small, regional house that had published it in hardcover went out of business shortly after the book was released. That had been three years before. It was only just coming out in a trade paperback....

A whooping in the distance distracted my attention. I looked north. Now that the fog had burned off I could see as far as the access road. A clutch of kids in bright sweatshirts were heading for the beach. They didn't seem to notice us. Nelson had been shrewd to move the cop car to the driveway.

"Are you going to do something about Cleo's body, Dale, or are you going to stand here all morning chewing the fat?" Lindquist's tone sharpened. He had seen the kids, too.

The deputy said, "Now, Tom, you know we're short-handed. I sent for the ambulance out of Kayport and they'll be here pretty quick. Ms. Bell, if you and Mrs. Dodge want to leave, I reckon I know where to find you. I'll need to take your statements sometime today, though."

Bonnie said, "I'm not going anywhere except the grocery store."

I had to run in to Shoalwater, too. I said, "If you want to ride to town with me, Bonnie, I'll fix us lunch afterward and we can wait for Deputy Nelson at my house."

Bonnie agreed to the plan a little too fervently. I think she was afraid of being alone, and I didn't blame her. I had a strong reluctance to watch the removal of the body. It was a relief that we had permission to go, though a bit puzzling at that point in a murder investigation.

Deputy Nelson shook our hands and thanked us in a semicourtly way for being good citizens. For all he knew, we could have bashed in Cleo Hagen's head.

We walked back to the beach approach and homeward on the paved county road. An elderly woman in the yard of the mobile home across the street from the McKay place stared at us as we passed by her. I gave her a big smile.

We walked homeward on the roadway because neither Bonnie nor I wanted to tackle the stretch of dunes to the south. In any case, Nelson had intimated that he was going to have the area searched. There was no weapon at the scene and Cleo Hagen's handbag was missing. None of us thought a woman of her obvious wealth and polish would have been strolling on the dunes without some kind of purse. She would have had a car, too. There was no abandoned vehicle on either side of the road.

"Maybe the killer took her bag," Bonnie muttered as we trudged along the street, "but if he was a mugger, he would have stolen her rings. Did you see the size of that emerald?"

I had. Cleo Hagen's left hand, bearing the sandy mark of Bonnie's shoe, had displayed, undisturbed, a wide gold wedding band and a square-cut emerald in a more ornate setting. The emerald was so large I had thought it was fake—until the sun broke through. "Maybe you startled him off."

Bonnie did not like that idea. We walked on.

"Tom Lindquist," she mused. "I actually bought a house next to Thomas Lindquist. That was the funniest book I've read in the last five years."

I gaped at her. "You thought *Starvation Hill* was funny?"

She stopped in the roadway. "*Starvation Hill*—what's that? I mean the one that came out in May. *Small Victories*. It was about growing up in a northwestern town...holy cow, Kayport. It must be. I wonder why the man is still alive. Maybe somebody got confused in the fog and whacked his ex by mistake."

"What do you mean?"

"I don't imagine the book's popular around here. It's satire and wickedly funny, and the people are so real you know he had to have somebody definite in mind. Even if he didn't, everybody must be trying to guess who..."

"You have to be thinking of another writer." I explained about the Western Book Award and the publishing house that had gone out of business. "*Starvation Hill* came out three years ago. There can't have been more than five thousand copies. It was lyrical and tragic, a terrible story in some ways. About an old woman whose father traded her to a band of Indians for food when she was ten years old."

"Historical?"

"Obviously," I said crossly. We were approaching our driveway. "It's a tour de force of narration—a female-viewpoint story told to a great-grandson who doesn't understand what the woman means half the time. My mother—she's a poet—said the control of Victorian language was dazzling."

"Huh." Bonnie sounded skeptical. "Maybe he's schizophrenic—Lindquist, I mean. Not that *Small Victories* isn't dazzling, too, but it's definitely modern. Set in the sixties." She gave a chortle. "The ultimate answer to *Leave It to Beaver*."

"I think we'd better exchange books."

"Okay." She stopped by the entrance to our driveway. "I'll duck across and take a quick shower. Half an hour?"

"Sounds all right."

"What should I do with the carpetbag?"

I'd half forgotten it. "Better bring it over. Tell Nelson about it. It's a pity you lost the note."

"I'll look again." The vivacity drained out of her. "My God, what a mess. I hope he didn't do it."

"Tom Lindquist? Me, too." I didn't add that most women who were victims of murder were killed by their husbands. Or ex-husbands. I wondered how much Lindquist had made from his books, and how much Cleo Hagen had offered him for the old McKay place, and whether any of that was relevant to the murder.

THREE

THE AMBULANCE BEARING Cleo Cabot Hagen's body to the hospital in Kayport, where the autopsy was to be performed, met us going the other way as we returned from Shoalwater. The driver was taking his time.

When Bonnie and I went off to Shoalwater, Freddy was in the shower. When we returned he had already left. A note on the refrigerator informed me that he and Darla had gone to the Oregon beaches. He'd be home late. Poor Freddy. I was fairly sure Darla would, at most, permit a little hand-holding as they leapt over tide pools or scrambled up cliffs. As far as I could tell, she was not a sexual tease. She just didn't understand the depth of Freddy's attachment. I hoped she wouldn't make him too miserable.

Bonnie and I chewed over the events of the morning, along with our pastrami sandwiches. She had found *Small Victories* for me, and I could hardly wait to get to it. Unfortunately, my copy of *Starvation Hill* was stored with the rest of our books until such time as we set up decent bookshelves. The house's former owners had not been readers. I reflected that I ought to dig the book out and ask Lindquist to autograph it before he was arrested.

Dale Nelson showed up around one-thirty. I fed him a sandwich and a cup of coffee, and he took our statements with a minimum of fuss and redundancy. He had gone by three. Bonnie went home—to take a nap, she said. I curled up on a lawn chair on the balcony outside the master bedroom so I could read and still keep an eye on what was happening at the old McKay place. Not much, apparently. I could see the roof of the blue Toyota pickup if I squinted. It didn't move.

Although the fog had finally burned off, the air was cooler than the day before, even in direct sunlight. I put on a pair of sunglasses and turned to the back cover flap. The

author bio was disappointingly vague. Thomas Lindquist
was a native of the Northwest and had been educated at
UCLA. He had published a number of short stories, most
of them in literary magazines, in addition to "award-
winning" *Starvation Hill*. Apart from that I knew no more
about him after I read the blurb than before. There was no
photograph.

When Jay came home an hour later I was so deep in the
story I didn't even hear the car pull in. He stuck his head out
the French door and said, "I hear you've found another
body."

I jumped and dropped the novel. "Uh, yes. What do you
mean, another body? I don't find bodies . . ."

"They find you. Right."

I stood up and gave him a kiss. "How did you hear about
it?"

"Sheriff's office. They want me to oversee the evidence
team."

"Are you going to?"

"I don't know. It sounds routine to me. The deputy can
probably handle it."

I held out Bonnie's copy of *Small Victories*. "Remember
Starvation Hill?"

"Sure. Good book."

"The victim was Lindquist's ex-wife."

He whistled. "Maybe not so routine."

I went down with Jay and told him everything while he
unwound over a bottle of Portland Ale. I drank a beer, too.
One of the advantages of our move north was the number
of first-rate microbreweries in the area. We were sampling
our way through the local products.

I avoided summarizing the plot of Lindquist's second
novel. Jay deserved to discover the fun himself. The book
was strong, many-layered satire, and all too obviously set in
Kayport and Shoalwater. I put it aside with reluctance.

It was a luxury to have Jay to myself two dinners in a row.
I hoped Freddy and Darla would take their time. I threw
together a prawn stir-fry. Afterward, I read and Jay put in
a couple of hours on his textbook. We watched the sunset
together from our balcony and went inside to make an-

other modest attempt at generation. Eventually we drifted back out to watch the fog roll in. I had no idea what time it was. Bonnie's lights were off and the Cramers' were on. I didn't see Bonnie's little Ford Escort. She had been threatening to drive to Astoria. I did make out a light in the second-story window of the McKay place.

I stretched and yawned. "I think I'll go finish *Small Victories.*"

"Is it another historical novel?" Jay was leaning on the rail. He straightened.

"No, unless 1965 is historical."

"Feels more historical all the time."

"Well, it's not. I was eight that year. We spent the summer checking out Civil War battlefields for Dad. Tod got into some poison ivy at Antietam." Tod was my brother.

"I remember it well," Jay said absently. He was peering north.

"Tod's poison ivy? If you're not going to listen..."

He stood straight, whirled, and plunged through the door to the bedroom. "That house is on fire. Call 911."

I dashed in after him. "What house, the McKay place?"

"Yes." He was pounding down the stairs. "Hurry!"

I stopped in the hall, retraced my steps, and dialed 911 on the bedroom extension. The phone had a long cord. I was standing on the balcony squinting in the direction of Lindquist's house by the time I got through to the dispatcher. I could see flames leaping along the dark rim of the roof.

When I was sure the woman at the other end understood me I hung up, threw the phone on the bed, and ran down the stairs three at a time. The front door banged shut behind me. I gained the road and ran flat out.

I could not have been more than a minute behind Jay. When I reached the edge of the McKay property, I could see Jay's head and Lindquist's against the glow of the fire. That was a relief. The house was old and had wooden siding and shingles—silvery cedar. I had been worrying that Lindquist might be trapped upstairs.

When I reached the drive I saw that he had already turned a garden hose on the flames. He and Jay were arguing. I couldn't hear what they said over the roar of the fire, which seemed to involve the northeast corner only, the side porch, kitchen, and whatever lay above the kitchen.

Jay shook his head violently and jumped back as Lindquist reached for him one-handed. The inadequate spray of water wobbled away from the flaring shingles, steadied, and returned. Jay took two swift strides in my direction. When he saw me he stopped.

"The bastard almost took a swing at me." Jay had to shout to be heard.

"Why?" I was yelling, too.

"Wanted me to hold the hose on the fire while he went into the house. I told him no dice. He'd die of smoke inhalation. That fire is dirty."

"Can't we do anything?" As I watched, Lindquist yanked the hose savagely and tried for a different angle.

"He's on a pump," Jay was shouting. "Not enough water pressure."

"What about the neighbor across the road?"

"Good idea."

A disadvantage of rural living was no city water. It stopped about three blocks up toward the crest. The rest of the houses, including ours and Lindquist's, had their own wells and septic tanks.

Jay was across the road banging on the door of the neat single-width mobile home. I followed.

At that distance the fire was quieter. I could see Tom Lindquist's battle silhouetted against the glare of the fire and the dimmer porch light, which was still on. The flames turned the fog orangey yellow.

I heard doors slamming and voices shouting elsewhere. People were beginning to notice. After much pounding, the light above the front door of the mobile home went on and the door opened.

The elderly woman who had stared at Bonnie and me earlier that day looked up at us. She was wearing a sweatsuit. The shirt front was covered with embossed pansies on a field of black. I could hear a television, rather loud, through the open door.

"What's the matter? Oh . . ." She spotted the fire.

"Do you have a garden hose, ma'am?" Jay, always polite in a crisis.

"I sure do." Once roused, the woman moved with vigor. She led us to a tap at the west end of the house. A coiled green hose with a spray nozzle lay in the grass.

Jay hooked the hose up, I unwound it, and the woman turned the water on. By the time I got the spray adjusted I had dragged the hose to the edge of the road. Jay took it from me. I straightened it while he jogged to the east end of the drive. That was as far as the hose reached.

Jay aimed high and the thin arc of water landed with a puff of steam on the edge of the smoldering roof.

Lindquist must have noticed. He glanced once in Jay's direction, then moved his own stream of water lower, to the roof of the porch.

I was standing in the road.

"Wow, lookit that, them shakes are burning!" An excited voice at my elbow. I looked down. A boy of about ten was standing beside me.

"Yeah, wow, there she goes...."

I laced into the little beasts. There were half a dozen of assorted sizes and both sexes. I managed to bully them back across the road to the yard of another mobile home, where several adults were standing, mouths agape, watching the show. I was about to approach the gawkers to ask whether *they* had a garden hose when a fire truck, siren wailing, lights flashing, jolted up the access road from the beach and crunched into the drive. Firemen leapt out. The brats cheered. Jay and Lindquist kept their hoses going.

Almost at once things got orderly. The truck was a tanker with its own water supply. While the fire captain directed a strong stream at the flames, shadowy figures in fire hats and heavy coats advanced on the house in a determined way, axes and pikes at the ready.

It was a good thing the Fire Department showed up when it did. Only a few minutes after the tank truck began to do its work, the light on Lindquist's porch dimmed and went out. The fire had reached the wiring. His pump apparently went, too, for he dropped the hose and ran over to Jay.

At that point another, regular truck arrived and the crew began stretching a very long hose up the road to the nearest fireplug, which was three blocks east.

A fire is a great crowd pleaser. People were clumped in every yard by then, and quite small children, whose parents should have been neutered before the fact, ran shrieking up and down the road. I have to admit I was just gawking myself, now that my presence served no purpose.

Several cars had pulled off on the shoulder of the county road. The drivers stood on the sandy verge and watched the fun, among them a blond woman clutching a notebook. For a moment I thought I recognized her, but I couldn't see her clearly in the shadows.

When the second fire hose kicked in, Jay and Lindquist began dragging the helpful neighbor's green hose back across the street. I ran to the mobile home and shut the water off at the tap. There was no point in draining her well dry.

Jay and I began to try our hands, not very effectively, at crowd control. Lindquist went back to his property. I could see him talking to the fire captain. A sheriff's car arrived with its lights flashing and the children suddenly became manageable.

The Shoalwater Fire Department might be a volunteer outfit, but they were well trained and efficient. Within half an hour the fire had been reduced to a stink of smoke on the thickening fog. Jay and I stood with the woman in the pansy sweatshirt and watched.

"I told old Tom McKay he should get asphalt shingles," she mourned. "I never did trust them cedar shakes. He was a stubborn old cuss, though."

Jay said, "I'm grateful to you for acting so fast, ma'am. I'm Jay Dodge . . ."

"At the Jorgenson house?" She held out her hand. "Ruth Adams. You're the quick one, kiddo. I never hear nothing while I'm watching the TV. House could burn down around me." She had a hearty, full-throated laugh with a wheeze at the end. "That's a good one. I'm sorry for young Tom, though. He don't have very good luck."

"First a dead body, now a fire," Jay said cozily.

"That, too." The woman turned to me. "Some day, huh? I'm glad it's over. You his wife?"

I introduced myself and we shook hands.

"Come over in the morning," the woman directed. "You and me can help with the cleanup. Bound to be a mess."

She was right about that. I agreed to come, rather doubtfully. I could see that the house was still standing, but I wondered how severe the damage was inside.

Jay said, "They're starting to wind down. I'm going back over. Lindquist will need a place to stay. He can use the guest room."

"I'll go home and make a pile of sandwiches," I offered, but I wasn't ready to leave. The sightseeing drivers, among them the woman with the notebook, had removed their cars. People on the lawns were beginning to drift back into the mobile homes, though the children were still whooping and shouting at a safe distance from the uniformed deputy. He was not Dale Nelson.

Jay walked across the road to where Lindquist was standing, now alone, by the board fence. Jay touched his arm. Lindquist listened and said something, shaking his head.

Ruth Adams and I chatted and watched. The fire captain and two of his men were conferring at the edge of the reeking porch. They had turned on the powerful lights of the tank truck to illuminate their task, so watching them in their dark outfits as they probed at the structure was a little like watching a film set. The scene took on an air of dramatic importance. Fog and smoke coiled everywhere like the special effects in a 1950s horror flick.

"What is that boy doing now?" Ruth stood on her tiptoes and craned.

Since I was a head taller I could see. Tom Lindquist had gone over to the fire captain and was arguing with him. Both men's gestures looked emphatic in the cold light. After some shrugging and headshaking, the captain appeared to make a concession. He beckoned to another fireman, who removed his hat and breathing mask and handed them to Lindquist. Lindquist put the gear on and took the fireman's coat as well. Then the captain walked with him to the front entrance of the house. They went in together, the fireman leading the way and probing the darkness with the beam of a heavy flashlight.

Jay drifted back across the road.

"What're they doing?" I asked.

"Lindquist needs to get something from the second floor. The chief decided the far end of the house was probably not dangerous, but he wasn't happy that Lindquist insisted on going in. Damn fool wanted to go back in when I first got there."

"Whatever it is he must want it badly."

"No lie."

"Was he already outside when you got here?"

"Had the hose out and the water on." Jay sounded terse and unhappy. "I thought you were going to go home and make sandwiches, Lark."

"Yes, massa." I was far too curious to leave before I saw the two men come back out of the house.

The firemen continued to prod at the charred shingles. Two of them got up on the south end of the porch and tried the door. They, too, had powerful flashlights—and axes and portable extinguishers. When the door swung open they entered the kitchen.

"Looking for hot spots." Jay sounded glum.

Finally the fire captain and Lindquist emerged from the front door. Lindquist was carrying a small box. He removed his gear and handed it back to the waiting fireman. Then he looked around. One of the other firemen touched his arm and pointed in our direction.

He came over to us, stumbling a little in the alternate bright light and blackness.

Ruth Adams said, "I told your granddad to get rid of them cedar shakes, Tom."

Lindquist's teeth flashed white in his grimy face. "So you did. Thanks for the use of your hose, Ruth."

"This lady and me will help you muck out tomorrow."

"If the fire department lets anybody in, I'll take you up on it. They're going to investigate, though."

"Arson?" Jay asked.

"It was a fucking Molotov cocktail," Lindquist said grimly. "Sorry, Ruth. I heard it smash against the porch. I thought it was kids or vandals."

"Did you see the arsonists?"

"No, but I heard the s.o.b.s drive off onto the beach. Sounded like a four-wheel drive."

Jay rubbed the bridge of his nose. His eyes didn't leave Lindquist's face.

"Did you go back in to turn off your word processor?" I asked. I had been doing some simple reasoning.

Lindquist registered my presence. "Mrs. Dodge..."

"Lark."

"I was about to say Robin and something stopped me."

"Fortunately."

His brief grin flashed again. His face was a mask of grime. "Yeah, I turned the computer off." The smile disappeared. "I pulled the disk out and chunked it into the box along with a couple of others. Will you keep them for me?"

I took the small box. I wanted to say it would be an honor, but there are some occasions when a smart mouth is a dumb idea. "Do you think you saved it?"

He shrugged. "I hope so. I tend to save rough drafts to a floppy automatically. If I didn't, I just lost that chapter. The rest of the book's on the hard disk. The smoke..." He cleared his throat. "I may have lost the whole fucking novel."

I said, "I'll take your disks home with me. Bring him, Jay. I'll fix the sandwiches."

Jay said, "I'll be awhile."

"I know."

Lindquist looked from Jay to me to Ruth Adams. "Thanks."

Ruth patted his arm.

About halfway down the unlit road I began to jump at shadows. The nearest streetlight, like the nearest city water, was three blocks east. Fog transformed the ordinary darkness into a threatening presence. I could make out our house lights, though, and, as I approached the driveway, I saw that the figure lurking at the edge of the road was just Matt Cramer. I went up to him.

"Did it burn to the ground?" He sounded excited the way nice people do at a disaster.

I told him my guesses about the damage and that Jay was bringing Lindquist home for the night. I didn't mention the novel.

"That's good, that's good." When he was agitated, Matt was apt to repeat himself. He was a burly man of medium height with mild, rimless glasses and receding gray hair. "I was putting Lottie to bed when I heard the siren—you know, the one they use to call out the volunteers."

I hadn't heard it at all. I was probably too close to the fire by that time. "They came fast."

"Good department. The siren worried Lottie. I had to stay there with her until her pills worked." The reflection of our porch light glinted on his glasses. "I feel like a rotten neighbor."

"There was nothing you could do, Matt."

"Well, tell Tom if I can do anything just to ask."

"I'm sure he'll appreciate that." It took me awhile to disengage. Matt's distress was real and he repeated his message several more times, with minor variations of wording. He kept saying that he was a bad neighbor, that he should *do* something.

Finally I announced in firm tones that I had to go check the guest room. Then I went in.

There was nothing wrong with the guest room that removing the green flocked wallpaper and putrid green shag rug wouldn't cure. I had changed the sheets several days before. I did place fresh towels on the foot of the bed. I also caught a glimpse of myself in the mirror above the bureau. My face was smeared with soot and my curly black hair looked as if it had been coiffed by a helicopter. I dashed upstairs, showered, and changed into fresh clothes. As I was coming down to make the sandwiches I heard Freddy's car in the drive. He always squirreled the Trans Am in the loose gravel.

It was a good thing I had gone to the grocery store. I was laying sandwich bread on the butcher block counter when Freddy thudded into the room. Freddy is not fat, just short and chunky, but he walks like Godzilla trampling Tokyo. I bit back my annoyance and smiled at him.

His round face was a mask of woe. "Darla wanted to go home early."

I wondered what I could say to console him.

"What's the excitement?"

"Did you see the emergency lights?" I described the fire and remembered he hadn't heard about the murder either. By the time I had told him everything and built a stack of sandwiches, Freddy looked almost cheerful. Then I thought of Lindquist's disks. If there is one thing Freddy understands it's computers, so I also mentioned the inaccessible novel.

"What does he have, a Mac?"

"I didn't ask. Hey, what're you doing?"

"I'm hungry." He had snaffled a turkey sandwich. He got a Coke from the refrigerator and sat down to encompass the food. "Where are the disks?"

"In the guest room and no way am I going to give them to you. We are talking Pulitzer Prize here, Freddy. The man is a *good* writer."

He looked hurt. "I was just going to volunteer to clean them."

"Clean!"

He took a bite of sandwich. "Somebody will have to clean them or they'll gum up the heads on the disk drive."

"Are you sure?"

"I'm not going to run a magnet over them."

"Well . . ."

"Let me clean them. I have this great stuff I got in Palo Alto, and I can put new sleeves on them, too."

I felt myself caving in. Freddy did know computers.

"When I find out what his word processor is I can do a printout."

I thought that might be a morale builder, even if the disks didn't contain the whole novel. Freddy cajoled. I resisted. Finally I gave them to him.

I made more sandwiches. As I was setting them out on the kitchen table, the front door opened and I heard Jay and Lindquist talking in the hall. I went out to them.

Both men were filthy with soot and grime. I told Jay to find Lindquist something clean to wear and sent them to the showers like a coach with a pair of players who had broken training. Our bathrooms, like the kitchen, were state of the art. When we bought the house neither Jay nor I felt like coping with plumbing and wiring, so we had had that work done professionally. There was plenty of hot water.

Jay came into the kitchen first. "Jesus, I'm thirsty."

"Have a beer."

He took one and leaned against the kitchen counter. "This is a damned bad business. An arson investigation on top of murder."

I said, "He didn't do it... then." I wasn't sure.

Jay looked troubled. "I hope not." He didn't say anything more because Lindquist dragged in wearing one of Jay's old sweatsuits and looking like death warmed over. I fed them both and hoped that Lindquist wouldn't ask about the disks.

In fact, he didn't say much of anything. Jay made a few vague remarks about the likelihood of the insurance company sending in an investigator and, when Lindquist didn't respond, added rather sharply, "The house is insured, isn't it?"

"Yeah. Standard policy." He looked into his beer.

"When did you take it out?"

"Uh, when...oh. Five years ago." He took a swallow. He had eaten two sandwiches.

I watched Jay's tension ease and regretted that I could read his mind. He had been thinking that Lindquist could have set the fire to collect on the insurance. I don't believe Lindquist understood him. Our neighbor had the unfocused look of a man at the end of his physical endurance—and no wonder. I was about to suggest that we all go to bed when Freddy's characteristic clomp sounded on the stairway. He entered the kitchen and Jay introduced his brother to Lindquist.

"What kind of computer do you have?" Freddy asked when the brief courtesies were over.

Lindquist blinked and said a name I had never heard of.

Freddy nodded. "An IBM clone. Good machine. Of course it's kind of slow."

"I had a hard disk installed in April."

"Good. What word processor?"

A brief gleam of amusement lit Lindquist's dark eyes. "Wordstar."

Freddy grimaced.

Lindquist raised his glass in ironical salute. "I like it. I'm used to it."

"If you'll bring me the computer tomorrow I'll see what I can do. Meanwhile I've cleaned your disks."

Lindquist stared. "For Christ sake, that was the fifth chapter of..."

"I didn't say I *erased* the disks. They were all sticky with smoke. I *cleaned* them."

Lindquist looked marginally relieved. "Okay, sorry. I'm brain-dead. You cleaned them but you didn't erase them. Thanks."

Freddy smiled a benign smile. "That's all right. Night, guys." And he was off.

I said, "I'm sorry I didn't ask your permission, Tom. Freddy is something of a genius with computers. He wouldn't have hurt the disks."

Lindquist set the beer down. "I think I'd better hit the sack. Where...?"

Jay led him off.

We went to bed soon afterward. I could hear Freddy's laser-jet printer humming.

FOUR

THE WIND CAME UP in the night. With it came one of those low fronts from the Gulf of Alaska that sweep rain into the Pacific Northwest at a rate drought-stricken Californians envy even as they make rude jokes about the climate.

I woke around nine when the wind gave our French doors a sharp rattle. Jay mumbled something and rolled over. After a drowsy pause I got up and wedged the doors tighter. Rain spattered the glass. I closed heavy winter drapes over the privacy curtain. The big room was black as night. Jay made a satisfied noise and burrowed deeper in the covers.

We had got to bed around two. I lay for a while beside my warm husband hoping I'd fall back asleep, but it was far too late. I'm usually up by six-thirty. I rose, showered, and pulled on jeans and a thick plush top. I had not yet reached the point of wanting to go for a run in a downpour.

Freddy had finished the printout. It lay in a neat stack on the kitchen table.

Human nature is very weak. I started a pot of coffee brewing and went back to the sheaf of papers. I read a couple of paragraphs, enough to realize I was looking at a story that was already well under way, before conscience smote me. I had never known a writer of fiction but I knew poets. They did not like to have people read their manuscripts until they were ready for criticism. Never, in some cases.

I riffled absently through the sheets of paper until I became aware that I was no longer looking at pages of manuscript but at personal correspondence. Cheeks burning, I let the papers flop into place and squared the stack. It is one thing to peek at someone's manuscript, another to read a stranger's mail.

The coffeepot was burping away. I stepped back into the kitchen and began mixing pancake batter by way of atonement. The letter I had focused on was addressed to the state historical society. At least I hadn't intruded on anything very private. I shoved the batter aside and got out a bottle of maple syrup. I was setting it in a pan of hot water when the front door opened on a gust. The draft rattled every door in the house.

The hair stood up on the back of my neck. Jay was asleep. I had heard Freddy snoring. I went into the hall. Tom Lindquist was closing the front door. He wore a yellow rain slicker and carried a bundle under his left arm. When he turned he saw me and stopped.

"Good morning."

"I went for a walk."

"So I see. Nice day for it."

He made a face. "Rotten. There's a guard on my house. The deputy let me get my wallet, though. And some clothes."

"Couldn't sleep?"

"I slept like the dead until seven-thirty." He came toward me and I could see that his hair and face were soaked.

"So you took a little stroll in the rain. Good idea."

"I had a lot to think over."

I took the damp bundle from him. It reeked of smoke. "Phew! I'll put these in the washer for you."

"Thanks."

"You can hang your slicker on that coat tree by the hall closet. Coffee's made." I headed straight back to the utility room and loaded the colored things—mostly well-worn jeans and sweatshirts—into the washer. When I returned to the kitchen he was sitting at the table staring in a dazed way at the printout. I poured him a cup of coffee. "I told you Freddy was good with computers."

He took the coffee and said nothing.

"Is it all right?"

He cleared his throat. "Yes. I saved it. . . ."

"Drink your coffee, Tom. And make the cops give you your computer. If anybody can get it working again, Freddy can."

His eyes were closed. "I'm beginning to believe it. I thought . . ." He didn't finish the sentence.

"I'm taking breakfast orders," I said brightly. "Pancakes or pancakes?"

After a moment he blinked and smiled at me. "I guess I'll have pancakes." He shoved a hand through his wet hair. "I hope I didn't startle you. I was trying to be quiet but the door got away from me."

"It's windy." I poured another neat pancake. Bubbles formed on the surface. I poured another. I had flipped that batch over when the doorbell rang. "Damn."

"I'll get it."

"Will you? Thanks."

He was already at the door to the hall. "It's probably the insurance investigator. I told the deputy where I was staying."

I slid the pancakes from the griddle to a plate in my nice warming oven. I could hear a woman's voice from the hall—agitated. It sounded like Bonnie. For a stiff moment I willed her to go away. Then the kitchen door opened again and Bonnie burst in.

"My house has been trashed."

"Oh, Bonnie. Have some coffee." I poured a cup.

She took it but her hands were shaking. "I can't find Gibson anywhere."

"That's your cat?"

"Y-yes." Her mouth was trembling.

I poured myself a cup. "More, Tom?"

Lindquist got his cup and warmed it. He said, "Is anything missing other than the cat?"

Bonnie sat. "I don't know!" Her voice rose on a wail. "I stayed in Astoria last night and got up early. When I reached the house half an hour ago, the front door was ajar. And Gibson's gone."

I indicated the telephone extension on the wall between the kitchen and nook. "Better report it to Deputy Nelson. Tom had a fire last evening...."

"Oh, no. How awful! You didn't lose—"

"It's too early to tell." Tom sat back down by the plate of pancakes I had served him. "The power's still out." He poured syrup and glanced up at me. "Do you want a dozen or so thawed crabs?"

"But surely an electrician..."

"It's a crime scene. I have the feeling I'm about to become the neighborhood food bank. Unless the crabs are evidence." He drank coffee. "Come over to the house with me, Bonnie. You can report your break-in to the deputy on guard duty. He's an auxiliary and looks just about bright enough to tie his shoes, but he can call it in for you."

She nodded miserably and drank her coffee. He cut his pancakes into methodical squares and began eating.

I poured more batter. "When did you leave for Astoria, Bonnie?"

"I dunno. Four-thirty? I was going to nap but I kept thinking about things, so I threw a suitcase in the car and f-fed the cat and just left. I stayed at the Red Lion."

"Jay and I were out on the balcony most of the evening. We didn't see anyone at your place. I know—Matt Cramer." Matt might have seen something. I told them about him waiting for me by the driveway. I checked my watch. It was half-past nine. Lottie would have eaten breakfast and be sitting at her station in front of the window. I dialed Matt's number. When his answering tape clicked on, I left a message for him to call me back.

At that point Jay stumbled down and had to be introduced to Bonnie. He still doesn't drink coffee, so I brewed his herb tea while the others explained the break-in. Outside the wind was slamming rain at the windows straight off the ocean. When the storm passed there would be a scum of salt on the south-facing glass.

Jay was late for a committee meeting, a fact that didn't seem to depress him. He called in Bonnie's incident and ate breakfast. I kept grilling pancakes while the others talked. At ten the doorbell rang again. Deputy Nelson and the insurance adjustor stood on the rainswept porch. That took a while to sort out and I poured more coffee. I also tossed Tom's jeans into the dryer and started the other batch of laundry, mostly underwear and cotton sweat socks. Jay left for the college, Bonnie and Nelson went across the street, and Tom took the adjustor off into the gale. Freddy was still asleep. Just a simple morning *chez* Dodge. Matt Cramer didn't call.

After a while I decided to do a little investigation on my own. I put on nylon rain gear and ventured out. A blast of cool water hit me in the face. The wind was blowing from the south at what felt like forty miles an hour and was probably twenty-five. I leaned into it and made my way to the door of the super-deluxe double-width mobile home the Cramers lived in. Our house faced west but theirs, on a wide curve of the road, looked due south, down the beach. I could hear the doorbell ringing but nobody answered. I peered into the front window. There was no sign of Lottie, and that worried me. Her routine hadn't varied since we moved in. Matt's Pontiac was missing from the carport.

I stood for an irresolute moment in the Cramers' driveway. The county car was still sitting behind Bonnie's little red Escort. She would need neighborly consolation but not yet. A gust slapped my face with a pint of salty rainwater, so I turned my back on the wind and started to go home. Then I remembered Ruth Adams. I'd promised to help her with the mucking out, whatever that might entail.

She was standing on Tom's porch waiting for me. "Took you long enough."

I apologized. Through the window I could see Tom talking with the adjustor. They were inspecting the smoke-blackened kitchen.

Ruth opened the door. "Tom wants us to get rid of the stuff in the freezer."

"Throw it out?"

"Lordy, no. No point wasting good food. Can you drive a pickup?"

I followed her into the kitchen, which smelled even worse than the clean clothes I had laundered for Tom. The men had moved through the arch into the living room. The whole north end of the kitchen was a charred mess. I could see daylight through the eaves. "What's this about a pickup?"

"I can't drive no more. Eyesight's going. We got to haul all that food around. Tom said we might as well use the truck."

"Oh." I'd never driven a pickup but Jay had owned a Blazer when we first met. "Sure. Is there a lot of stuff?" I had thought Tom was joking when he offered me the thawed crabs.

"Plenty." Ruth, whose workaday sweatsuit was more utilitarian than the embossed pansies of the night before, led me into a small square pantry. The tiny room was actually the north end of the porch, enclosed as an afterthought, and it had suffered heavy damage. The door led from the kitchen. The room stank of smoke, the walls were blackened, a corner of the roof was missing, and both small windows had been broken, either by heat or by the actions of the fire crew.

The shelves were lined with discarded appliances and empty fruit jars, and an old-fashioned chest-style freezer squatted beneath one small, high window. The surface of the freezer was black with smoke, stain and soot. Ruth dusted it with a rag.

She had also brought a neat stack of paper grocery bags. "I guess we can use these. Better double-sack." She began thrusting one bag inside another.

I picked up two bags and followed suit, less skillfully. "Where do we take the food?"

"Well, let's see, there's the Gundersons and old Pat Ryan..." She reeled off half a dozen names I didn't recognize. "You have a freezer?"

"Uh, gosh, yes. I don't use it much. There are a few TV dinners and some extra ice in it. I can store anything that hasn't melted yet."

She inserted another bag and snapped the double sack open, setting it on a low table beside the freezer. "That's good. The stuff in the bottom's probably okay. Still, it got pretty hot in here. The lid was open a good twelve, fourteen hours, Tom said. Fireman must've popped it. It's too late to save the vegetables."

"Can't they be refrozen?"

She made a face. "Ruins the taste." She unlatched the lid and lifted it, grunting. The chest was almost full of plastic bags, all neatly labeled. Apart from one limp carton of Raspberry Swirl ice cream I saw no commercial packaging. The garden was apparently bountiful. The idea of Tom blanching kettles full of veggies in his country kitchen ought to have been comic but wasn't.

I poked at a sack of green beans. The top layer of food had indeed thawed. "How are we going to decide who gets what?"

She flitted from the pantry and returned with a couple of dish towels. "Better swab off the melted ice."

I took a towel and repeated my question.

Ruth shrugged. "You take what you want. I'll take what I want. You put the stuff that's still frozen in your freezer. Then we can let folks take their pick of what's left. Look at them huckleberries. Darned if I don't think I'll bake me a pie. I do like huckleberry pie." From the gleam in her eyes I gathered huckleberries were a rare treat for her. I had once seen a punnet of huckleberries at an upscale foodmart in San Francisco with a price that made my eyes whirl in their sockets.

We mopped wet plastic, and stuffed the bags—of peas, beans, broccoli, baby carrots, blackberries—into our double grocery sacks. The bags contained far too much for one person to eat at a sitting. When I said so, Ruth explained the technique of freezing each piece separately on a cookie sheet and filling a large bag from which the cook could pour a single portion.

"Twist the tie and pop the bag right back in the freezer," she said cheerfully. "Big sack of corn lasts me all week. Maddy—that was Tom's grandma—used to freeze huckleberries and blackberries in a pie tin so they was already the right shape for a pie. She'd just pull a slab of berries from the bag, slap it in the crust, pour on the sugar and whatnot, and bake it. Maddy made real good pies." She bent over the freezer and prodded a bag of yellowish blobs. "Razor clams. They're about half thawed, darn it. You make clam fritters?"

"Uh, no, I once made chowder." Not a success story.

"With razor clams?" She sounded appalled.

"Just the regular canned kind."

"Well, that's all right. You can chop up your geoducks for chowder, too—they ain't much good for anything else— but a razor clam, now, that's prime eating. Dust it with a little flour and fry it in butter, or whip up a batch of fritters.''

"Maybe you'd better give the clams to somebody who's used to them. I'm from California, remember?"

"It don't show." She smiled. "Okay, we'll give the clams away. It's almost time for the fall season anyhow. You should try 'em fresh first time around. How about crabs?"

I was swabbing clam packets. "Are they cooked?"

"Lord, yes."

"Then I'll take a half dozen. I can feed Tom crab for dinner tonight." Six crabs. I could ask Bonnie to dinner, too.

"Good idea. You'll have to back 'em, of course."

"Of course." I had no idea what she was talking about. The Dungeness crab I had eaten at restaurants had come atop a bed of lettuce or swimming in some exotic sauce. It was shellfish to die for. If I had to back the crabs I'd back them.

Ruth hauled the crabs out, one by one. They had been frozen in brine, one to a bag, and there must have been a dozen. They were indeed thawing. In California, shelled crab meat had sold for $15 a pound that spring. Ruth was mining gold.

I helped her load the crabs into two empty cardboard boxes from a stack of boxes in a corner of the pantry. Tom was into recycling as well as gourmet delicacies. Long, white-wrapped packets lay a foot deep in the bottom of the freezer.

"Salmon." Ruth was not very tall and she bent almost double over the chest, prodding the top layer. "I guess these are still okay, but we'd better move them soon."

Chinook salmon, I reflected, dollar signs obscuring my vision. Not quite as expensive by the pound as crab but also gourmet fodder. Salmon I had cooked. Once a week since we moved to the peninsula, broiled, with lemon or dill sauce. I wondered what several hundred pounds of prime Chinook salmon would fetch on the open market.

I dragged three of the largest boxes over to the freezer and we loaded the salmon in. The boxes were too heavy for Ruth to lift. I staggered under them when we began carrying our spoils to the pickup, though I trusted spoils was the wrong word. We tossed the melted ice cream into the garbage can behind the house.

At that point Tom apparently registered our efforts. He came out of the house, trailed by the glum adjustor and handed me the keys to the truck.

I explained that I could store the still-frozen salmon for him.

"Thanks." He looked relieved. "Sure it won't crowd you?"

"Nope. Crab for dinner tonight, though."

He smiled. I wondered if he knew how to back crab. And whether he would be available for consultation. Dale Nelson was bound to want to interrogate Tom as soon as the insurance man had made his inspection.

I backed the Toyota with exquisite care past the insurance man's passenger van. When I found the windshield wipers, I pulled onto the road and drove over to the house. My upright freezer, which had come with the place, stood in our decrepit garage. That made downloading the salmon easy. I just backed in, opened the freezer door, and slid the damp stuff from the bed of the pickup to the shelves. The salmon took up most of the empty space. I should have dried the freezer paper off again, but we were in a hurry. I'd have a defrosting job later.

Ruth came in to admire my kitchen while I stowed crabs and sacks of vegetables in the refrigerator. Freddy was sitting in the breakfast nook. I introduced Ruth, who shook hands and explained our mission. Freddy was unmoved by the thought of thawed veggies.

"Are they going to let Tom bring the computer over?"

I admitted I'd forgot to ask.

He took a moody sip of coffee.

"He was pleased with the printout, Freddy."

"Maybe I should go over and offer to bring the machine here for him."

"You could try. The adjustor's still there. I suppose Tom will have to let him examine the computer first, in case the repairs are costly...."

"I'll fix it for free."

"Are you sure you can?"

He took a final gulp of coffee and rose. "If I can salvage the motherboard..."

"That's great," I interrupted, not wanting to get embroiled in a discussion of computer innards. "You may have to get the deputy's permission to remove it. He's at Bonnie's house...."

"Okay." Freddy gave Ruth a polite smile and clomped out, so intent on his mission I didn't have a chance to tell him about Bonnie's break-in.

I told Ruth instead, as we climbed back in the pickup and headed out into the storm.

She made distressed noises. "Regular crime wave, ain't it? Take a left here. It's that blue trailer with the windsock."

I told her about the seagulls and Bonnie's threatening message as I parked on the grassy verge in front of the small mobile home.

"That's downright shameful!" She sounded honestly shocked. "Welcoming a new neighbor that way—I never heard of such a thing. Why, there's people come in here from California and Canada and Seattle and all kinds of places. It ain't Christian."

I set the brake and switched off the ignition. "We haven't had any trouble."

She shook her head sadly and climbed out.

We made five stops on the flat, all at mobile homes. The owners were elderly, about Ruth's age, I thought, and happy to relieve us of our groceries, though two declined clams on the grounds that they'd already stocked up. Blackberries, beans, and broccoli were popular. I had to admire Ruth's tact. All of our customers seemed to be in what the English call reduced circumstances, but Ruth managed to suggest their taking the food would be a favor. All of them knew Tom.

At each stop Ruth retailed Bonnie's sad story. I could have sworn her auditors were shocked, too. I had met none of them before and they seemed friendly enough, even when I admitted I'd come up from California. All of them were curious about our plans for the old Jorgenson place. The last, a sharp-faced woman who had been a grade school teacher, expressed frank relief that we were going to refurbish, not tear the bungalow down to build a modern beach house. I assured her the thought had not occurred to us.

"It's happening all along the dunes, Mrs. Dodge. Perfectly good houses—not shacks by any means—being torn down and replaced with big monstrosities like something out of *Sunset Magazine*. Pretty soon we'll look like Los Angeles. The new houses block the view for the people on the crest, too." She shook her head. "I don't know why anyone would need a house that big to retire to."

I ventured the possibility the owners weren't thinking of retirement.

She snorted. "Thinking of renting the places out by the week, more likely. It used to be quiet around here, no traffic, no crime. Now we've got murder and arson and idiots driving sixty miles an hour up and down that road from town."

Ruth cut in at that point, on the grounds that we still had thawing food in the back of the pickup, and we made our escape. I wondered how I'd react if someone tore down Bonnie's little house and replaced it with a two-story palace with cathedral ceilings. Or with condos.

Ruth directed me up the road to a small, handsome house on the crest. "Clara Klein lives up there. She's a painter. Tom said to take her a crab and some huckleberries." Ruth was hoarding the huckleberries.

I decided I wanted some, too. I am not a baker but I recalled the existence of frozen pie shells. Might as well give it a try and stun Jay with my domesticity. We had been married six years and I was beginning to learn how to cook.

Clara Klein didn't answer the doorbell at once, so I had time to look the place over. It was small and discreetly landscaped with native evergreens in bark dust mulch, and the architecture fit the pine-covered slope. The view over the dunes was a panorama, wider than ours and almost as dramatic. I could see the insurance man's van pulling away from the old McKay place a quarter mile below to the south. I thought Tom was standing on the porch.

The door opened to reveal a stately woman of about my mother's age. She wore a paint-smeared smock over the ubiquitous sweatsuit, and she had drawn her grizzled hair back in a knot at the nape of her neck. She was smoking a cigarette.

Ruth introduced me and explained our mission.

Clara Klein's eyes widened. "Tom had a fire? I went to a showing in Cannon Beach yesterday and I didn't get back until this morning." She came out onto the encircling deck and walked to the edge, peering west through the billowing curtains of rain. "Yes, yes, I see. How terrible for him. I hope he didn't lose the book he's working on."

Ruth looked confused.

I said, "I think it can be saved. The main damage seems to be confined to the kitchen and front bedroom. He said the computer was in the back bedroom."

"Yes, he works there—has a view of the beach and that iniquitous resort they're building."

I cleared my throat. "Did you hear about the murder?"

That got her full attention. She said slowly, "I heard something on the radio coming home but I was switching stations. Who...?"

"Cleo Cabot Hagen."

She crushed the cigarette out in a planter box. "Tom's ex-wife? My God, what a complication."

"A friend and I found the body. It was in the dunes, but fairly close to his house."

"No! No, that's awful! Tom wouldn't..." She seemed to gather her wits or perhaps the still-gusting rain penetrated her awareness. "Come in and have a cup of coffee."

Ruth said, "I'll get the crab and the berries, Clara. Leave the door open."

"Okay, thanks." Clara Klein led me through a truncated hallway to a room that seemed all glass. It was one of those spaces that serve the functions of living room, dining room, and recreation room in one open plan. A high bar with teak stools separated the small, casual kitchen from the living area. She directed me to a stool and poured coffee. Her easel was sitting by the huge west-facing window.

"Tell me about it," she demanded, and poured a cup for herself.

I gave her a terse account of the previous day's events while I looked the room over. There was a lot of bare wood, and the floors were dotted with found objects and area rugs in shades of cream and beige. The north wall had a Franklin stove with a grouping of easy chairs in interesting fabrics. A low bench edged the west and south walls. It was cluttered with comfortable cushions, papers, baskets, books, and sculptural odds and ends. Nothing disturbed the ocean view except the easel. The clutter convinced me Klein was a real artist, not a dabbler. Most creative people I've known, including my mother, like to live in mild chaos. It was a comfortable place and attractive in a funky, unplanned way.

I finished a brief account of the fire and said that Tom was staying with us.

"I gather you know he's a writer."

I nodded and sipped coffee, watching her. She was frowning at the ocean.

Ruth entered with a paper bag at that point and had to be given coffee and thanks.

Ruth shrugged. "You can thank Tom. I brought you some vegetables, too."

Klein was sorting through the sack. "Huckleberries, yum. Thanks, Ruth, I'll make a pie and vegetable soup. It's a soup day."

"I just open a can of Campbell's myself."

Klein smiled at her. "I do, too, when I'm in a hurry, but there's nothing like homemade soup with hot bread when it's raining out. Half the pleasure is smelling it while it's cooking."

Ruth had to allow she was right. We drank our coffee and the painter shook our hands and thanked us again. "Tell Tom I'll clean that print I framed for him. I hope it wasn't scorched."

"Killerwhale?" I asked.

"That's the one. He bought it in San Francisco, of all places, but it's Tlingit work."

Not Kwakuitl after all. I assured her I'd convey her offer.

We were standing on the rain-swept deck by then. Clara peered toward the McKay place. "There's a cop car in the drive. Poor Tom, what a mess. Why couldn't the stupid woman get herself killed on her own territory?"

There was no answer to that and the rain was driving almost horizontally, so Ruth and I sprinted for the pickup. Clara waved to us from the deck.

Our next stop lay on the far side of the crest, down a wooded slope. The road down was unpaved gravel and sand, mostly sand. I hoped I wouldn't get stuck.

"What's this about a book?"

"Tom has published two novels." I shifted down. "Didn't you know?"

"He said something. I told him he should get a regular job."

I laughed.

Ruth defogged the windshield with her sleeve. "Where...oh, yes. Turn into that road to the right."

I obeyed, and pulled up in front of a rusty shack that could not have been called a mobile home without gross distortion of the language. It was nearly engulfed by brush and overhung by enormous spruce and cedar trees. At some point a drunken carpenter had built a shed over the aluminum trailer. An ancient tricycle lay on its side by the door. Only a dim light through the window suggested the presence of life within.

"The Johnsons," Ruth said tersely. "Tom said Melanie's old man left her last week. Good riddance." She rang the bell and gave a sharp rap on the door for good measure. The wind was quieter in that dank hollow, but the rain sheeted down through something approaching primeval darkness. I clutched my damp sack of food and shivered.

Ruth banged on the door again and after another pause, during which I could hear a child wailing, the door opened.

"Oh, hi. I thought it was the welfare." A dull-eyed woman of about my age stared at us without curiosity. She was pregnant and wore a man's gray sweatshirt over her protruding belly. A toddler with a runny nose clutched at one jeans-clad leg and sucked his thumb. "What do you want?"

Ruth went into her explanation for the seventh time and the woman held the door open.

"Yeah, I can use the food, though the brats probably won't eat clams. C'mon in."

We entered the dark, cramped space bearing a sack apiece. A girl of about five was watching cartoons on a snowy television screen. She didn't look at us.

Melanie Johnson cleared a space on the filthy counter with her arm and we set our sacks down. "What's in 'em, beans? Maybe the kids'll eat beans." She gave a short, un-amused snort of laughter. "They can eat beans or cereal, that's about all I have left."

"You got a car, Melanie?"

"Naw, Kevin took the pickup, the bastard. My mom's coming over tomorrow." She lifted the plastic bags out and set them by the sink, which overflowed with unwashed dishes. The air in the trailer smelled sour and almost moldy. "We can't move in with her but she'll get us some milk and stuff and take me to the welfare office."

"Better go to the Methodists," Ruth said. "They've got canned food for emergencies. What're you going to do?"

A spark of anger lit the woman's dull face. "How the shit do I know?" The spark faded and she shrugged. "Time to move on, I guess. I used to work for Blanco over at the dry cleaning place in Kayport. Maybe he'll give me my job back. But I need a car..." Her voice trailed as if finishing the sentence would take too much effort.

Ruth sighed. "I'll call the Methodists for you, if you like. Maybe they can bring you some things for the kids."

"Yeah. Thanks."

Ruth seemed disinclined to linger and we went back out into the storm. I was as appalled by Melanie's resignation as by her poverty.

I turned the ignition key and the engine roared to life. "Isn't there a shelter for women like that?"

"I dunno. Kevin didn't beat her or nothing. I expect the welfare will send somebody out in a couple of days. The trouble is, there's no work around here any more for peo-ple like them. He don't have an education and neither does she, and the logging's dead. My husband was a logger, made a good living at it. We raised four kids on what he made logging and had us some good times, too. Used to drive down to Reno in the camper whenever the Forest Service closed the woods. Two of the kids went to college over to Kayport, but my oldest boy's a logger and he's out of work half the time."

We emerged on the county highway that ran east of the crest.

"Your man, now, he's a professor."

I said, "Jay used to be a cop. He's running a training program for police officers."

"Yeah," she said. "A professor. Does he know anything about retraining loggers and such? I tell Ben he ought to try something else and he keeps saying he don't know nothing else."

"I can ask, Ruth. But that woman, Melanie, needs help right now."

Ruth said calmly, "Her mother will drive her in to the welfare office and I'll call the Methodists. She'll get by for now. And she'll get on welfare as long as Kevin stays away from her. Could be why he left."

We stopped at two other, less horrifying places and disposed of the last of the food. I asked Ruth how she had chosen the recipients and she shrugged.

"You live here long enough you'll get acquainted. Tom mentioned a couple of names, including Melanie's, and I thought of a couple. I figured Clara would want to know what was happening."

I drove down the west-running road to the McKay place and parked in the driveway.

As I killed the engine, Ruth said, "Part of Melanie's problem is that no-good mother of hers. Never taught her how to cook. Cereal, my foot. When Mel has money she feeds the kids junk food. She could save a bundle if she'd learn to do something besides open a can. And she ought to clean that shack up.

I wondered whether I would have the energy, had I been pregnant, penniless, and stuck in a rusting tin trailer with two toddlers. My mother hadn't taught me to cook, either.

Ruth opened the door and got out. I followed suit. The cop car was gone. So was Tom. We stood for a while looking at the shambles of his kitchen.

Ruth heaved a sigh. "Well, I guess we've done what we can for now, honey, seeing as how the power's still out. You go on home. Thanks for driving me."

I gave her a hug. "Don't forget your huckleberries."

Her face brightened. "I'm going to make me a pie."

When I got home I noticed that Bonnie's lights were on. I ran across to her small house and knocked.

She opened the door and gave a big smile. "Gibson came back. I put out a can of tuna and pretty soon there he was. Come in, Lark."

I ducked out of the rain, spraying water. Bonnie's living room, just big enough for a couch, a chair, and the tiny Franklin stove, looked as if she had already tidied it. She had built a fire in the stove.

"The real mess is in the kitchen," she called over her shoulder. "Have a chair."

I followed her instead and peered into the efficiency kitchen. Everything from the cupboards and refrigerator had been dumped on the floor. "Ick. I just dropped over to say you'd better come to dinner." I explained about the thawed crabs. "And I'm going to make a pot of vegetable soup. Come about six."

"Will Tom be there?"

"If he's not sitting in the county jail."

Her face clouded and she picked up the broom and dustpan. "How likely is that? I know the cops always look at husbands, but they haven't been married for a while. Didn't he say she remarried?"

I sighed. "I don't know anything at all, Bonnie. Come to dinner and maybe Jay will be able to fill us in. Or Tom."

She gave a short, sharp nod. "Okay. Now, clear out, friend. This kitchen is just big enough for me and Gibson."

I hadn't noticed the cat. He was sitting in a basket atop the refrigerator and he looked surly. He was a big tabby with gray green eyes. He glowered at me as if I were the villain who had disturbed his universe.

Freddy's Trans Am was gone and I didn't see Matt's Pontiac in the Cramers' driveway either, so I had no excuse not to go into my kitchen and face the crabs. I hung my sodden raingear on the coat tree and went in search of *The Joy of Cooking*.

FIVE

THE ROMBAUERS appeared to be better acquainted with Maryland blue crab than with Dungeness. The description of what they delicately called removing the coral sounded like major surgery to me. I took a crab out and looked at it. I won't say it looked back, but I felt a real disinclination to cut it open. Instead, I rummaged in the cupboard for soup makings.

I had canned chicken broth and Italian plum tomatoes, garlic, onions, and a packet of wheel-shaped pasta. With a judicious mixture of Tom's produce I could create a decent soup. There was fresh-grated parmesan cheese. I called the college. Jay was in a meeting so I left a message for him to bring home baguettes. I would make lots of soup, and if Tom was still at liberty he could demonstrate crab backing. If not we could eat soup. I had forgot to salvage a sack of huckleberries.

It was three by then. I hadn't had lunch so I fixed a sandwich and took it upstairs in search of *Small Victories*. I opened the curtains of our bedroom, plunked a pillow on the floor, and had a little picnic while I watched the storm. Then I curled up on the bed with Tom's novel. I surprised myself by falling asleep in chapter twelve.

"Must be a dull book."

I jolted awake. "Jay! What time is it?"

He bent and gave me a kiss. "Four-thirty, sleeping beauty."

I pulled him down onto the bed and undid his necktie. He always wore neckties to meetings with the dean. "I bet you don't know how to back a crab."

"Into a corner?" He removed Tom's novel to the end table, tossed his jacket on the floor, and began twining. The crab issue receded from my consciousness.

We went downstairs around five, languorous but freshly showered. I showed Jay a crab.

He turned the orangy pink shell over, inspecting the pale carapace on the underside. "Beats me. I once helped a buddy clean abalone but I've never dealt with a crab before."

I shoved the crab back into its bag and replaced it in the fridge. "I guess I'd better start the soup. Did you get my message?"

"About the bread? It's in the box." Our handsome, old-fashioned bread box was almost the only relic of the kitchen as it had been when we moved in.

I approved the baguettes and took cans from the cupboard. "Want a beer?"

Jay was already rummaging in the refrigerator. "Ballard Bitter or Full Sail?"

I went for Full Sail and he opened beer while I opened cans. "Still no lights at the Cramers'. I hope Lottie's all right."

"Shall I call?" Jay set my glass on the work surface and pulled a chair from the nook.

"I left a message."

The front door opened and shut on voices. Jay and I exchanged looks. "Freddy," he said. "And Darla."

Freddy came thumping in with his girlfriend in tow. "Hi, Jay. Where's Tom, Lark? I got the specs for the computer."

Jay was offering Darla a choice of beer, wine, Coke or coffee. She chose Coke and took a can for Freddy, too.

As I put ice in their glasses, I was wondering what had provoked Darla's presence. She rarely visited, and she treated Jay and me with polite reserve when she did. Since she was trying to dampen Freddy's ardor, I thought that was understandable, but it didn't make for jolly spontaneity. I said hello.

She took the glasses and gave me a brief smile, then said with abrupt intensity, "Where's Tom? They haven't arrested him yet, have they?"

I blinked. "Do you know Tom Lindquist?"

"He's my cousin."

"Good heavens."

Darla was 100 percent Native American, a fact she was apt to fling at people's feet, like a gauntlet, when she first met them. She was also the youngest member ever elected to the Nekana tribal council, an office she took very seriously, as indeed she should. When Darla passed the bar, she intended to work in a firm headed by the tribe's lawyer, a distinguished local attorney and former congressman who had promised to groom her to deal with Nekana legal affairs. She was working three days a week in the law office that summer as a paralegal.

Darla took her Coke into the nook and began pressing for details of the investigation. I let Jay and Freddy bring her up to date while I minced garlic and readjusted my perceptions. There was no reason Darla should not be Tom's cousin, of course, and no reason his name would have come up during her infrequent earlier visits either. We hadn't known him then. I peeled an onion and began chopping it with my trusty French knife. Still, the coincidence surprised me.

They didn't look much alike, though Tom's hair and eyes were dark. Darla had the fairer complexion. The real difference lay in body structure. Though she was not at all fat, Darla was short and wide, with a round face. She was a good three or four inches shorter than Freddy, in fact, which probably contributed to his attraction to her. Tom was about Jay's height—five eleven—and slighter. Jay has wide, solid shoulders and a deep chest (which probably contributed to my attraction to *him*). I thought Tom was pleasant-looking, but Darla was really pretty, and there was certainly no family resemblance.

The onion was getting to me, so I finished chopping it and washed the juice from my hands. When I had wiped my streaming eyes, I measured olive oil into the kettle.

I sipped at my beer while the oil heated. No way could Jay allow the sheriff to co-opt him for the investigation team. Freddy was already Tom's partisan, having bonded over the computer. If Tom was Darla's cousin, he was more than just a neighbor with literary credentials. He was practically a relative. I wondered if Jay appreciated the complications.

I tipped the garlic and onions into the oil and took out a wooden spoon to stir with. The oil bubbled gently. I love the smell of fresh garlic. I opened the other cans and listened as Freddy and Jay filled Darla in on the fire. Freddy was explaining how he had cleaned the disks when I heard the front door open again. I was not surprised to see Tom stick his head in the kitchen.

"Smells good." He was wearing jeans and a sweatshirt I had washed for him and he looked frazzled.

"It's vegetable soup." I dumped broth and tomatoes into the kettle. "You have company."

"Who...?"

"Hi, Tom." Darla got up and gave him a cousinly hug in front of the refrigerator. "Grandma told me to get my butt over here and find out if you need a lawyer."

Tom ran a hand through his damp hair. "Possibly, brat, but I don't think you're experienced enough to take me on yet."

"Cut it out. This is serious."

Amusement lit his eyes. "You can tell Aunt Caroline I'm still a free man. I spent the afternoon reviewing my last forty-eight waking hours with Dale Nelson, and I signed a statement."

Darla groaned.

"Then he warned me not to leave the county and brought me back from Kayport. They found Cleo's car at the construction site while I was trying to remember her exact words to me for the thirtieth time. I think the car distracted Dale."

I poured a cup of white wine into the soup. "You must be thirsty, Tom. Have a beer."

"Thanks." He nodded to Freddy and Jay, who had watched the drama from the nook, and opened the refrigerator door. "Jesus, there are crabs in the beer."

"I hope you know how to back them because I don't."

"No problem. Want me to do it now?"

"Drink your beer first. I'm making soup"—I glanced at Darla—"and we might bump elbows or something."

"I can back crab," she said seriously. She was a serious young woman. However, she took the hint and they both retired to the nook.

I opened the miniature door of the spice cabinet and began pulling down herb jars. Bay leaf, tarragon, peppercorns, rosemary. I thought oregano might make the soup taste like pizza sauce so I left it where it was. "I'll bet you have fresh basil in that garden, Tom."

"Sure. Do you need basil?"

"Not now, but I might get ambitious one of these days and make pesto." Pesto was one of my more successful culinary experiments.

I tossed herbs into the soup with what I hoped was a nonchalant air. The stuff was beginning to smell wonderful. I wondered if six people would fit in the breakfast nook. "Can you stay for dinner, Darla?"

"I . . . yes. Thanks."

"Terrific. Jay, you and Freddy go in and clear the crud off the dining room table. Bonnie's coming, too, so set six places. And *dust* it." The dining room was a bit cramped because the living room furniture was stored there along one wall.

Jay and Freddy rose to the occasion.

I had put the pasta wheels in the soup and was watching Tom clean the second crab when the doorbell rang. "Coral" was a euphemism for crab guts, and since Tom was busy removing the top shell, not the bottom, I didn't understand the term back either. I said so.

Darla was watching her cousin with critical attention. "I suppose we say back because only the back is left when they're cleaned. The coral's a delicacy."

"I'm sure it is."

Tom glanced at me and grinned. "Where should I toss the delicacy?"

"The garbage can's under the sink."

Before Darla could protest, Bonnie opened the kitchen door. She was carrying a covered dish in her left hand. "Hi, Lark. Your husband said to come on in. This nice lady I don't know just brought me a pie. She said it was huckleberry. Can you believe it?"

Ruth had a very soft heart. She must have baked two pies. I took the glass pie plate from Bonnie and set it on the table in the nook. The plate was still warm and the pie smelled almost as good as my soup. Gourmet dinners were easy.

I introduced Darla to Bonnie and the two women shook hands. Tom said hello and went on backing crab with professional deftness. I got Bonnie a glass of wine.

"The soup smells great."

"It will be magnificent," I said modestly. "Do we need to crack those, Tom?" I got down a platter of the sort turkeys repose on at Christmas.

"It's a friendly gesture."

"What with?"

"A nutcracker will do the job—or a hammer, or pliers."

"Or a monkey wrench?"

"You have the idea."

I found my nutcracker and handed it to him. "It's a good thing they didn't toss you in the pokey. Horrors, the veggies!" I had forgot to add vegetables to my creation. Without them, vegetable soup would have seemed a little odd. I pulled the sacks from the refrigerator. Since I took only a handful of stuff from each of four bags, there were a lot of vegetables left. Tom told me to put them in the freezer.

"But Ruth said that ruins the flavor."

He cracked the last heavy claw of the sixth crab and set it on the platter with its fellows. "Ruth's a purist. They'll taste okay in soup."

I loaded Bonnie and Darla with plates, bowls, and silverware and sent them off to the dining room. Then I told Tom about our food distribution system. He rummaged in the refrigerator for the ingredients of a dill tartar sauce he said would go well with crab and listened without comment. I was still worried about the Johnson woman.

"She'll get by." He mixed mayonnaise and plain yogurt, and chopped up a dill pickle.

"Ruth said that, but—"

"You can't change the universe, Lark. Mel doesn't know you, and she'd probably resent what she'd think was nosiness. I'll drive over tomorrow and see if she needs to go into town."

"She said her mother was coming."

"That's good."

"How do you know all those people?"

"I worked with Kevin Johnson off and on. Mostly I bump into people on the beach or in Shoalwater. It's a small place and I've been back five years now." He smiled. "And I'm related to half the old-timers on the peninsula."

I took out baguettes and butter. There was blackberry jam, too, so I spooned some of that into a bowl, though jam was probably redundant. "That may be true, but only one of the people I talked to seemed to know you're a published author."

He shrugged. "They're not great readers and my first book sank without a trace."

"No, it didn't. I read it and so did Jay."

He had picked up the platter of crabs. He stared at me over the cracked carcasses. *Starvation Hill?*

"That's the one. It's a splendid novel."

He flushed. "I spent a lot of time on the research."

Jay stuck his head in. "Oh, good, you're almost ready. The table's set. I put your scrapers and chisels and so on in the living room, Lark."

"Shucks," I said crossly. "I was going to use them to make a centerpiece."

The meal was a triumph, though I forgot the grated parmesan. Darla was kind to Freddy and was clearly moved by his efforts to rescue Tom's computer. Jay ate two bowls of soup. So did Tom, while Darla explained that she was a member of the Nekana tribal council and that her father, uncles, and two brothers were fishermen. Bonnie listened respectfully and shelled her crab. Then she segued smoothly from a discussion of politics of salmon fishing to a comic account of her own family's preoccupation with fish. Before he retired to Arizona, her father had been an avid deep-sea fisherman. Over her mother's protests, he had mounted a stuffed tarpon on the living room wall. "Not for nothing am I called Bonita," she concluded, straight-faced.

When the laughter subsided, Tom asked whether she had a brother named Marlon. We might have degenerated into real silliness had the telephone not rung. I answered it in the kitchen. It was Matt Cramer. He said Lottie was in the hospital. The doctors thought she had suffered another stroke.

I listened to Matt for quite a while. I think talking helped him. There was a possibility that Lottie would have to go into a nursing home, and Matt was resisting the idea fiercely. He could take care of her, he said several times. She would hate a nursing home. She wanted to sit in her own living room and watch the ocean. That was true and so sad my eyes teared. I said something inadequate and reached for the Kleenex box. Jay came in with the crab platter as I was wiping my eyes.

"What's the matter?"

I covered the mouthpiece and explained.

"That's bad news. Give him my sympathies." Jay shook his head. "What do you want to do with the leftover crab?"

"Refrigerator." I said into the receiver, "I beg your pardon, Matt. Jay distracted me. What did you say?"

He replied, rather plaintively, that I had asked him to call. For a moment I couldn't remember why. "Oh, the break-in." I explained what had happened and asked if he'd noticed anything, but he was so preoccupied with Lottie's condition he couldn't remember. He said he'd think about it and hung up.

By then my guests were clearing the table and shuttling dirty dishes into the kitchen. Ruth's pie, to which I added the option of vanilla ice cream, made a big hit. Darla explained the secrecy that shrouded her family's source of huckleberries. I hadn't realized they were a wild fruit. No wonder they cost a bundle.

Tom said, "Those are LaPorte huckleberries."

Darla flushed. "Yes. I meant Grandma's patch, not the Sweets'. Mom and my sister know where it is, but I was away at college before Grandma would take Mom or Ella to it. Grandma says there are black bears out there, but Ella didn't see any sign. Maybe I'll go picking with them next year."

Tom waved a fork. "If the bears let you."

Darla made a face at him. Freddy looked from her to Tom and back with something like wonder. It had probably never occurred to him to tease Darla.

When the pie had vanished, Freddy raised the question of the computer. He wanted to start working on it right away.

Tom raised his eyebrows. "Tonight?"

"Sure. Right now."

"Okay—after the dishes are done."

Freddy groaned.

I said magnanimously, "That's all right, Tom. Jay will do the dishes."

Bonnie said, "You wash, Jay. I'll dry." And they did.

Darla went with Tom and Freddy, and I shelled the un-eaten crab, of which, owing to the popularity of my soup, there was plenty. A whole crab is a lot of crab. I wondered if crab soufflé was hard to make.

The computer crew had taken the components of Tom's system upstairs to the extra bedroom when the phone rang again. It was the insurance adjustor and he wanted to talk to Tom.

I went up and led Tom to the telephone in the master bedroom so he could have a little privacy. Darla and Freddy were deep in technical conversation over the bones of the computer. I left them to it and went back downstairs. Jay and Bonnie had finished the dishes, so I brewed more cof-fee and made Jay a pot of herb tea. We took our mugs to the breakfast nook. The storm was easing. I could see a light at the Cramers'. Poor Matt had to be near distraction.

Jay said he'd drop by the hospital the next morning with flowers. Lottie liked flowers. Jay had one more committee meeting. Then he was free until after the holiday. I told him he could rip out the living room carpet.

"Thanks a lot." He smoothed his mustache. "I'd almost rather go talk to the sheriff."

Bonnie was watching us with the interest unmarried peo-ple sometimes show in spousal exchanges.

I stirred my coffee. "Do you have to help with the inves-tigation?"

"Only if I want the largest department in the area to feed students into my training program." His eyes narrowed. "What's the matter, Lark?"

"Conflict of interest?"

"You mean prejudice. I doubt that my advice on the preservation of physical evidence can be twisted one way or the other. If he's guilty, he's guilty. I don't think he set the fire.''

Bonnie was fiddling with her glasses. ''Tom didn't kill anyone.''

Jay opened his mouth.

I jumped in. ''If you say 'anybody can kill' one more time, James Dodge, I'm going to be seriously bored.''

Jay smiled. ''Lark's dangerous when she's bored, Bonnie. I think it would take a lot to make Tom kill, but I don't know who the other suspects are, so I'm not making judgments.''

''I am. He didn't do it.'' Bonnie shoved her glasses on. ''I guess we'll just have to find a fall guy. How about Darla?''

''No motive,'' I said regretfully.

Footsteps sounded in the hall and the door opened. It was Tom. Bonnie blushed. I waved a hand at the coffeemaker. ''Help yourself.''

He poured a mug. ''They found a witness.''

Jay sat up straight. ''Somebody saw the arsonists?''

''No. The woman in the mobile home north of me heard the vehicle driving away, though. Thought it was teenagers. When she looked out her window the house was on fire. She saw me come out and grab the hose.''

Jay shoved a chair out for him and scooted his own closer to mine. ''That's great. It's a shame that fire truck came up the beach approach. It obscured the tread marks.''

Tom was staring out the kitchen window into the dark, mug in hand. The rain had stopped but it was still overcast and windy. After a moment he sighed and came into the nook. ''I suppose that's why they blocked the approach last night—to look for tread marks. The adjustor says the electrician can come in the morning.''

''That's a relief. Ruth and I will help.''

Tom took the chair and smiled at me. ''I appreciate the offer, Lark, but I'm going to have to hire a crew anyway—carpenters and painters and so on.'' He looked down at the mug. ''The adjustor said he'd put me up at a motel, too, so you can get back to normal tomorrow. I'm grateful for your help.''

''Which motel?''

"The one in Shoalwater."

"Then you can forget it until after Labor Day."

He looked at me, frowning a little.

"Even if they have a room available it'll be no place for a writer this weekend. Roomsful of kids shrieking and running in and out all day. Teenagers with boom boxes vibrating the walls all night. I think you'd better stay here."

"I can't just move in on you...."

Jay said, "It's not a problem, Tom. The house is huge."

After a long moment, Tom nodded. "If I won't inconvenience you...."

I said, "Freddy will have hundreds of questions for you."

"If you're sure...." Tom cleared his throat. "Thanks."

Jay turned to Bonnie, smiling. "We can put you up, too. We haven't had a full report on your damage yet."

Bonnie beamed at him. "I feel a lot better just knowing you guys are across the street, but I think I ought to stay with Gibson. He wasn't used to the place and now he's really twitchy. And one advantage of *not* having a huge house is that it doesn't take long to clean. I already cleared a path to my bed."

"Will you feel safe?" I felt a little guilty that I hadn't made the offer.

"Probably not, but I didn't feel safe in Santa Monica either. Feeling safe is a luxury."

"That's a hell of a note." Tom set his mug down. "Did they mess with your computer?"

Bonnie shook her head. "I haven't bought one yet. I decided to wait until I'd unpacked everything. There's not much room in the cottage and my old machine took up a lot of space."

"You could get a laptop," Tom suggested.

"That's an idea."

We talked computer for a while. It was a good thing Freddy was still upstairs. He had grandiose notions. After ten minutes or so Darla drifted down. She said Freddy had promised to drive her home in half an hour.

Darla wanted to talk about the murder. Tom didn't. When she probed he evaded. There were undercurrents in the conversation I could sense but not analyze. It was clear that Darla had disliked Cleo Hagen, or perhaps she just disliked what the dead woman had represented. The resort, on the literal level; on another, an alien style of living.

After a while Tom said, rather wearily, "Cleo or no Cleo, the resort will be built. They've broken ground."

Darla looked mysterious. "Legal questions will be raised after Labor Day."

Tom snorted. "I suppose the tribal council's going to file an injunction."

Darla scowled at him. "Why not? It's Nekana land."

Tom looked at her over the rim of his coffee cup. "So's the McKay place. Are you going to sue me, too?"

"Your title's clear." She raised her chin. "Chief Nisqua deeded your land to Captain McKay."

"Yeah—in exchange for what? Blankets?"

"It was a recorded transaction."

Tom leaned toward her. "Be real, Darla. Captain McKay was a scoundrel and I have my doubts about old Nisqua. After all, the land belonged to nobody or to the Great Spirit or whatever, and it was the people's territory, not Nisqua's. How could he sell it? It wasn't his."

Darla cocked her head. "You sound as if you want that abomination down the beach to go in."

"I don't. I'll have to look at it every day when I sit down at the computer. But at least the builders are going to extend the sewer line. The worst pollution along this approach comes from septic tanks like the one under my garden."

"Pollution's only one issue."

Tom sighed and leaned back in his chair. "Once you grant the idea of land ownership at all, you're asking for large-scale litigation. The corporate big boys can beat you at that every time. It's their law, Darla."

Darla said intensely, "I can make the law work for us."

"Not yet, brat."

Jay had been sipping his tea and listening without expression. He said mildly, "The law's an ass."

Darla looked bewildered but Tom laughed.

He raised his mug in salute. "The first thing we do, let's kill all the lawyers."

Darla flushed a deep, unbecoming red.

Bonnie had gone to the kitchen to pour herself another cup of coffee. She said over her shoulder, "Don't let them pull your leg, Darla. They're just quoting Shakespeare."

Darla's mouth quivered. "It's not a game."

"No?" Tom shoved his hair off his forehead. "Isn't the tribal council playing games, too?"

"What do you mean?"

"I hear they just passed a law defining a member of the tribe as anyone with one-quarter Nekana blood."

Darla's fist clenched on the table. "There has to be a line."

"My grandmother was Nekana. She was always proud of that." Tom looked up at Bonnie as she came back to the nook, then glanced at Jay and me, too. "My grandmother and Darla's, my great-aunt Caroline, were sisters. They thought of tribal membership as a matter of kinship."

"I don't see your point." Darla's voice was cold.

Tom met her eyes. "Their grandfather was a Frenchman, Darla. Pierre LaPorte. The marriage was registered with the diocese of Nisqually. Believe me, I've seen the records. I figure that makes me something less than a quarter Nekana. What's more, unless you *and* your children are into endogamous marriage, your little membership rule is going to exclude your own grandchildren from the tribe."

Darla wasn't about to concede but the sullen set of her jaw suggested he was hitting close to home. "There has to be some kind of definition."

"Why?"

"Why! Voting rights, property..."

Tom leaned back in his chair. "Property?"

Darla's eyes dropped.

"You're buying into racism."

"Why don't you speak up, then?" she flared. "We held a big hearing. Everybody was invited to speak."

"I thought you'd want me to take a blood test first."

I began to feel sorry for Darla.

Jay sipped tea. "Is there a lot of tribal resentment against the resort?"

Tom shrugged. "There's bad feeling, yes. There's bad feeling among a lot of local people. My grandfather made a living, sort of, from an oyster bed in Shoalwater Bay. I lease out the rights to that and my tenants tell me they can't pay the rent, the oysters are dying off. The crab boat operators claim they can't keep going either. Not enough crab. The salmon runs are dwindling. Logging's on its last legs. Farmland is being covered with mobile homes. All the traditional ways of making a living around here are threatened by population growth.

I thought of Ruth's logger son who was out of work half the time.

Tom went on. "Even the retired people, whose mobile homes are part of the problem, are raising a fuss. They don't want noise and heavy traffic. The resort symbolizes all that. People like you and Annie McKay will have an easy time mounting a crusade against it, Darla. But stopping construction of the resort won't solve the problem of growth. It's here to stay."

"Annie McKay," I murmured. "Surely she's not related to you, too."

Tom's expression lightened. "She's not, but her husband's a cousin." He grinned. "On what my grandfather always called the cadet branch of the family. Successful branch is another way of looking at it. Those McKays own the paper. Annie's just the editor."

Darla said, with spirit, "The McKays own the paper, and two fish-processing plants in Kayport, and a chain of building supply outlets that covers half the state."

Bonnie said, "If they sell building materials, isn't fighting a development a bit inconsistent?"

Darla shook her head. "McKay Construction Supply caters to do-it-yourselvers—like Jay and Lark. The McKays probably see a big professional resort as cutting into their potential market. The real reason, though, is the Enclave."

I had encountered that term. "Is that the private development at the tip of the peninsula?"

Darla wrinkled her nose. "The one with the wall and the security guard."

"And the private ferry across the bay," Tom added. "Some of our rulers commute from the Enclave to Olympia."

Olympia was the state capital. I rubbed my forehead. "I suppose the McKays own one of those gorgeous Victorians in the Enclave."

Tom nodded. "Pure Carpenter Gothic."

Jay ruffled his mustache with one finger. "Are the Enclave people opposed to the resort?"

"Most of them," Tom said. "They don't want their playground cluttered with strangers."

"Annie McKay is a strong environmentalist. I think she's sincere." Darla sounded as if she were trying to convince herself.

"Sure she is." Tom's mouth twitched at the corners. "She comes from a sincere family."

Family again.

I looked from Tom to Darla for an explanation.

Darla shrugged. "Annie was a Reilly. They run the only funeral parlor in Kayport."

Tom said, "I went to high school with Annie. That branch of the McKays are summer people, but she was just a local. For all I know, Annie's a committed environmentalist now. Running the McKay paper gives her the power to do something about issues that interest her."

I got up. "I'm getting a headache. More coffee?"

There were no takers.

Jay drank the last of his tea. "I can see why Dale Nelson rolled his eyes when I asked who had a grudge against Cleo Hagen."

"And why he wanted me to be guilty of murder," Tom said wryly.

"Trying to simplify things?" I asked.

"I told him Cleo wasn't a simple woman." Tom shoved his chair back and stood up. "I'll go check on Freddy's progress."

That turned out to be unnecessary. Freddy had promised to take Darla home in half an hour and he was a man of his word. He thumped down the stairs before Tom reached the hall. Freddy and Darla left with a minimum of formality. We all went to the door to see them off.

As the Trans Am churned out of the graveled drive, Tom said, "I don't know why it is, but whenever I'm around that kid—Darla, I mean—we wind up bickering."

"Maybe you should stop calling her 'brat,'" Bonnie murmured.

He digested that. "You're probably right. She was a cute little devil when she was five."

Bonnie said abruptly, "It was a great dinner, Lark, and even better company, but I think I'd better trot on home to Gibson."

Jay said, "Shall I go across with you and double-check for thugs?"

Tom said, "I'll go. I need a walk."

SIX

I RAN THE NEXT MORNING.

I woke early. No one else was stirring, and the storm had left the air like crystal. I ran five glorious miles, almost to the Enclave, trotting the last half mile back along the tide line. It was great to be alone.

The storm had tossed debris, most of it natural, onto the firm sand. Fat gulls poked at bits of crab, kelp strands, broken razor clam shells, sand dollars. Vessels were prohibited from dumping plastics at sea, but an assortment of nautical bags and bottles had also washed ashore. I reflected that I ought to bring a garbage bag down and start collecting, but there was a beach cleanup, sponsored by the Kayport Jaycees, scheduled for September, so I let the thought go.

A droning to the south resolved into the sound of helicopter blades. I watched the oncoming craft and wondered whether it was Coast Guard or commercial. It swung over the dunes south of Bonnie's house, hovered for a moment like a huge fly, then settled at the resort site. The one tiny airport on the peninsula was too small to handle business jets, so the resort's corporate supervisors flew in and out in helicopters. I wished they wouldn't. Owing to a youthful tour in Vietnam, Jay had bad associations with the noise. It made him edgy and had triggered a nightmare, though he said he was getting used to the racket after a summer of almost daily whop-whop-whop.

I slowed to a walk and followed the path across the dunes to the road. Bonnie's car sat in her drive, but Matt's Pontiac was missing. I deduced Matt had already gone to the hospital, and I spared a thought for Lottie.

Jay had left, too. He had a breakfast meeting with the training program's advisory committee. As I entered the house I could hear the downstairs shower so Tom was awake. I made coffee and went upstairs for my own shower. Freddy was snoring. He had taken Darla home, returned, and gone right up to Tom's computer. He was still busy with it when Jay and I went to bed.

When I came back down from my shower, Tom was on the phone in the breakfast nook. I poured a cup of coffee and drank half of it while I glanced through the Shoalwater *Gazette*. It was a weekly paper. It had come the night before and had apparently gone to press before the murder and arson stories broke. That would give us a break from gawkers and invasive reporters—unless the wire services stimulated the dailies in Portland and Astoria to investigate.

The editorial dealt with an upcoming bond election. There was nothing new on the resort. I thought about turning on the radio. We had not subscribed to cable television, the only kind available, and I was grateful not to have to watch the TV news.

Tom was obviously talking to a repair person—a carpenter or painter or electrician. He uh-huhed several times, said a glum good-bye, and hung up.

"More coffee?"

"Thanks. I'm keeping a log of these phone calls."

I smiled and poured him a cup. "Don't be so scrupulous. They're local calls, aren't they?"

"I made two to Astoria. It seems there's a building boom."

"If so, it's probably the only building boom in the continental United States."

"You may be right. I'm having one hell of a time locating an electrician." He sipped hot coffee. "You said something about tearing out carpet. Need some help?"

"It's kind of you to offer but unnecessary. I was looking forward to mutilating the stuff myself."

"Two can rip faster than one."

"That's true. But—"

He said, "If I'm going to have to stick around here waiting for a kindhearted electrician to return my call, I might as well make myself useful."

Who was I to argue? The thought of all that nasty pink carpet was tempting. I offered breakfast first, but Tom said he wasn't hungry and did I have claw hammers or crowbars. I had both. We went into the living room and began ripping.

The chore went fast, especially when I discovered that the flooring beneath the rug was solid, if somewhat scarred, oak. The vandals who had installed the carpet had removed most of the molding from the baseboard, but Tom thought we could find something to replace it at the McKay Supply outlet in Kayport.

I was exuberant. I called the college and left Jay a message to rent a sander. Tom and I hauled the moldy roll of carpet to the garage. I showed him his salmon while we were out there, and Bonnie ran across to ask if I needed anything from Kayport. I said no and she took off in her little red car.

Tom and I went back into the house. We ate breakfast. We discussed the probability of all the flooring in the house being oak—he had played with the children of the owners when he was growing up—and the phone finally rang. It was for Tom, an electrician. I promised to field his other calls and saw him off, looking hopeful, to supervise the rewiring of his house.

The sight of all that bare wood fired me with ambition. By the time Jay came home with the sander around eleven, I had vacuumed up the debris and scrubbed the surface with Green Stuff. Jay was duly impressed. Also a little guilty, until I told him how fast our job of destruction had gone. He went upstairs to change into work clothes and I surveyed my living room.

I should have been daunted. Tearing down the wallpaper had revealed a cracked, plaster surface full of nicks and gouges that would have to be filled and covered with a coat of sealant. All the woodwork, including the window frames and the oak mantel above the brick fireplace, needed to be repainted. The brick was red and uninteresting. Covering it with plaster would create a southwestern effect, trendy that year, but not suitable to the architecture or climate. I thought I'd better just paint the bricks white.

If I also painted the walls white, I'd have lots of nice blank space on which to hang artwork—my great-grandmother's handwoven coverlet, for instance. Then I could find an area rug to evoke the indigo and beige of the coverlet and arrange our living room furniture in a comfortable grouping around the fireplace. I had enough antique odds and ends to fill the remaining space. It would be a congenial, interesting room, a place to entertain friends. I could hardly wait.

I inserted paper in the sander, plugged it in, and cut a wide arc on the surface of the floor. Just testing. As I swung the machine around for a second swath the doorbell rang. At first I thought it was the telephone, but I switched the sander off and the bell pealed again. Definitely the doorbell. I hoped Bonnie hadn't suffered another disaster and remembered she had left for town.

I went to the door, dragging the heavy sander. The long electric cord followed me. I hoped whoever it was, whether carpenter, reporter, or huckster, would gain the impression that I was a busy woman.

A thirtyish business executive—his buttoned down costume left no other interpretation possible—gave me an unsmiling stare. "Mrs. Dodge?"

"Yes."

"I understand that Thomas Lindquist is staying with you. May I speak with him?"

I hesitated. I was about to tell him where Tom was, but something in the man's manner repelled me. I swung the sander around to my side, thumbing the switch, and adopted a tone my mother would have applauded. "Who shall I say is calling?"

"Donald Hagen."

I opened my mouth. Cleo Cabot Hagen's husband. An incredibly clean-cut Republican, if looks were any indication, and probably five years younger than his wife. That was interesting.

I heard Jay's footstep on the stairs. "He's not..."

The man didn't wait for me to complete my sentence. He leaned into the door, shoving it wide, and strode past me into the hall.

"Just a damned minute!"

"I want to talk to Tom Lindquist."

"Really, Mr. Hagen . . ."

"Lark . . . ?"

"You dirty half-breed!"

"He isn't—" I was about to explain that Tom wasn't home, but the man drew a handgun from the pocket of his jacket. Jay was halfway down the stairs.

"Hey!" I yelped.

Hagen's chiseled features registered no known emotion. "Think you can kill my wife, you bastard? I'll show you. . . ." He raised the gun.

Instinct took over. I swung the sander up, two-handed, aiming for his gun hand. I connected with his right elbow. The gun fired as it flew out of his hand, the din bouncing off the walls.

Jay leapt down the stairs, and we both fell on Donald Hagen like a tower. We knocked him flat.

Jay twisted the intruder's arm behind his back. "Who the devil . . . ?"

"Hagen." I gasped. "Looking for Tom." My head was still ringing from the sound of the gunshot.

Jay gave a sharp jerk of his arm. "What do you want?"

The man groaned. "Fuck you, Lindquist."

Jay straddled Hagen, keeping the arm pinned. "You're off base, buddy. I'm not Tom Lindquist, and you're under arrest. You have the right to remain silent . . ."

I couldn't believe Jay was Mirandizing Hagen there before my very eyes, but he finished the whole warning, word perfect, and added, "Any comment?"

"Lindquist killed my wife."

"I doubt it," Jay said, and gave another jerk.

Hagen moaned again.

Plaster was still sifting down. "He knocked a hole in the ceiling!" I heard a thud upstairs. Freddy. I swallowed a giggle.

"Go call 911, Lark," Jay instructed, irritation sharpening his voice.

I abandoned the sander where it lay and ducked into the kitchen. The dispatcher didn't understand me until I calmed down enough to speak coherently. She assured me help was coming. I went back into the hall.

Jay still held Hagen's arm in a twist and was frisking him, one-handed. Jay does not like being shot at. I didn't envy Hagen. On the other hand, I didn't feel sorry for him either. I watched with interest as he squirmed and protested.

The gun had come to rest by the archway that led into the dining room. I despise guns. I nosed the weapon the rest of the way around the corner with the toe of my sneaker. The air reeked of cordite. "Shall I go find your handcuffs?"

Jay grunted. He kept a pair of handcuffs in his briefcase. God knows why, so the question wasn't entirely idiotic. He had a knee in Hagen's back, the arm in a lock, and was thumbing, left-handed, through the man's wallet. "Donald C. Hagen, the Hagen Group, San Francisco. No shit."

Hagen was saying something about his lawyer.

"Wait till your fancy corporation hears from *my* lawyer," Jay snarled. "What do you use for brains, Hagen, tofu?"

The bell rang.

I sidled over to the door and peered out the little glass window alongside it, which I should have done when Hagen rang, though the sight of him wouldn't have stopped me from opening the door. I don't know what I expected to see. Corporate goons? A middle-aged man in a gray three-piecer and Lee Iacocca glasses stood on the porch, wringing his hands.

I opened the door. "Yes?"

"Is Mr....oh, no." He stared past me, eyes bulging behind the spectacles. "Oh, dear, what have you done, sir?"

"Who are you?"

"I...uh, I beg your pardon, madam. I'm Clinton Walls. I'm the Pacific Northwest vice president of the Hagen Group. Mr. Hagen, he...oh, dear."

"He just tried to kill my husband." I had gone from adrenal surge to wrath. "Is that how you people do business?"

"Oh, dear, I'm sorry, madam, believe me. He's distraught. I heard the gunshot. Did he hurt...?" He was trying to see past me and took a step forward.

"If you knew he was armed, Mr. Walls, you're an accessory. Step back onto the porch, if you please."

Behind me I heard Freddy thudding down the stairs, questions rattling out in his light tenor. I met Walls's worried eyes. "Out, Mr. Walls. We are going to stand on the porch together and wait for the police."

Walls made a choking noise but he did step back. I joined him and pulled the door shut behind me.

"Is anything wrong?" Matt Cramer was edging across the lawn.

"Just a little misunderstanding, Matt. I've called the cops."

"Anything I can do?"

I clenched my teeth on another giggle. "No, thanks. We're fine."

"Lottie really appreciated the flowers." He was coming over to the porch.

Walls looked as if he might burst into tears.

"I thought I heard—"

I said, "It was a gunshot, Matt, but nobody was injured."

Matt was standing on the front walkway, looking up at us. "Oh my, oh my. Who...?"

"The shootist claims to be Donald Hagen. He mistook Jay for Tom Lindquist."

Mr. Walls made distraught clucking noises. "Please, madam, I don't think...I'm sure Mr. Hagen won't..."

I said to Matt, "I do hope Lottie's better."

"About the same, about the same. I came home to get her fresh nightclothes. Who's that?"

I introduced Walls to Matt, wondering how Eugene Ionesco would have dealt with our dialogue. A siren yelped in the distance.

"I really didn't think he meant to harm anyone," Walls assured Matt. The vice president was beginning to regain his composure. And to think about self-preservation.

A sheriff's car rounded the corner and wheeled into our driveway behind an alien BMW that had to belong to Hagen. I wondered if he kept fresh BMWs at every construction site.

Dale Nelson jumped out and ran toward us, hand on the butt of his gun. This time he had backup. Another deputy, older and fatter, got out, too. He stood on the far side of the cop car and aimed his gun at us, two-handed, over the roof.

Lest they imagine Walls was the culprit, I said hastily, "Jay's inside with Hagen."

Nelson gained the porch. "Is he armed?"

"Hagen? Not anymore. He fired one shot."

Nelson jerked his head at the other deputy. The gun disappeared.

I opened the door. Jay was still sitting on his assailant and Freddy was watching both men from the stairway, one hand on the newel, his eyes bright with excitement.

I ushered Nelson and the fat deputy in. Walls and Matt tried to follow but I shut them out.

Nelson had Hagen handcuffed and sitting in the back of the sheriff's car within five minutes, in spite of Walls's anguished protests. Hagen was sputtering threats by that time and red in the face, whether from anger or embarrassment it was impossible to say. I wondered if he was on something, coke perhaps. The fat deputy stayed by the car to keep an eye on him and Nelson returned with us to the house.

I showed Nelson the gun and let Jay do the explaining, which saved time. They said the weapon was a .38, but even I could see it was no Saturday night special. Hagen's initials were engraved on the butt.

Waiting for the evidence team to show up consumed a good hour. They had to drive over from the county seat, which was forty miles away on the east side of the bay. Well before they came, a local car appeared and Nelson sent the prisoner off to be booked. Then Nelson took our statements.

Walls hung around in the BMW. He was making calls on a cellular phone, so it was probable that Hagen's attorney would meet his client at the courthouse. By the time the evidence team came, children from the mobile homes on the flat had spotted the excitement. They flocked around Walls's car and watched him telephone. Their parents gathered in knots down the road, or across it, in the dunes.

Bonnie drove up and stood on her porch watching, and Matt joined her. Finally, Tom Lindquist also appeared.

The deputy in charge outside wouldn't let Tom come in at first, or so Tom said when he did enter—via the back door and the utility room. He was appalled when he heard what had happened and offered to move out immediately, but Jay was having none of that. Jay was angrier than I've ever seen him in a long time, though he was concealing it well. I suppose Nelson and the technical people saw a cool, critical professional. I saw a volcano. I waited for the eruption.

The telephone kept ringing—Tom's craftsmen returning his calls and one enterprising reporter. Tom spoke with the craftsmen and hung up on the reporter. Once Freddy figured out that the exciting part was over, he went back upstairs to work on the computer. I made crab sandwiches.

The cops finally left after marking up my floors and walls, covering various surfaces with fingerprint powder for no apparent reason, and measuring trajectories. They pried the slug, intact, from the ceiling, and of course they photographed everything. We were lucky the bullet hadn't fragmented or ricocheted, so I tried to be philosophical about the hole in the plaster.

When we had seen Nelson off, Jay turned on me. "What the hell do you mean, letting that freak in the front door?"

I held onto my temper. "Is that any way to talk to the woman who just saved your life? I didn't let him in, Jay. He shoved his way in."

"But—"

"You're upset. I understand. So am I, but don't take it out on me. Go for a run."

His mustache whiffled.

I touched his arm. The muscles were tight as cable. "A long run."

He drew an uneven breath and wrapped both arms around me. "He was down there with you. I thought..."

I hugged back. "Never mind. It's over."

Eventually Jay took my advice and went for a run. I drifted back to the kitchen where Freddy was consuming crab sandwiches and telling Tom about the state of the computer. Disassembled, from the sound of it. The phone rang again and Tom answered.

"For you, Lark." He held out the receiver.

I said hello.

A female voice I didn't recognize said, "Hi, Lark. I hear you had a little excitement over there."

That was one way of putting it. I almost hung up.

The woman went on in a cheery, oblivious voice, "This is Jean Knight. Are we still on for Labor Day?"

Labor Day. Good God, I had forgotten that we were set to entertain the Knights. "I...uh, yes, as far as I know. The weather..."

Jean laughed. "It's nice today, so it'll probably be miserable by Monday. If you're set on a barbecue..."

"Well, I thought I'd do salmon. I can roast it in the oven, if need be. I warn you the house looks like a hurricane struck it." I described the denuding of the living room.

"It'll look great when you're done. Is Lindquist actually staying with you?"

"Yes. I expect we'll have Tom and Bonnie Bell, our neighbor across the street, as well as you two and Freddy. Possibly Freddy's girlfriend."

"That sounds like a crowd. I was going to ask if I could bring Annie McKay, too, but—"

"The editor?"

"Yes. She and I work for the Nature Conservancy. When I mentioned I knew you, she said she'd like to meet you."

I had the feeling Annie McKay's interest in us was motivated by curiosity about the biggest news story on the peninsula. I hesitated, but I was fairly curious myself, so I said, "Sure. The more the merrier."

"If Annie's husband, Bob, is in town, I imagine he'll want to come too."

I wondered if we had enough chairs. "That's okay."

"Great. I'll bring the dessert, Lark. Anything else I can do?"

"Dessert will be extremely helpful."

"What time?"

"Around five, I thought. See you then."

We hung up simultaneously. "Whew," I said. "Is it okay with you if I activate the answering machine, Tom?"

"Sure. I have the workmen pretty well lined up."

I explained about the Labor Day fest. Tom said he had been planning to go out on a boat but he supposed he'd have to cancel that anyway. He thanked me for the invitation and offered me a frozen salmon. I accepted. Freddy promised to invite Darla.

I looked at Tom. "You know Annie McKay, don't you?"

"Went to high school with her."

"Good. She's coming."

His face took on a strange expression. "Have you read *Small Victories?*"

"Oh, no. The Prom Queen?" The Prom Queen was the object of the teenaged protagonist's hopeless infatuation.

Tom nodded. "Maybe I should go fishing."

"Not on your life, sir." I felt the bubble of laughter I had been suppressing rise in my throat. "Not on your life." I was beginning to sound like Matt Cramer.

SEVEN

MY AMUSEMENT EVAPORATED as soon as I took a deep breath. I had ten people coming for dinner on Labor Day and it was already Thursday. Ten people and eight dining room chairs. I could put half of us in the dining room and half in the nook...no.

"What's wrong, Lark?" Freddy took a slurp of Coke. Tom frowned.

I opened my mouth to say "Nothing," but a commotion from the front of the house distracted me. Tom stood up.

I heard Jay, and Bonnie's lighter voice responding to him, and I shook my head.

Tom sank back on his chair. "I could get jumpy hanging around here."

Freddy laughed. I didn't. I hadn't realized I was jumpy, but I was. Twitchy as Bonnie's cat.

Jay swung the door open and Bonnie preceded him, carrying a ceramic casserole dish. "Scalloped oysters for dinner," she said. "What's the matter, Lark?"

Jay was watching me, too. "Something wrong?"

I burst into tears.

I hate it when I do that. Even as I blubbered, I knew I was just reacting to too much adrenaline. I have always been far more apprehensive about social crises than about physical danger. I could tell myself I was foolish to disarm a maniac with one cool sweep of my sander, then fall to bits because of couple of strangers were coming to dinner, but I can't help being that kind of fool.

Though my little nerve storm blew over almost at once, it lasted long enough for Freddy and Tom to disappear. Jay patted me. Bonnie murmured soothing phrases as she set her dish on the counter. I leaned against Jay's sweat-soaked jersey and hiccupped out an account of my disastrous dinner plans.

Bonnie said, "You could stash everybody upstairs on that nifty balcony."

"The balcony is off our bedroom," I moaned. "Besides, we can't eat outside. Jean Knight says it's going to rain."

Jay gave my shoulders a squeeze. "I guess we'll just have to do the living room."

Bonnie set the oven to preheat. "I can paint woodwork."

"But we can't finish . . ."

Jay kissed my ear. "Sit down at the table, darling, and make a list. I smell like a stalled ox so I'm going up for a shower now, but I'll be right back."

I sat. Bonnie made me a cup of tea, and found paper and a pen in the drawer by the telephone. I wrote PAINT and stared at the word. The tea smelled good. Bonnie kept up a light chatter about her casserole.

One of the happier consequences of being a woman is that you can cry like a baby and forgive yourself. After a couple of calming sips I began to think. "You'll help?"

"Sure. I'll enjoy it."

"But there's so much to do. I still have to sand the damned floor, and now the hall looks like hell, too . . ."

"Leave the hall," Bonnie said firmly. "The bullet hole will make a great conversation piece."

"God, Annie McKay is the *newspaper* editor."

"So let her photograph it. Give her an exclusive."

I snickered.

The back door opened and Tom stuck his head in. "What's the joke?"

"Just basic goofiness," Bonnie said airily. Tom had visited his garden. "Salad stuff. That's great, Tom." She shoved him at the sink. "We're going to paint Lark's living room tomorrow."

"Good idea." He turned on the water and started rinsing bibb lettuce. "That's a high ceiling. How are you fixed for ladders, Lark?"

"One stepladder." I had used it when I painted the kitchen. "And some rollers and pans."

"We'll need a couple of extra ladders if we're all going to pitch in." Tom took my salad spinner from the shelf and started loading it with lettuce. "And tarps. Extensions for the roller handles."

I scribbled on my list.

"I have piles of remodeling gear locked up in my garage. My grandfather did repairs on summer people's houses."

"Won't your crew need the ladders?"

"Those bozos don't come until Tuesday."

"Frustrating," Bonnie said.

"A little." Tom glanced at me warily as if I might burst into tears again. "But the power's on and at least they threw a tarp over the hole in the roof. Let's deal with Lark's living room. You won't need to buy hammers or a saw...." He gave the spinner a whirl.

"Geez!" I remembered the molding. And I still hadn't sanded the floor.

"I have carpenter's tools and fifty years' worth of nails." Tom twirled the knob and the spinner rattled away. "You should apply a clear acrylic to that floor."

"I was going to use oil and wax," I protested.

"Nice theory." Tom peeked at the lettuce and put the lid back on. "Sand from the beach would chew up an oiled surface inside a week. Not to mention what water and mud will do when it starts raining again. Also you'll need to let the acrylic season thirty-six hours or so."

"Oh." Thirty-six hours!

"What colors are you going to use?" Bonnie interjected.

"White."

"Hmm." Bonnie sounded polite. Tom frowned and spun the wheel.

I stuck out my jaw. "I am going to paint everything in that room white except the floor."

"Why not let me call Clara Klein?" Tom gave the spinner a last twist.

I moaned again. "And invite her to dinner?"

He laughed. "Invite her to look at your living room. She has a great eye."

"We need to get started right away."

"Sure. I'll drive you over to Kayport tonight in the pickup, if you like. McKay Supply stays open until nine. Meanwhile, let me call Clara."

I rolled my eyes. "Okay, but you'll have to ask her to dinner on Labor Day. I'd better call Ruth Adams and Matt, too."

Bonnie cleared her throat. "That's thirteen people, Lark."

I waved my hand in a grandiose gesture, slopping tea. "Who's superstitious?"

Tom called Clara. I was relieved to hear she already had an invitation for Labor Day. She was on her way to the bar of the Blue Oyster for a drink and dinner—they didn't allow smoking in the dining room—and she'd pop over on her way.

When Tom hung up I took over the phone. Ruth thanked me but her kids were coming with the grandchildren, and was it true a crazy man had taken a potshot at Tom in my front hall? I gave Ruth an exclusive. She sounded as if she might ask for my autograph. Matt Cramer wasn't home, so I left a rather confused invitation on his recorder.

By the time I rang off, Jay had come down in jeans and a work shirt. He and Tom took a steel measuring tape into the living room.

Bonnie set her oysters in the oven and turned on the timer. "*Early* dinner. The painting's going to be fun."

"Chaos," I said with affected gloom, but I felt much more cheerful. I am a creature of action.

I got up and finished making salad. Tom had brought two tomatoes from his hotframe. Bonnie's scalloped oysters were delicious, though we scarfed dinner in record time. I started parceling out tasks at the table.

Jay and Freddy had built Jay's log house in Monte when Freddy was only fifteen, so Freddy couldn't claim inexperience. He did point out that if he wasted his time daubing my walls the computer would languish. I excused him only after he promised to deliver Tom's chapters in time for the party. Also he would have to forage for himself. I had no intention of cooking.

It was clear from the way they exchanged dimensions that Jay and Tom were the logical ones to lay in the painting supplies. I intended to sand the floor. Bonnie said she'd vacuum after me—and clean up the kitchen.

Shortly after the men took off in Tom's pickup, Clara Klein rang the bell. She was wearing a wild batik with a matching turban and narrow tan trousers. She waved a cigarette at my couch and sofa—they were still shoved against the dining room wall—and when I showed her the living room, told me it had great proportions.

I said I wanted it all white. Clara didn't even try to argue. She just nodded and smoked, making little hmmms. Finally she said the red brick fireplace should definitely disappear under at least three coats of white. There was a special paint for bricks. When I repeated that I wanted the walls white, she smiled and admired the mantel. It *was* rather nice. She tossed her cigarette in the fireplace and looked at her watch.

I knew I was being surly. I gritted my teeth. "I really appreciate your coming over, Clara."

"No problem. See you in the morning."

I hadn't bargained on that. I told her the men had orders to bring home four gallons of white latex.

She gave me a pat on the shoulder and made for the front door. "Great proportions. Night." She hopped into her Karman Ghia and drove off.

I put on the mask the rental company recommended, grabbed my old Walkman and a couple of Springsteen tapes, and started sanding. I sanded the floor three times with different grades of sandpaper. Every pass I took was another swipe at Donald Hagen. It felt good.

Bonnie was true to her word. Each time she heard the sander stop, she trotted in with my vacuum cleaner and shooed me off to the kitchen for a break. By my first break the kitchen was clean. By the second I found she had hauled out my ancient crockpot. I lifted the lid and sniffed. Soup for the troops. A good idea—it could cook all night and all day.

Bonnie and I were scrubbing the floor with Green Stuff when Tom's pickup turned into the drive. Long strips of wood hung out the back of the truck. Tom and Jay unloaded it and came in to admire our handiwork. It was ten o'clock. We had a last cup of coffee and Bonnie went home. Jay and I were in bed by eleven, and I fell into sleep as if I were falling down Alice's rabbit hole. I think Jay was exhausted, too. He didn't thrash around the way he often does.

To my surprise Darla showed up the next morning before eight-thirty. Freddy had called her the previous night. She was wearing a long-sleeved blue work shirt and jeans, and she said she wanted to help. She had taken a day off work. I was touched, though I did wonder whether she was hot to paint or hot to be at the center of the action. I had heard the story of the shooting on the Astoria radio station when I listened to the seven o'clock news. Five reporters of assorted media had left messages on the answering machine.

I set Bonnie and Darla scrubbing woodwork. Clara Klein breezed in fifteen minutes later. She accepted a cup of coffee and I dug out my lone ashtray. We strolled, cups in hand, to the living room. Bonnie and Darla looked up and Clara gave them a big smile. Then she turned on me. She explained, very gently, that white fireplaces were okay and even white woodwork. She could tolerate a white ceiling. But acres of white wall? No. The room would look like a very old-fashioned hospital—a TB sanatorium, perhaps, as in Thomas Mann, or selected scenes from *A Farewell to Arms*.

She had set the ashtray on the mantel. "Trust me, Lark." She flicked an ash. Her eyes gleamed.

"Not mauve." I was wavering.

Clara's eyebrows shot up. "Mauve would be stunning."

"I don't want stunning. I want comfortable."

She grinned. "Trust me. I've seen your couch."

"My mother-in-law gave us that sofa and the matching chairs. They're ghastly expensive." They were real suede, pale cocoa-colored and squishy with cushions. There was also a very large hassock.

"I can believe it. Expensive and boring. Never mind. Everything will look great." She stubbed out her cigarette, plunked her coffee cup on the mantel, and held out her hand. "Receipt?"

What could I do? I found it for her and even helped her load the four gallons of flat white latex into the Karman Ghia.

Jay and Tom were bringing in Tom's extra stepladders. They spread tarps over my sanded floor and went into the kitchen for coffee. Then they stood in the living room with their mugs, making male planning noises, while Bonnie and Darla scrubbed. We had filled all the cracks in the ceiling within half an hour and were ready to start in on it with long-handled rollers.

Jay had bought a white paint thickened with sand for the ceiling. To my surprise, it covered the ceiling in one coat plus daubs. It was dry by eleven-thirty, and Darla and Bonnie had scrubbed everything in sight, including the fireplace. We were ready to attack the walls.

Clara hadn't returned so I called time and we took a lunch break. Darla pointed out that I ought to remove the salmon from the freezer if I wanted it thawed by Monday. I would not have thought of that. I dashed out for the salmon and Darla dashed upstairs to get Freddy.

All of us repaired to the kitchen where we built enormous sandwiches and talked strategy. Darla and Bonnie argued over whether to strip several coats of paint from the woodwork or just to sand. Tom and Jay rumbled over the relative merits of rollers and sponges for painting walls. Freddy gave us a computer update in his light, eager tenor. Listening to them, I realized I was enjoying myself hugely.

So were they. Jay had lost the look of tooth-grinding tension. Tom, whose black hair was speckled with bits of plaster, kept making the kind of wisecracks that are hilarious in context and make no sense otherwise. We laughed and ate. We were full of energy.

For a mad moment I considered suggesting Tom fire his laggard crew. We could finish my living room and move on to his place in a kind of pioneer barn raising. Fortunately I kept my thought to myself. Tom didn't need to think about his charred belongings. Bonnie didn't need to brood about her prowler, or Jay about his close call with an urban cowboy, or Darla about her coming injunction. None of us needed to think about the murder. I had inadvertently created an island outside of time. I wished it wouldn't end.

Clara showed up as we straggled back to the living room. She declined a sandwich but took a cup of coffee and my ashtray. She had bought taupe paint. Gray, she assured me, would look cold in the normal Northwest overcast. Taupe was much warmer. It was pale taupe, she said.

I associated taupe with panty hose, but I decided to keep my mouth shut and see what the walls looked like before I squawked. I could always cover them with white later.

Clara eyed me defensively through her protective cloud of smoke. So I thanked her. When she discovered we were about to open the cans of sealant, she took off for home. She was allergic to the fumes, she said, but she promised to come back early Monday to supervise hanging my great-grandmother's woven coverlet.

Before we covered the powdery residue of the defunct wallpaper with sealant we had to patch more cracks. That took all five of us and two hours of creative spackling. Then we opened the sealant and I understood Clara's flight. The stuff smelled like a World War I gas attack.

Tom made us open all the windows and doors—he had used the sealant before—and we worked in teams. Tom, Jay, and I used the long-handled rollers on the upper reaches. We took a break and headed for the dunes to air our lungs while Bonnie and Darla finished off.

Jean Knight's rain had not yet begun but a gusty wind was blowing from the southwest. The three of us stood on the crest of dune behind Bonnie's house and looked south. There were no helicopter noises from the resort site and no signs of life. The stillness had an air of expectation, of dread, possibly. I shivered in the rising wind.

Jay said, "I talked to the sheriff. He agreed to let me off the hook."

"Great." I was relieved. "When did you call him?"

"Yesterday—after I ran."

Tom squinted in the fitful sunlight. "What do you mean, off the hook?"

"I'm not going to take part in the official investigation."

"I thought you wanted to."

"Not particularly. I have a textbook to finish, remember? I just didn't want to offend the police."

"Don't you get your students out of the high schools?"

"Some. The best are working cops, though. I pointed out to the sheriff that getting shot at by one of the suspects was likely to compromise my testimony. I've already given Nelson guidelines. He's pretty sharp, so the evidence should be okay. The main problem with that department is lack of organization."

They talked for a while about the kinds of physical evidence a forensics team ought to evaluate. Tom got interested in insects. He sounded as if he were taking mental notes. I would have laid a bet that his next novel would involve a crime with a bug-ridden corpse.

Writers are weird people. My mother once told me she was collecting images for one of her better-known poems at her grandfather's funeral. I can't manage that degree of detachment.

After perhaps five minutes of investigative theory, I steered the conversation back to the events of the previous day. "How much do you know about Donald Hagen, Tom?"

He shrugged. "We've never met. After yesterday, I can't say I want to meet him."

"Was he younger than your... than Cleo?"

"Four or five years. Cleo and I were the same age, but she always had an eye for younger guys."

"I thought Hagen was pretty stupid."

Tom said cautiously, "I gather he's no genius, but he doesn't have to be. The Hagen Group is a family firm—privately owned."

"A sinecure. He must be a rich man."

"Cleo had an eye for the main chance." He sounded more amused than bitter. "But she always pulled her weight. She earned more than I did the whole time we were married, though I was making a good salary."

Jay said, "What did you do?"

"Wrote advertising copy."

"Ugh!" That boggled my mind. Nothing in the style of either book suggested advertising, and *Small Victories* satirized TV hype. Debasement of language was one of the book's major motifs.

Tom smiled. "As long as you can look at it as a game, like Scrabble or acrostics, writing copy's enjoyable. I had interesting accounts—couple of Napa valley wineries, a software firm, a chain of Mexican restaurants."

"But you quit to write novels full time?" Jay hunched a shoulder against the wind.

Tom sighed. "Not just like that. I came north when my grandparents died. They were killed in a car wreck."

I said, "I'm sorry, Tom. That must've been awful."

"It was a shock. They were getting on, of course, and I'd thought about illness—cancer or heart trouble. I wasn't ready to lose them both." He rubbed his forehead. "Hell, I wasn't ready to lose either of them, and not that way. My mother was killed in a car wreck when I was twelve."

We stood silent for a while, then Tom added, "My grandparents died five years ago, the year after I divorced Cleo."

So he had initiated the divorce. I wondered if Jay found that as interesting as I did.

Jay is a professional interrogator. He changed the subject. "How did you get started writing?"

Tom blinked. "I dunno. I guess I've always been a storyteller. It runs in the family." He laughed. "The LaPorte family anyway. Grandma was famous for her tall tales. My grandfather was a reader, a great patron of the Shoalwater Public Library. I remember him reading me Forester's Hornblower stories when I was really young."

Jay turned his back on the wind. "Did you study writing?"

Tom nodded. "At UCLA, after I got out of the army. I'd published a couple of stories by the time I graduated, and I thought I could write fiction on the side. Most writers do."

I rubbed my arms. "Couldn't you get a fellowship?"

He shrugged. "Maybe, if I'd applied. I needed a job with a decent salary. My grandparents were getting older. Grandpa shouldn't have been out in all kinds of weather harvesting oysters—not that he was going to listen to me. I thought I ought to help them out. Besides, I wanted a piece of the action myself. Poverty is overrated. I got through

UCLA by cleaning rich people's swimming pools and eating a lot of beans. I don't like beans."

I knew that. He liked salmon, and crab at $15 a pound. I sighed. "Did you meet Cleo in San Francisco?"

"Yeah, at a party. She looked good through the haze of dope. She looked good when the smoke cleared, as a matter of fact. She was a beautiful woman...." He shoved a hand through his hair. "Cleo knew how to make her beauty vulnerable. I'm usually intimidated by beautiful women, but she got past that. I have no idea why she decided I'd make a good investment."

"Maybe she liked writers," Jay suggested.

"A groupie?" Tom snorted. "Cleo never read anything but annual reports and the *Wall Street Journal*. And she was jealous as hell of the time I spent writing *Starvation Hill*."

Jay's eyebrows rose. "Did you write that in San Francisco?"

I was surprised, too. The book was pure Pacific Northwest—culture, language, geography.

"Partly." Tom made a face. "Took me seven years, counting the time I spent on it in college. Chapter two was my senior thesis."

A four-wheeler loaded with kids jounced down the beach, well in excess of the 25-mile-an-hour speed limit. We watched it out of sight.

"Shitheads. They're driving on the clam beds." Tom sighed. "People think novelists just whip stories out. Maybe some do, but *Starvation Hill* took a lot of digging."

I was thinking about Cleo. "And your wife didn't like your preoccupation?"

Tom said slowly, "I don't know which she resented more—the amount of money I spent on research, or the time. At first she was enthusiastic. She even came up here with me a couple of times, though she hated Shoalwater. I guess she thought I'd write the kind of novel that gets you on *Geraldo*. That rarely happens, especially not with a first novel, but she kept talking as if I was going to turn into Tom Wolfe or Norman Mailer. She had unrealistic expectations, which is strange because otherwise Cleo was as hardheaded as they come."

"Did you have problems selling the novel?"

He laughed. "Freddy tells me you're a bookseller. What do you think?"

"That books like *Starvation Hill* come along once a decade." I added, with reluctant truth, "And that you probably had a hard time placing it. Publishers don't like risks." I hung on doggedly. "The house that did print it . . ."

"Wheeler Incorporated." He looked as if the name tasted sour. "They went out of business. The receivers remaindered *Starvation Hill* about three weeks after it was published. Since I'd never seen a check for the advance—"

"What!" That stunned me, though it shouldn't have. Jay was scowling.

Tom looked away as if the confession embarrassed him. "I was a patsy." He dug at a clump of beach grass with the toe of his sneaker. "When the committee told me *Starvation Hill* had won that book award, I had to tell them it was already out of print. They were sympathetic but it was a damned awkward situation. I felt like a fool."

Jay made a growling sound.

"What did Cleo think of that?" I asked. "Were you divorced by then?"

"We split six years ago, one of those no-fault California divorces. If she'd known about the book she would have felt vindicated." He smiled a small, wry smile. "I was damned glad she didn't. It was not a good year for me. The IRS audited my tax returns and reclassified writing as my hobby."

I drew a sharp breath.

Tom's mouth twisted. "Technically, I'm not a writer at all, I'm a fisherman."

"Can they do that?" Indignation sharpened Jay's voice.

"Can and did. I wasn't earning enough from writing. Until I sold *Small Victories* last year I couldn't even have got a hearing."

I said, "*Small Victories* has to be doing well now."

Tom nodded. "It's selling. When the critics liked it, the secondary rights people put the paperback rights up for auction. That brought in a nice chunk of cash, or it will when everything's ironed out. The film rights sold, too. I can file as a writer next year."

I cleared my throat. "Are you going to?"

He grinned. "I thought it would be more entertaining to see if the feds audit me again and insist I'm a fisherman."

"Maybe they'll classify fishing as a hobby this time," I offered.

"Did Cleo Hagen know about *Small Victories?*" For the first time Jay sounded like a cop.

There was a long pause. A car passed our house going south. The driver craned to look at us. We were due for the Siege Curious.

Tom said, "Cleo's information was out of date. I didn't enlighten her."

Jay's face stayed neutral. "She thought you were broke?"

"People with Cleo's resources have no trouble doing credit checks on peons like me. She knew what I made last year to the dollar, and she knew I'd sold *Small Victories* for a modest advance. She hadn't heard about the rest."

"So she offered to buy your house out of the kindness of her heart?"

Tom was watching Jay with dark, wary eyes. "She knew how I felt about the place and she thought she could take it from me."

Jay raised his eyebrows. "A motive for murder?"

"It would have been last year. This year I can afford a lawyer."

I had been doing some adding up. "When you said you were going out on a boat on Labor Day, you meant working."

Tom nodded. "Yeah, Darla's Uncle Henry lets me crew when I need cash. It gets a little uncomfortable in winter, but I've been working on the boats off and on since I turned fifteen."

If you fell into the ocean off the Shoalwater Peninsula you would die of hypothermia within twenty minutes. In summer.

Tom was saying, "At least fishing doesn't do weird things to my head."

I kicked at a clump of dunegrass. "You're being inconsistent. You said writing copy was like a game . . ."

"I said as long as I could think of it as a game I could go on doing that, but writing anything else while you're in a book mucks up your sense of language. I'm better off fishing." He added, when he caught my unbelieving stare, "Maybe not financially. Better off as a writer. *Small Victories* was a fairly cynical attempt to produce a commercial novel."

I scuffed the sand. "It's a good book!"

He said coolly, "It's solid contemporary satire and the research cost $17.42 counting a library fine."

"Cost-effective. The IRS should love it."

"That's what I thought. It's my IRS book."

I said, "The next one's not satire, is it?"

"No. I'm doing this one for myself, which means I'll have one hell of a time selling it. I hope and trust *Small Victories* will not win prizes."

"For God sake, Tom, why not? I keep saying it's good. Bonnie thinks it's the best thing she's read in ten years. Why are you putting down your own success?"

He flushed. "I don't want to be locked into contemporary satire."

"I suppose that could happen." It did happen. I had seen too many writers imitating themselves to doubt it.

Jay frowned. "What's wrong with satire?"

Tom bent down and pulled a strand of beach grass. "You have to stay angry."

"That's bad?"

"Every time my outrage slackened, I'd think about the IRS auditor and tough it through another scene. I don't like forcing that kind of anger." Tom twisted the grass blade into a knot. "*Small Victories* was a cardiovascular accident waiting to happen, and thanks to the Wheeler fiasco I couldn't afford health insurance."

Jay was rubbing his arms against the chill breeze. "You aren't joking."

"No."

"So Cleo Hagen knew about your financial troubles."

"That's right. And she was going to push me to sell the house."

"Do you think the Hagen company will keep after you?"

"I doubt it. They don't need my place. If they'd needed it, they would've wanted Bonnie's, too. The cottage was on the market almost a year."

"At $35,000?" I still found the prices incredible.

"Is that what she paid for it?" Tom didn't even sound interested. "Cleo offered me $75,000. Just enough to stay within the limits of probability. If she'd wanted land, she'd have snapped up Bonnie's place, and grabbed for this one and Matt Cramer's lot, too. But she didn't. She was just trying to get at me."

Jay tugged at his mustache, eyes on Tom's face. "If I were you, I wouldn't repeat what you've said to Dale Nelson. He thinks the offer for your house meant you had to want Cleo Hagen alive and dealing. That's the only reason he didn't arrest you."

"Do you think I killed Cleo?"

"No." Jay didn't hesitate.

Tom scuffed sand. "I wish to hell I knew who did it."

"Want me to try to find out?"

I stared at my husband. Ordinarily he despises what he calls civilian interference in police cases. I had underestimated his outrage.

Tom drew a long breath. "If you're serious, yes. Strange as it may seem, I loved Cleo. I didn't like her, mind you. I couldn't live with her. But I did love her."

"Will you cooperate?"

"Yes. I can't say it'll break my heart if the killer turns out to be Donald Hagen."

Jay's face closed. "If he is, I'll find out. I called my mother yesterday. My late stepfather—Freddy's dad—had a lot of connections in California real estate. I told Ma to cash in her favors. She keeps in touch with those people—or her lawyer does."

The thought of my mother-in-law, Nancy, playing detective tickled me so much I was ready to call her myself.

Jay was saying, "Of course you realize I'll have to give whatever I find out to Nelson—if it seems relevant to the official investigation."

Tom shrugged. "I have no beef with Dale. He's trying to be fair, and he isn't the sort to make an arrest without a strong case."

Jay stuck out his hand. "I'll do what I can, then."

Tom shook it. "Thanks. I keep saying that...."

"Uh, I think Bonnie wants us across the street," I said.

When we got to the porch, Bonnie announced that she and Darla had finished and that Matt Cramer had called from the hospital. Lottie was going into surgery to remove a bloodclot in her brain. That cast a pall.

We waited an hour for the sealant to dry on the walls. The taupe paint went on fast. It looked awful. When I saw the grungy brown I almost had another fit of weeping. However, the paint did dry lighter. Tom and Jay nailed the strips of wood to the baseboards in short order while the female contingent gave the fireplace its first coat. The disappearance of the red brick almost convinced me the walls needed color—but not taupe. Though we spent a lot more time painting the woodwork, the chore went surprisingly fast with all of us working. I kept my eyes averted from the taupe walls.

Jean Knight called again, horrified to hear of the shooting. She volunteered to cancel, but I had got the bit between my teeth. Besides, if Jay was serious about doing an independent investigation, he would want to meet the McKays. They represented an important focus of hostility to what Cleo Hagen had stood for. In a sense, Cleo and Annie McKay had been rivals for power in the community. I wondered how seriously Annie took her leadership role. I wondered how she felt about Tom's book.

We painted and grazed in the kitchen and painted some more. Bonnie's soup was tasty, though less interesting than mine. Jay took a couple of official calls and Tom one. Two reporters left messages. We kept painting. By ten I had to admit that everything except the floor was looking as good as it was going to look. Tom thought we might get away with two coats of acrylic. Jay held out for three. Bonnie yawned. I sent her home and we headed for our bedrooms. Darla and Freddy were still brooding over the computer.

As Jay and I snuggled into the big bed, the first rain hit the French doors. I listened, drowsing.

"You ought to drive to the hospital tomorrow," Jay murmured.

"To see how Lottie's doing?" Rain rattled the windows. "You're right. It's my turn."

"Flowers."

I nestled against him. "She'll still be in intensive care. Jay?"

"Mmm?"

"I don't like taupe."

He didn't answer. The wind gusted and the rain poured down. I decided to let my grievance ride.

EIGHT

I DROVE TO KAYPORT in my old Toyota, which was rapidly approaching classic car status, around nine Saturday morning. At that hour, Darla hadn't yet appeared and Freddy was still asleep. I had no idea how late he had worked on the computer. We had touched up the walls and woodwork, and Tom, Jay, and Bonnie were gearing up to finish the floor when I left.

I had decided to leave the final transformation to them, partly because the sight of the taupe walls depressed me and partly because I needed to shop. We were out of Coke, beer, bread, cold cuts, coffee, and butter, and I had my holiday meal to buy for. I also decided to stop at the hospital. Matt would appreciate the gesture.

The previous night's rain had blown inland, but it was still overcast and whitecaps scalloped Shoalwater Bay. I took the county road that paralleled Highway 101. On weekends, the main route attracted a maddening combination of RVs, sports cars, high-wheel pickups, ancient Lincolns, and rusty beaters. This was a holiday weekend.

The Ridge Road, as it was called, ran along the bay. Thick groves of pine and spruce, intermingled with laurels and other evergreen brush, grew up to the narrow shoulder. On either side of the road, bulldozers had shoved out clearings for mobile homes. More pretentious dwellings dotted the bay side. Where the forest gave way to open pasture or cranberry fields, very deep drainage ditches hugged the asphalt.

There was little traffic. I kept the Toyota at the speed limit. About three miles south of the town of Shoalwater, I had to slow to forty for a tiny old man driving a long, long Cadillac, vintage 1975. As I waited for a straight stretch where I could pass, a jacked-up pickup drew in behind me and began tailgating.

I gritted my teeth and kept a respectful distance from the Cadillac's bumper. The pickup nudged closer, so close I could see little through my rear window but the truck's electric blue bug shield. The old guy oozed down to thirty-seven miles an hour. I kept my distance.

Finally we rounded a blind curve dominated by tall spruce, and the road stretched ahead, clear for half a mile. I depressed my turn signal, glanced back, and hit the accelerator. As I began to pull left, the pickup roared past me, horn blaring. He almost knocked my side-view mirror off.

I braked, swearing, glanced ahead and passed. The old man peered at me through the steering wheel.

I settled back at the speed limit and took a long, calming breath. I hadn't seen the license number of the rapidly vanishing pickup, though it had Washington plates. It was silver blue and muddy, and I had caught a glimpse of a driver, a passenger, both wearing baseball caps, and a gun rack. Not exactly a rare sight on Ridge Road. Reporting the incident would be a waste of energy. AAA ought to propose a new category of reckless endangerment, DIT—driving under the influence of testosterone. Fat chance. The driver had not been a teenager. I chugged along, nerves sparking.

At its south end, the peninsula widens. Ridge Road crosses the state route that leads east along Shoalwater Bay and west to Kayport. I turned west and entered a sluggish stream of tourists.

Kayport is technically a river port, fronting the mouth of the Columbia where the ship channel crosses the treacherous bar. From the marina, which shelters commercial fishing boats and private pleasure craft in democratic juxtaposition, you can just see the long bridge south and the odd, upthrust mountains beyond Astoria. I should have crossed the river to shop in Astoria because the prices were lower there, but I didn't feel like wasting an hour driving back and forth.

I entered the lot of the shopping mall and pulled into a parking spot near McKay Construction Supply. Jay wanted a packet of fine-grain discs to sand the first coat of acrylic.

I found the discs, savoring the aroma of raw wood that permeated the big building, and got in line behind a man

with an armload of deck stain and a woman lugging a new
toilet seat. Then I spotted the latex paint. The sight was too
much. I bought a gallon of antique white, the same color as
the enamel we had used for the woodwork. I told myself the
latex was for the hallway, but I knew I was going to cover at
least one of the ghastly taupe walls with it.

McKay Supply was all business—no chatty clerks or
cracker-barrel spectators. Five cashiers ran the customers
through like logs on a green chain. Outside, I stowed paint
and paper in the trunk, then moved the car across the lot to
the huge new Safeway.

I was pushing a cart along the produce aisle looking for
mushrooms when Jean Knight hailed me. We exchanged
greetings and Jean bored in on the shooting, avid for details.

She was shorter than I, most women are, and a few years
older, with a short, curly perm and bright brown eyes. Jean
was a pleasant woman but I didn't care for this new avidity.
I gave her the bare facts.

"Yes, but what was he like?" Her eyes gleamed.

"Hagen? Armed and stupid." I spotted mushrooms.
"Listen, Jean, I have a prejudice against blocking super-
market aisles. I'll meet you at Aho's in half an hour and give
you the skinny on the shooting over coffee, okay?" Aho's
was the bakery.

She agreed, grinning, and we moved on.

Since Tom's garden produced everything but obvious
California objects like avocados, I didn't dally. I selected
chanterelles and fresh brown mushrooms for a pilaf, got a
couple of lemons and a lime, went on to the deli, and
through the checkout line.

Aho's was the only professional bakery on the peninsula, but it was world class. I had already used their baguettes to good effect. I chose a couple of sandwich loaves—
sourdough and oat bran—and drooped over the croissants,
then moved on to dinner rolls. In the end I bought two
dozen dill rolls, because dill and salmon go together,
thought of Freddy, softened, and added a bag of tollhouse
cookies and a dozen hazelnut biscotti. Then I ordered a

caffe latte and went in search of Jean. She hadn't come in yet, so I took a small booth and sat down to sip.

I was wondering if I ought to break into the biscotti when Jean materialized, trailed by a woman out of L.L. Bean. It had to be Annie McKay.

Sure enough, Jean was making the introduction. She must have called the *Gazette* office as soon as I moved on to the chanterelles.

Annie McKay shook hands and settled opposite me in the booth while Jean went off to get coffee. The editor was about Jean's height, and her cotton cardigan coordinated with the dominant salmon pink of her Madras plaid shirt. Her sunglasses rode on the top of her head like an Alice band for trendy grown-ups. I was glad I'd taken the trouble to shed my sweats in favor of stirrup pants and a big cotton sweater.

"So you're Lark. You've had a strange introduction to the peninsula."

I explained that we'd been in the area three months and made amiable generalizations about the scenery while I tried to puzzle out who she reminded me of.

"We delude ourselves that our bit of wilderness is unspoiled. God knows it's beautiful, even as it sinks under the weight of mobile homes and tacky construction." As she raised her hand to smooth her already smooth blond hair, the large gem on her ring jogged my memory. Annie McKay reminded me of the corpse. She was also the blond woman I had seen at the fire, clutching a notepad.

I listened to Annie filling me in on the consequences of uncontrolled growth, compared her to Cleo Hagen, and thought strange thoughts.

After my first wild leap of imagination, I realized Annie had had at least one solid reason to appear at the scene of the fire. She was the editor of a small paper. Probably her reporters lived in Kayport. She lived in the Enclave, much closer to Tom's house.

When Annie concluded her impassioned denunciation of clearcuts, I murmured, "I imagine you're right. They're certainly ugly. Say, didn't I see you the night Tom's house was firebombed? At the fire, I mean."

Her face went blank.

"On the edge of the county road. You were holding a notebook and watching the fire crew hitch up the long hose."

Jean had returned with two coffees. She laughed. "Were you at the scene of the crime, Annie?" She plunked down beside the editor and beamed at me. "Jim says Annie has a great nose for a story."

Annie took a sip of the hot coffee, grimacing, then set the mug down. She gave me a tight smile. "Reporter's instinct. I didn't stay long."

That was true.

Jean was chattering about the *Gazette*'s coverage of local news events and got off on the sports reporter's brilliant account of the state basketball tournament. When she wound down, I asked about her plans for the school year. I sipped cooling coffee. Annie related an amusing story about a boatload of sport-fishing tourists, and Jean cross-examined me, but nicely, about the shooting. Annie didn't take notes. In fact, there was no sign of the notebook.

When I reached the part about the graffiti the evidence team had left in our hall I noticed the time. I had spent nearly an hour in Aho's. I might as well have driven to Astoria. I disengaged as gracefully as I could and took my purchases to the car.

The small, two-story hospital stood on a knoll above Highway 101. Because of the peninsula's large population of elderly residents, the hospital had a good cardiac unit. It provided general care as well, though it was always in economic peril. A nursing home lay to the north. I found the hospital's visitor lot and went into the reception area.

As I had supposed, Mrs. Cramer was in Intensive Care and not allowed visitors or flowers. I thanked the volunteer at the reception desk and was about to leave when Matt entered from the east corridor. I went to him.

"Lark...." His face brightened. "Did you come to see Lottie?"

"Yes, but they told me she's still in Intensive Care. How is she, Matt?"

"Better, better." He blinked several times. His eyes were bloodshot. "She said my name when she came out from under the anesthesia. She's much better."

I congratulated him and said I hoped she'd be able to come home soon. Apparently that was the right wish. He began to tell me all about the excellent home care he would give his wife, how she was looking forward to seeing his dahlias and the ocean. I listened, impressed by his optimism and saddened by the possibility that it might be misplaced.

Eventually I remembered the invitation I had left on Matt's answering machine, so I translated that for him. At first he didn't think he could make it, but when I mentioned that Annie McKay was coming, he brightened again and said he'd try to drop by. Annie was Matt's local hero. I told him to be sure to come and gave his arm a pat.

"Thanks, Lark." He beamed at me. "Lottie and I are glad you moved in next door. Glad. We'll see you Monday."

As I pulled onto 101 what he had said registered and I shivered. "Lottie and I . . . we'll see you . . ." Matt rambled a lot. Was he getting worse? I hoped the "we" was just a manner of speaking.

The traffic on 101 was exasperating but less threatening than the pickup on the Ridge Road. I reached home around one.

Freddy was up and working at the computer. Darla had phoned to say she'd come over Sunday. The others had beavered away, though, and the first coat of acrylic was almost ready to sand.

My ravenous crew fell on the groceries while I gloated over the floor. It, at least, looked splendid. The taupe walls loured. Bonnie restrained me from slapping antique white on them by volunteering to help me paint the hall. We covered the smears and diagrams with one quick coat while Jay, in stocking feet, sanded the living room floor for the last time. Tom was laundering his clothes.

Dale Nelson drove up as Bonnie and I were agreeing on a second coat and contemplating the woodwork. I answered the door.

"Ma'am." He touched the brim of his hat.

"Come in. We were just destroying the scene of the crime."

His invisible eyebrows shot up and he peered into the hall. "Oh. Guess it's okay. Husband in?"

Jay had been carrying the sander out to the car. He came into the hall from the back of the house. "Hello, Nelson. Did the sheriff tell you I was off the case?"

"Yeah." Dale entered and shook hands with Jay, looking glum. "I can't say I'm glad. We still haven't found a weapon in the Cleo Hagen murder. The m.e. says there was sand and salt in the wound, so we're looking for likely driftwood. The killer probably tossed it in the surf. There were some stray fibers on her clothes. Her handbag turned up in a dumpster outside the Pig'n Stuff." The Pig'n Stuff was a drive-in near the Shoalwater approach. Near the resort site, too.

Jay offered the deputy a cup of coffee and they went back to the kitchen. Bonnie and I looked at each other.

"I need a coffee break," I said.

She grinned. "Me, too. And I bet Tom could use a cup." She stuck her head in the utility room. Dale seemed a little alarmed when the three of us entered the kitchen, but Jay wasn't on the case, after all. I saw no reason why we should be excluded. Bonnie and I *had* discovered the body.

We munched biscotti and sipped coffee and let the gents talk. Tom's presence seemed to constrain Dale more than Bonnie's and mine did, which probably meant Tom was still high on the suspect list.

Dale was euphemistic when he described the rest of the m.e.'s findings. That was all right with me. Jay didn't press for details either, though he said he found the time of death interesting. Cleo Hagen had been killed between eight p.m. and midnight the evening before we found her body. It was a wonder the crows hadn't done more damage than they had.

Donald Hagen had been released on bail—substantial bail, as far as the judge was concerned, but probably peanuts to Hagen. He was staying at the Fisherman's Rest in

Kayport. I hoped he would hate it. He had been told not to leave the county.

Tom's arson case was being handled by another deputy—the fat one who had come with Dale when he answered the 911 call. Nelson said they were still trying to identify the perpetrators' four-wheel-drive pickup.

That reminded me of my little contretemps on the Ridge Road. I told Dale about it and he looked thoughtful. Jay listened in grim silence and the muscle at the hinge of his jaw jumped.

Nelson said, "Two guys—what color were the baseball hats?"

I closed my eyes and visualized. "Green with a gold logo. At least the passenger's was. I couldn't swear to the driver's."

"Softball league," Nelson murmured. "How tall was the driver?"

"Heavens, I don't know. Pretty tall." I thought about the tiny man who had peered at me through the steering wheel of the other car, the Cadillac, and did a mental comparison. "Probably six feet."

"Skinny?"

"Heavyset. I didn't get a good look at his face but it was kind of red. I think he wore a Levi's jacket. But the guy was surely just another tailgater. He didn't try to run me off the road. He just passed too close. It was probably some innocent logger or fisherman in a hurry to get to Astoria for a Saturday on the town."

Nelson took a bite of coffee-soaked biscotti. "Mmm. Metallic blue pickup, probably GMC, blue insect screen, gun rack, buddy riding shotgun. Remember any of the letters on the license plate?"

I closed my eyes again and tried but I couldn't get a clear picture. "Sorry."

"That's okay, Lark . . . Mrs. Dodge."

"You can use my first name."

He said ruefully, "I shouldn't. Not on a case. Ms. Bell, I'm damned sorry we haven't got anything on your vandal. You hear noises at night, call 911. We're keeping a car in the area for the time being."

Bonnie said, "Gosh, that reminds me. I found the message. You know, the one that was with the dead seagulls. It blew into the grass beside the road, so most of the writing's washed away. Shall I get it for you?"

Nelson stood up. "I'll come across with you. That could be useful, real useful. Thanks for the coffee, folks. Tom, keep your nose clean, hear?"

He and Bonnie left, Bonnie looking pleased with herself. I went back to my paint roller, and Jay and Tom got out their lambswool applicators, took off their shoes, slid on kneepads left over from my basketball days, and started the final coating of acrylic in the living room. Bonnie was gone quite a while. I was just heading back to wash out the rollers and pans when she slipped in the front door.

"He says they can probably do a lot with the message. Isn't that terrific?"

I agreed. There was a feeling in the air, as if the wheel of events were about to turn. Toward solutions, I hoped.

We worked quickly and so did Jay and Tom. Freddy came down, freshly showered and duded up, as we began to clear away our equipment.

He blinked at the bright hallway. "It looks great, Lark—but I'm glad you left the bullet hole."

He was off to join Darla's family for the afternoon and evening. At any other time, the invitation would have sent Freddy into transports of delight. Now he just wanted to work on the computer.

I wondered if Darla's access of hospitality had anything to do with the fact that Freddy had given most of his attention to the computer the day before. I almost said something about playing hard to get but refrained. He wasn't yet ready to be teased about Darla.

Tom said he was going clothes shopping in Astoria when the dryer finished its last cycle. It turned out that his wardrobe consisted of the contents of his laundry basket—everything else had burned in the bedroom closet. The loss was at least partly covered by insurance, but Tom hated buying clothes. He hoped I was going to appreciate the sacrifice when he showed up at my party with the price tags hanging out.

I gave him a kiss on the cheek that raised Jay's eyebrows and said I didn't mind sweats, but Bonnie was energized. She *loved* shopping for clothes, even men's. They drove off together an hour later in Bonnie's Escort. Tom looked a little white around the eyeballs but Bonnie was cheerful. I hoped she wouldn't make him buy Day-Glo spandex.

Jay and I had the house to ourselves for the first time in days. We did not neglect the opportunity, and I think we worked through his little twinge of jealousy. We also found ourselves admiring the living room, from time to time. Jay liked the taupe. *Chacun à son goût.*

That evening we lay in bed together reading. I finished *Small Victories*. Tom was right about the tone. Funny or not, it was a very angry book. He was wrong about the quality. He had avoided the clichés of contemporary satire with the deftness of a sapper negotiating a minefield. Half the comedy derived from the reader's disappointed expectations. I liked the novel almost as much as Bonnie had, but I didn't love it the way I loved *Starvation Hill*.

Jay was blue-penciling the latest chapter of his textbook. He had got reading glasses that year. They made him look like a terribly sexy scholar. He finally ripped them off and laid the manuscript on the end table beside them. I was about to suggest that he put the glasses back on, so I could remove them, when the phone rang.

We had deactivated the answering machine at eight on the off chance that Jay's mother would call from L.A. with information about Donald Hagen. Jay picked up the receiver. I could tell from the frozen expression on his face that the news was bad, and my heart thudded into double time. He slid out of bed and carried the phone across the room, still listening. "Yeah. Okay. Be right there." He hung up.

"What is it?" I was envisaging Bonnie and Tom, who had not yet returned, at the bottom of the Columbia. That was a narrow bridge.

"Freddy," Jay said. "He's at the hospital in Kayport. Darla, too. Somebody ran the Trans Am off the road."

"Oh, God." I was on my feet and reaching for my jeans. "Was he . . . is he . . ."

Jay said with careful calm, "Nelson says he thinks they're just shaken up. Cops had to use the jaws of life to get Freddy out, though. I'm off, Lark. I want you to stay here in case Ma calls."

"Jay!"

"Please."

I swallowed my chagrin. "Okay. Give him my love."

Jay was throwing on his clothes.

"And don't drive too fast." That was a feeble attempt at humor. Jay is compulsively law-abiding.

He peeled out, spraying almost as much gravel as Freddy had. I went into the kitchen and brewed coffee. My mother-in-law didn't call and I didn't call her, though I was strongly tempted. There was no point in frightening Nancy unnecessarily.

Half an hour later Bonnie and Tom returned. I heard the doors of the Escort slamming and went to the front door. Bonnie was loading Tom's arms with paper bags and oblong boxes, and they were laughing. Tom made his way across the road with his pelf. I opened the door for him.

He grinned at me around a large sack. "Waiting up?"

I explained about Freddy and the smile vanished. Tom headed back to the guest bedroom to dump his purchases. I was pouring coffee for both of us when he entered the kitchen.

"Do they know what happened?"

I gave a careful summary of the little information I had, adding, "Freddy wanted to stay home tonight and work on your computer. I wish he had." I was near tears.

"He's a good kid. Did they say anything about Darla?"

I'd half forgotten Darla was Tom's cousin. I shook my head. "Jay will call as soon as he has definite news."

We sat for a while, sipping coffee and thinking our own thoughts. I didn't doubt Tom's were even darker than mine. His family had bad luck with automobiles.

The phone rang and I leapt for it.

Jay said, "It's okay, Lark. I'm bringing him home."

"Thank God." I asked him about Darla and he said the hospital wanted her to stay overnight for observation. She was complaining of a stiff neck. That didn't sound life-threatening and I let my breath out in a long sigh. Jay said he'd call his mother in the morning and we hung up.

Tom rang Darla's parents. When he had finished talking, I said, "Is she..."

"Marie said the doctor on duty thought she was fine."

"Phew."

"If they find the driver of the other vehicle, I'll strangle the bastard myself."

NINE

MY SALMON WAS THAWING. I took it out, knocked off the slush, and inspected it. It didn't stare back at me with little beady eyes, fortunately. The head and tail had been removed. The flesh was bright pink. The roast weighed fifteen pounds, so the fish must have been a twenty-pounder. I wondered how long Tom had taken to reel it in, or did commercial fishermen do that?

I had been broiling salmon steaks and filets all summer, but I had never roasted a whole salmon. The prospect was making me apprehensive, so I got out the Rombauers to see what they recommended. Ten minutes per inch at 350 degrees. Wonderful. That would have been very clear if the salmon had been square. Parts of it were thin and parts thick. It was more than a foot long, and three inches wide at the tail.

I brooded. I had time to brood. Jay and Freddy were sleeping in, whereas I had come wide awake at six-thirty, and, when I returned from my run, Tom had already made coffee and vanished. The day before I had relished solitude. Now I wanted company.

Freddy was sore all over, or so he had said when Jay brought him home. He was worried about Darla and mournful over the Trans Am. The police had told Jay the car was totaled. Since Freddy was on pain medication, we shoved him into bed almost as soon as he walked in the door. Then we tried to sleep. I succeeded, after half an hour of tossing and turning, but I was drowsily aware that Jay lay too still beside me, the way he does when he can't stop thinking and doesn't want to wake me. I heard him get up some time around three-thirty, and I fell back asleep before he returned. So it wasn't surprising that he was still out cold at eight-thirty, when I finished my shower and dressed.

I slid the salmon back in the fridge and *The Joy of Cooking* back on its shelf. I drank another cup of coffee and nibbled biscotti with it. Then I remembered we'd unhooked the answering machine. I reprogrammed it so the phone wouldn't wake anyone with its ringing, and went to look at my beautiful floor and ugly walls.

The sun was shining in a dim watery way. The pale oak of the floor gleamed under its acrylic surface. It felt completely dry and I wished I could start moving furniture in. However, it was safer to wait until the next morning, so I ignored the taupe walls and contented myself with arranging things in the hall.

The hall floor had not been buried under a shag rug, so it looked dark and stained by comparison with the living room wood. My next project. I vacuumed the indigo runner with its conventional border. Bonnie and I had left the door to the coat closet stained dark. I thought the door was mahogany, and it had a beveled glass mirror. The white frame set the wood off nicely, but I gave the surface a polish, just to kill time. Our coat tree was also stained dark. I removed our bright jackets from it, hung them in the closet, and gave the rack a rub, too.

We had stored a small walnut table with an inlaid surface in a corner of the dining room. I dragged the table out and set it at the far end of the hall. Then I hung an oval mirror above it. I was admiring the effect when I heard Tom enter the back door. I joined him in the kitchen.

He was pouring coffee. "Morning. How's Freddy?"

"He seems to be fine—at least he's still out."

He gave me a serious once-over. "Couldn't you sleep? I saw you running."

"I slept better than Jay." I made a face. "I just wake up early. Sometimes that's a nuisance. I finished your book, Tom. I liked it."

"Thanks," he said absently. "Do you want flowers for tomorrow? I have asters and daisies, some dahlias."

"Have you been working in the garden already?"

He smiled. "You run, I garden. I woke about the time you went out—heard you leave."

I poured a cup of coffee. "Want a biscotti?"

"Sure. Is that the singular?" He took one from the jar. "Italian word."

"Heavens, I suppose biscotti is plural. What would the singular be, biscottus?"

He laughed. "I have no idea. They taste good."

We settled into the nook and talked about the salmon for a while. He had heard of the ten-minute rule and told me to measure the *vertically* thickest part. He also offered to make a special mayonnaise his grandmother had served with salmon.

"Is it a Nekana recipe?"

"I don't think the Nekana went in for mayonnaise. No chickens, no olive oil."

I flushed. "I'm pretty ignorant."

"Grandma called it Irish Mayo because it was green—lots of parsley and fresh tarragon."

"She must have been an interesting lady."

"She was a great cook—learned from the nuns. Her family was fourth-generation Catholic and always sent the girls to the convent for polishing. The LaPortes were not happy when their eldest daughter married a heretic."

"Your grandfather?"

Tom smiled. "His family were Methodists. His mother was a leading light of the WCTU, but Grandpa was a free thinker by the time I knew him. The Methodist ladies snubbed my grandmother because she was Nekana, so Grandpa snubbed them. He was a crusty old guy. Never forgave them."

"You didn't deal with the race issue in *Small Victories*."

The smile faded. "I wasn't ready to deal with it, and it's too complicated for a book like that anyway. There's still a lot of prejudice in this area, especially about fishing rights, and a lot of stereotyping of the usual drunken-Indian sort. Darla's probably on the right track with an activist program for the council. And speaking of Darla, I think I'll call the hospital."

"By all means." While he phoned, I took another look at the hall and decided to set a bouquet of Tom's asters on the table. I went back to tell him I'd take him up on the flowers and he was just replacing the receiver. "How is she?"

"Stiff and cranky. I talked to her. They'll release her as soon as the doctor makes his rounds. Her dad's going to pick her up." He expelled a long breath. "There are lights on that stretch of highway. She got a good look at the truck that ran the Trans Am off the road, considering she had to twist against the seat belt to see. Sounds like your side-swiper."

I gulped. I had been hoping the incident on the Ridge Road was idiocy rather than malice. "Somebody's out to get us."

"The thought had entered my mind."

That was depressing so I asked Tom to go with me to cut flowers, by way of distraction—self-distraction.

We came back with armloads of bright blossoms to find Jay grumping over a cup of tea. I knew better than to try to make conversation. Tom and I stuffed the extra flowers in jars of water until I could decide what to do with them. The asters looked just right at the end of the hall. Tom went for a walk and I started poking among the boxes in the dining room, looking for treasure.

I unearthed two framed eighteenth-century maps of the Pacific Coast I had found on a visit to London. I hung northern California to the right of the living room arch and the Pacific coast from British Columbia to Yaquina Bay to the left. Classy. I could barely restrain myself from dragging stuff into the living room, too. I found the woven coverlet.

Jay was on the phone to his mother when I poked my head into the kitchen, so I decided to run across to Bonnie's house. Tom was there drinking coffee. Some walk. He had filled Bonnie in on Freddy's accident and she was suitably shocked. We discussed the marauding pickup without getting very far. I had the feeling Tom was keeping something to himself—he had a brooding, inward look. I left after one cup, in case they wanted privacy.

As I crossed the road a carload of gawkers drove slowly past. Matt's car was gone. The sky was clear. I wondered if Jean had been wrong about the weather. If Labor Day turned out to be sunny, we had gone to a lot of unnecessary exertion. We could have held a barbecue in the backyard.

I pushed the thought from my mind and went into the house. Jay called to me from the kitchen.

"What is it?"

He thrust the phone at me. "Ma wants to say hello. I'm going up to roust Freddy."

I took the receiver and covered the mouthpiece. "That's cruel, Jay. Let him sleep."

"I heard signs of life. He's conscious."

I turned to the phone. "Hi, Nancy. How are you?"

"I wouldn't have a gray hair on my head if I didn't have kids."

I laughed. Her hair was the color of expensive champagne. "Freddy's fine, really."

"I'll believe it when I hear his voice. How about Jay?"

"He's a little tense."

She sighed. "Nightmares?"

"He'll be okay, Nancy. I'm going to make him move furniture."

"That's the ticket. You're my best daughter-in-law, kiddo."

"Your only daughter-in-law."

"At the moment. You're head and shoulders above that twerp Jay married the first time around."

I winced. I am a little sensitive about my height. Jay's first wife, Linda, had not been a twerp, just a psychology major who talked too much shop. At least that was what Jay told me.

"How's the girlfriend?" Nancy asked. "What's 'er name? Marla?"

"Darla. I guess she's okay, too. I haven't seen her yet."

"Is it serious, Lark?" She meant was the relationship serious.

I hesitated. I could hear thumps and groans on the stair. "I'm not sure. Freddy's serious, or was, and now she's showing promising signs."

"They're infants." She added hastily, "And don't ask how old I was the first time around. Jay says you're fixing the house up real nice."

Nancy had married at eighteen, borne Jay, and been widowed at nineteen. Her two daughters were the product of a disastrous second marriage. She was thirty-nine when Freddy came along, the child of her third husband, a successful real estate broker.

I told Nancy about my floor, and how well the taupe walls were going to go with her sofa and chairs. Freddy's arrival made further lies unnecessary. I said hasty farewells and placed the receiver in her younger son's hand. Jay put a mug of coffee in the other and we left Freddy to his inquisition. Jay approved the hall but reversed the position of the maps. He thought it was more tactful to put California on the left.

The afternoon was tranquil. Around three, a live reporter showed up from the *Oregonian*. He was a short, intense guy with a dark beard and hair. Jay gave him a brief statement about the shooting, and I allowed that finding the body of Cleo Hagen wasn't exactly pleasant. A pretty woman the reporter introduced as his wife took photos of us standing on the front porch. They were weekending at Shoalwater and thought they might as well get a color story. They didn't make pests of themselves, but we ducked inside and hid out.

Freddy slept a couple of hours in the afternoon, called Darla, and went back to the computer. Tom and Bonnie drove off to the Pig'n Stuff in Tom's pickup. They offered to bring hamburgers for us, too, but I declined and did a stir-fry for dinner. Nelson phoned Jay around seven to say nothing was happening. That sounded good to me. We all went to bed early.

I woke in the middle of a nightmare that entwined my total social humiliation with the body of Cleo Hagen. The corpse was wearing her sunglasses like a headband. I lay awhile in the dark, sorting things out, before I became aware that it was raining. There seemed to be little wind but the rain was pouring down in a steady, earnest way. It was a wonderfully cheering sound. Vindicated, I snuggled against Jay and fell asleep.

I woke at six-thirty, rested and conscious of happiness. It was still pouring. I sang in the shower, gave Jay a prod, and put on a set of mungy sweats that were made for moving furniture. Then I floated downstairs and brewed coffee. I took a mug into the living room and started making decisions.

By seven-fifteen, both Jay and Tom were staring into their mugs and muttering, Jay over herb tea. Neither man wanted breakfast. I let them absorb two cups apiece, then turned ruthless. When Bonnie came over at eight, already coffeed, we were placing the big couch where it would face the fireplace.

Between the couch and the hearth I had laid a Turkish rug, dark red with the usual flower border. Tom and Jay brought in my teak coffee table and set it in the center of the rug. That was the easy part. My grandmother's platform rocker, ugly but incredibly comfortable, I placed left of the coffee table, at an angle, with an occasional chair on the right. That made a good conversation area.

Bonnie eyed the arrangement critically. "Where are you going to put the hassock?"

"In the basement." There was no basement, owing to the high water table. I hated the hassock.

Jay said, "Poke it under the window for the time being." I helped him carry the hassock out of the way. It was a heavy sucker, two feet by four and knee high. It would have made some child a handsome bed. Our big west-facing window looked out over the dunes. The hassock slumped beneath it like a dead whale.

Tom was sitting in Grandma's rocker, head back, eyes closed. As we collected to admire the couch, he gave a single rock and opened one eye. "Dibs."

Jay laughed. "Too late, buddy. I married Lark to get dibs on that chair."

The doorbell rang. Bonnie answered it and returned, after a considerable delay, with Clara Klein. Bonnie's arms were loaded with bulging plastic garbage sacks and Clara carried a narrow parcel wrapped in brown paper. Both women were wet.

"Ho." Clara set her parcel on the mantel. "Coffee."

I went off to the kitchen for the necessaries and kept telling myself not to say anything about the taupe walls.

When I returned with coffee and the ashtray, Bonnie had plunked the garbage bags into a corner and Clara was waving a lit cigarette at the hassock. "What the hell is that?"

"A hassock."

"It came with the couch."

Jay and I spoke simultaneously. Tom was still in the rocker, eyes closed. The faintest of grins touched his mouth.

Clara growled. She paced the length of the hassock, glowering at it. I was about to say we didn't have to keep it in the room, but she forestalled me. "Do you have another of those Turkish rugs—a little one?"

"Uh, a small runner. But it doesn't match...."

"A runner. Just the thing. Bring it over here."

I went into the dining room and dug in one of the storage boxes. I decided I would damned well say what I wanted to say about the taupe walls.

I tossed the rug on the floor at her ladyship's feet.

"Great," she said, waving smoke from her eyes. "Now unroll it so I can see. Wonderful. Bonnie, where...oh, I see." She stubbed out her cigarette and set the ashtray on the windowsill. Two strides took her to the garbage bags. She rummaged in one and came up with three pillows. She strolled back, tossed the pillows on the north end of the hassock, and circled to get a better look.

I gaped. "It looks like a fainting couch!"

Clara grinned. "That's the idea, but something's missing."

"Uh, what?" I was admiring the pillows. They didn't match anything either but looked great with the hassock and the six-foot-long Oriental runner, which was dirty beige with the usual ornate border. The pillows were wild prints, one geometric, the other two chintz flowers, and mostly indigo and dark red with bits of white. The geometric one was large, the others smaller.

Clara brooded, head down. By this time she had a full audience. Both men and Bonnie were trying to see what was missing, too.

"That's it." She gave a sharp nod. "Tom!"

"Ma'am?"

"Don't be a smartass. I need a heavy hook, the kind that screws in."

"Like a plant hook?" Jay asked. "I have a couple in the garage. Shall I get one?"

Clara beamed at him. "That's the idea. What's your name?"

I was horrified and made introductions immediately. Jay must have been out of the room on her previous brief visit. They shook hands and I could see that Jay had fallen in love. He went off after the hook.

"Tom, you bring a chair or something and see if you can find the roof joist. Lark, your Boston fern."

My Boston fern was the pride of my kitchen but I was beginning to get the idea. I went to fetch it and Bonnie followed.

"The woman's a magician!"

I climbed up on a chair and unhooked the fern, lowering it carefully because I did not want to add repotting to the day's labors. "I'm beginning to feel hopeful about the walls."

"They'll look fine." Bonnie took the pot and I kept the wires that had held it from tangling. We edged back into the hall with our burden and brought it to Clara as Tom announced he had found the right spot for the hook.

The fern looked splendid hanging just north of the hassock. I supposed it would survive on western sunlight.

All of us stood in the archway the better to admire Clara's set piece.

"It looks as if Sigmund Freud were expecting a short patient," Jay murmured. "How about a small bookcase there on the south wall, Clara? We have one of those law office affairs with glassed-in shelves."

"Absolutely, but only if you put books in it. No *objets d'art*."

"Are we barbarians?" Jay's mustache twitched.

Clara chortled. "Now, where is this famous coverlet?"

That, I was eager to show her. I had already laid it, wrapped in an old bedsheet, on the dining room table.

Clara approved. "That fabric is older than your great-grandmother, my sweet. Eighteen forty or I'm a pickled herring. Natural linen and indigo wool in a whig star pattern. What a relief you have proper stretchers. I have seen people *nail* granny's hand-stitched quilt to the wall, speaking of barbarians."

The entire east wall of the room was a blank with the guest room behind it. I was pleased that Clara and I had the same spot in mind. She made the men set the proper hooks on the right studs, changed her mind once about the height, and finally allowed them to hang the coverlet.

"Oh," I said. "Oh, Clara."

The taupe wall was exactly the right color to set off the hanging. What was more, the focus of the whole room swung. No one could enter without admiring the coverlet.

"Oh," I said again, mute with gratitude.

Clara looked pleased. "Now, let's finish up. I have to be at this ill-omened arts council picnic at noon." She made us set the two squishy suede chairs below the coverlet with a low walnut table and a small lamp between them. What I really needed, she said, was proper track lighting for the hanging, but that would have to do. Then she dug out her garbage bags again.

Out came more pillows—smaller ones in assorted sizes and lovely clashing prints. She tossed them at the couch and it looked as if God intended suede couches.

The two small windows on either side of the fireplace were surmounted by heavy brass curtain rods, pitted and green with age. I had meant to replace the rods. Clara got up on the chair and tangled a swath of fabric over each of the eyesores and, lo, they looked like *Country Living*. The fabric had a cream field with a stylized rose pattern in the exact dark red of the Turkish rug.

"H-how did you find it?" I stammered. "It fits in exactly."

Clara made an impatient noise. She was tearing the paper off her thin parcel. "You mentioned the Turkish rug. That's turkey red, kiddo. Whatever you do, don't polish the rods. The patina's gorgeous."

It was. I had almost covered the rods with white enamel. "Wherever did you find the fabric?"

"Oh, stashed away in a closet. If you like it you can pay me for it later. I think it cost twenty bucks."

"I like it." I also liked the effect on the taupe walls. They were rapidly receding.

"Consider the pillows my housewarming present. I had them stashed away, too."

"Oh, Clara, thank you. I'll remember you in my will."

"I'll take the platform rocker," she said. "Tom, what do you think?" She had cleaned the handsome print of Killer-whale. She climbed on the chair and set the print in the center of the mantle.

"Looks great," Tom said. "Thanks, Clara."

Clara winked at me. "On loan from the Lindquist gallery." The print matched nothing in the room and looked exactly right. Clara jumped down. "Don't hang it. That's a great mantel. Just let the print lean against the chimney. And if anybody puts anything else up there, chop his hand off."

She whipped out a cigarette and lit it. I dashed to the windowsill and fetched her ashtray. I would buy her a large ashtray of her very own. Maybe I would save her butts as relics. She had saved mine.

Clara left in a flurry of thanks, tossing suggestions over her shoulder. If I wanted to be twee, I could hang photographs of ancient relatives in oval frames. Or I could put up some decent watercolors. She liked the maps in the hall.

I said she should at least stop by after her picnic was rained out and take credit for the room. Clara laughed. I stood on the porch and waved until the Karman Ghia disappeared.

"God, what a woman," Jay said.

Tom looked complacent. "I told you she has a great eye."

I gave him a hug. I hugged Bonnie. I kissed Jay on the mouth. Then I fixed breakfast. It was the least I could do.

TEN

JAY TOOK A LONG CALL from his mother that afternoon, about the time I decided I had done enough fussing over the dining room table. Tom went off to the garden for more salad makings, Bonnie was at home whipping up canapés, and Freddy, even stiffer than he had been the day before, was groaning over the computer.

Jay took the call upstairs. When I had double-checked the wineglasses, I decided to shower and get dressed, so I heard snatches of his end of the conversation. What I heard was not very revealing, but he looked interested. He was taking notes.

Since it was still gusting rain out, I set aside my optimistic California sundress and pulled a black-and-white geometric tunic over a black turtleneck and stirrup pants. I finished my eye makeup and got out a pair of dangly earrings.

Jay hung up. "You look more like a magpie than a lark in that outfit. Very forthright colors." He smiled at me.

I scowled. I laid the black-and-white earrings down and took out a set of fuchsia disks.

"No," he said. "Try the turquoises."

The turquoises were a birthday gift. I held them up. "They're too small."

"Trust me. They do great things for your eyes."

This manipulation never failed. I stuck the silver wires through my earlobes and got up from the vanity. "What did Nancy have to say?"

"A lot, but it'll keep. The Hagen Group is overextended. They got caught when the California real estate market sagged."

"Hooray! Maybe they'll pull out."

He shrugged. "Not if this is the last property they own that's appreciating in value."

"Maybe a rich benefactor will buy it and donate it to the Nature Conservancy. Are you going to wear those jeans?"

"Why not? It was supposed to be a barbecue."

I groaned. The jeans were covered with paint spatters. When Jay dressed for work he always looked creased and spit-shined, no doubt a consequence of his years in uniform. At home, though, he tended toward laid-back California Grubby. Since he was a reasonably laid-back Californian, that was not remarkable.

Downstairs I put on a chef's apron and started sautéing mushrooms and garlic for the pilaf. Tom returned, wet and windblown, washed the salad greens for me, then drifted off to get dressed. He was not talkative. I thought he felt apprehensive about meeting Annie McKay.

The Knights arrived at five-fifteen. Bonnie was arranging platters of crab puffs and cheese straws on the buffet, and Jay and Freddy had not yet come down. I ripped off my apron, tossed it on one of the storage cartons that still lined the dining room wall, and went to answer the doorbell.

I took Jean's exquisite tart of cranberry-glazed pears, babbling greetings as she made ritual kissing noises and Jim said something hearty. They hung their rain gear on the coatrack while I showed Bonnie the dessert. They greeted her like old friends and chose California wine over northwest beer.

We moved to the living room. Jay had laid a fire in the grate, so I lit a long match while Jean and Jim exclaimed over the room's transformation. Their approval seemed genuine and Jim, at least, had seen the room in its bordello apotheosis. Jean stood in front of the coverlet, sipping her wine and looking at it while I poked the fire. Bonnie was telling Jim about her break-in. He scrunched his broad, good-natured face into sympathetic lines.

The wind gusted and a puff of smoke set me coughing. "I thought you said the chimney was swept, Jim."

"So the Jorgensons told me." He reached around me and jiggled the lever that worked the draft. The air cleared.

"Thanks."

"No problem. You've done wonders with this room, Lark. I wouldn't have recognized it."

I explained about Clara Klein's magic act.

Jean said, "The painter? No kidding?"

"She's a friend of Tom's."

Tom and Jay came in as if on cue and another round of greetings followed. Jay had changed into respectable jeans and a sage green cotton pullover. I gave him a wifely smile.

I took their orders—Full Sail for Jay, Pinot Noir for Tom—and when I returned found that Jim was cross-examining Tom about the fire. They seemed to know each other at the level of politeness. The men took their drinks. As I turned to go back for the canapés I caught a glimpse of Bonnie. She was standing by the fireplace, nursing her wineglass, and she was looking at Tom with a gleam in her eyes. I slipped back across the hall in a thoughtful mood.

Bonnie had found Tom interesting from the first, and not just literarily. That night I could see why. He was wearing a white tennis sweater with a navy edging stripe over a navy turtleneck, tan slacks, and those hard-soled brown moccasins so beloved of menswear catalogues. Suitable and un-surprising for a casual holiday dinner, though Bonnie had forgotten to tell him it wasn't trendy to wear socks. The change from gray sweats and jeans was startling. I had the feeling Tom would look like a million dollars in an Italian silk suit. Just then he looked like an author. Bonnie could be pleased with her handiwork.

I hoped that was what the gleam meant. I felt protective of both of them. They had been thrown together by cir-cumstance, but they didn't know each other, and Tom was a murder suspect. There was no getting around that. I didn't believe he had killed Cleo Hagen, but I foresaw a lot of grief for Bonnie if he were charged. If I wasn't misinterpreting the gleam.

As I picked up the platter of crab puffs, the bell rang again, so I carried the canapés with me when I went to an-swer the door. Darla stood on the porch.

"Good heavens, Darla, are you all right? How did you get here?"

"My brother." She was wearing a white beaded head-band, an orthopedic neck brace, and a tan raincoat.

I peered past her. "Ask him to come in...."

"He has a date." She stepped in and began sliding out of her raincoat as I looked around for a place to set the crab puffs down. Under the raincoat, she wore a cream tunic with fringed sleeves and slim pants, very pretty, but the collar looked odd.

I gripped the platter. "I wish you'd called. I'd have sent Jay for you. Come in and get warm. We have a fire going. Would you like wine or beer . . . ?"

She hung her coat on the rack, wincing. "I'll have a Coke, thanks. I'm still on pain medication."

I led her to the living room. "Jim, Jean, here's Darla Sweet. Darla is Tom's cousin. She and my brother-in-law were at Stanford together . . ." I set the platter on the coffee table. The Knights shook hands and I explained to Darla who they were. Unnecessary. Jean and Darla had met at the hearings that dealt with the resort variances.

Jay installed Darla on the platform rocker. She gave a small grunt of pain as she sat, then smiled up at him. "Thanks. Everything looks terrific. I like the print on the mantel."

Tom said, "It's mine. On loan. Are you okay, kid?"

She grimaced. "I feel like a liability suit. Where's Freddy?"

Where was Freddy? I hadn't noticed his absence.

Jay said, "I'll go get him. He's probably still working on the computer."

"And I'll get your Coke." Bonnie was explaining the wreck to the Knights as I made for the kitchen. Tom was watching Darla.

I poured Darla's Coke into a tall glass and added a couple of ice cubes. Thumps from above suggested that Freddy would be coming down, too, so I poured another Coke. I glanced at the clock. It was almost six. Where were the McKays? Should I start the salmon? It was oven-ready, wrapped in foil in a glass baking dish. I removed it from the refrigerator and set it on the stove top, then stood, wavering. Should I preheat the oven? I decided to wait until the McKays showed up. I hoped my guests wouldn't be falling down drunk by the time the food was ready.

I delivered the Cokes and went back to the dining room for the cheese straws and the stack of little cocktail napkins. The crab puffs were disappearing rapidly. Everyone seemed cheerful, so I decided not to brood. The doorbell rang again. I caught Jay's eye and he slipped out of the room to answer it. He returned with Clara Klein.

"Hello, everyone. Looks like a party." She gave a comprehensive grin and whipped out a cigarette. I had cleaned the ashtray and set it on the bookcase. I retrieved it and brought it to her.

"Thanks, Lark. You're the Knights?"

Another round of greetings, a glass of chardonnay. I was glad to see Clara. Her picnic had washed out. She was starving, she said. I thrust the cheese straws at her and glanced at my watch. Five minutes.

Tom appeared at my elbow. He said quietly. "Go ahead with the salmon, Lark. It tastes good cold."

I gave him a grateful smile and went off to preheat the oven. I had just turned the knobs to the right settings when the doorbell rang again. This time I didn't run to answer it. I set the pilaf in my warming oven and strolled back to the hall. Jay and Bonnie were doing the honors, Jay removing wet rain gear.

Annie McKay spotted me and advanced with her hand held out. "Sorry we're late. Unexpected company. What a nice little house, Lark." At least she didn't say what a nice little bullet hole. She was wearing a raw silk pantsuit that reminded me again of the corpse.

I forced a smile and shook hands. "I'm glad you could come."

"Through the deluge. So hard on California transplants."

I said coolly, "Jay and Bonnie are Californians, but I'm from upstate New York originally. After seven years of drought, I relish rain. Is this . . . ?"

Annie placed a proprietary hand on the big man's sleeve. "My husband, Bob. Lark and . . ."

"Jay," I supplied. "And our neighbor, Bonnie Bell."

"Jay teaches law-enforcement classes at the college, Bob." Annie gave her husband a look that said behave yourself. She held out her hand to Jay. "Bob's on the Board of Trustees."

Jay shook her hand, rumbling a polite noise.

Bob McKay gave us a blurred smile, the men shook hands, and Annie and Bonnie nodded at each other. I told the newcomers to place their drink orders with Bonnie, excused myself, and went back to my salmon.

Bob McKay looked more like Jim Knight than like his own cousin. Slightly shorter than my six feet, he was blondish gray with thinning hair, and rather red-faced. He wore an expensively casual jacket that deemphasized his belly, and no socks with his moccasins. His eyes were watery blue. He looked as if he had been massaged within an inch of his life.

I formed no impression of Bob's personality, but I got the distinct feeling he wasn't thrilled to be where he was. I wondered if Annie dragged him to all her community encounters. I wondered what he did for a living.

I chunked the salmon in the oven and set the timer. As I went to the refrigerator for the salad, Bonnie entered. She almost bumped into me and she looked rather flushed.

"What is it?" I backed away to give her room.

"I found our fall guy."

"What?"

"For the murder. Bob McKay."

"Good grief...."

"He wants a Beefeater martini up with two olives."

"Uh..."

"And the s.o.b. pinched my ass."

"Oh, Bonnie, I'm sorry." I meditated. Neither Jay nor I drink the hard stuff as a rule, so my liquor supply was scanty. My mother's tipple is gin and tonic. She swears it's impossible to distinguish one gin from another in a mixed drink. She always buys whatever is cheapest. I had a fifth of Old Bathtub.

I took out a small glass pitcher and tossed in half a dozen ice cubes. "Get me the jar of olives from the door of the fridge."

"Right."

I measured two jiggers of gin onto the ice cubes. "The sherbet glasses are in the cupboard."

Bonnie set the olives on the counter and brought a glass. Fortunately it wasn't the kind with a hollow stem. "Where's the vermouth?"

"A martini takes vermouth? This one will be very, very dry." I strained the cold gin into the glass, stabbed a couple of green olives with a toothpick, dribbled a bit of olive brine into the mess, and gave it a stir with the olive-laden toothpick. *"Voilà."*

She went off, grinning, and I turned back to the salad. I was amazed at my calm. I was also aware that I was missing the main drama, so I checked the timer and my watch and bolted for the living room.

Tom and Freddy had ranged themselves behind the platform rocker. No way was Bob McKay going to pinch *Darla's* ass. She sipped her Coke demurely as Annie, who was sitting on the suede couch, said something earnest to her about injunctions. So Annie knew about that.

Jay, bless him, had taken Bob over by the fainting couch for a little conversation. Bob seemed to be listening. He took a swallow of martini. I didn't see him grimace. Jim was adding a stick of wood to the fire. Bonnie and Jean hovered around Clara as she pointed out the peculiar excellence of the whig star motif repeated, small scale, in the border of the coverlet. I drew a long, relieved breath and wondered where my wineglass had disappeared.

It was on the bookcase. I retrieved it and sat by Annie. She seemed tense, intent, but I had no way of judging whether or not that was her usual state. She was explaining an obscure point of property law in clear, simple language. I wondered why. Darla had been admitted to the law school, after all, and it was *her* injunction.

When Annie ran down, Darla just shrugged. "Yeah, I know. *State of Washington versus Engebretson,* 1974."

Annie frowned.

"The injunction may not work, but it's bound to create another delay. We've kept the crew leashed all summer. They didn't even try to start construction."

"They did rearrange the landscape." Tom took a sip of his Pinot Noir.

Darla glanced up at him. "They could have had the main lodge up and running by now, Tom."

"I suppose so. At least they extended the sewer and water lines."

Annie fiddled with a cheese straw. "You think that's a good thing?"

"It's the only course if the commissioners are going to permit new residences along the beach."

"They should freeze housing construction entirely."

Tom cocked an eyebrow. "Isn't that kind of radical?"

She gave a short laugh. "Don't quote me."

"I wouldn't think of it," Tom said, so mildly I wondered if she caught the jab.

She did. I felt her stiffen and glanced at her face. Her eyes had narrowed.

I jumped up. "Oh, my goodness, it's almost time for me to check on the salmon. Tom, you're the expert. Help!"

I thought he was amused. He set his wineglass on the coffee table and followed me.

"Well, look at that," I muttered when we were safe in the kitchen. "Twelve more minutes."

Tom laughed. He laughed harder when I told him about the Beefeater martini.

"Is Bob a lush?"

The smile faded. "He may be my cousin, but I don't know him very well. He's probably bored. Annie shouldn't force him to socialize with locals. He's not running for office."

"Good thing. He pinched Bonnie."

Tom swore under his breath.

"Will you go back and tell everyone dinner in fifteen minutes?"

"Sure. Take it easy, Lark. I promise not to pick a fight with Annie."

I sighed. "What if *she* picks the fight?"

He grinned and left. Bonnie returned almost at once with an order for another martini. Bob had a discriminating palate.

Dinner went well. Matt Cramer came as everyone was shuffling past the salmon, plates in hand. He said he could only stay half an hour. He had to go back to the hospital. I fed him and introduced him to Annie, who was so gracious I began to think kindlier thoughts about her. I also felt sorry for her. Bob absorbed three glasses of wine with dinner.

Matt ate two helpings of tart. He thanked me twice and went off looking almost chipper. Annie had made his day.

"Who was that?" Bob McKay asked. Nobody answered him. I had served coffee with the tart and been reminded of the old saw about wide-awake drunks. He pinched *my* ass.

Darla and Freddy creaked upstairs to the computer. The rest of us drifted into the living room and Tom built up the dying fire. Jay pulled one of the chairs from the pair below the coverlet into conversation range and offered it to Jean. Annie had resumed her place on the couch. She was talking about zoning laws.

Bob McKay, eyes glazed, wandered over to the hassock, as if distancing himself from the subject or the company. Jim pulled the other easy chair into the circle, and Jay and Tom fetched a couple of dining room chairs for themselves. I made a mental note to give smaller parties or buy more chairs.

Jay was explaining about Matt Cramer's wife in response to a question from Jean. I poured another round of coffee and sat on the couch beside Annie, who listened to Jay with every appearance of sympathy. She ignored Bob's withdrawal.

"Matt lives next door, doesn't he?" Clara had taken over the rocker as by divine right. She leaned back, rocking gently through her veil of smoke.

"In the mobile home just south of us."

"The one with the beautiful flowers," Bonnie murmured.

Annie settled deeper into her corner of the suede couch. Her nose wrinkled. "Mobile homes are a key to overpopulation, in my opinion. If we got rid of the trailers on the peninsula there'd be no problem."

"Now, Annie, you've been in the business." Jim hitched his chair. He looked uncomfortable. "Fifty percent of my sales are of mobile homes."

"Maybe that's why I gave up selling real estate." Annie smiled a perfunctory smile as if to soften the tart response.

Clara said, "Where would you put the people, Annie?"

Annie shrugged. "Mobile homes are mobile. That's the advantage, I assume."

Tom gave the fire a poke. "In other words, let somebody else deal with the problem."

Annie looked at him. "Somebody else is not trying to protect a hundred or so square miles of semiwilderness, including a stand of old-growth timber. This is a unique ecosystem. . . ."

"So is downtown Chicago."

Jim gave a salesman's laugh and Clara said, "Be fair, Tom."

Bonnie was watching from the chair opposite the rocker. "I can see Annie's point. Some of the mobile homes are well designed, and Matt's yard certainly looks nice, but, face it, those trailers on the flat east of you are real eyesores. I bet they weren't there when you were growing up, Tom."

"No, and I agree that their septic tanks cause problems, but Annie's solution is worse than no solution at all." He picked up his coffee cup from the teak table and took a swallow. "I notice your editorials have never suggested bulldozing the mobile homes, Annie."

She set her empty cup on the table. "You read my editorials?" She didn't sound flattered.

"Every week. Also the Police Blotter."

I hid a grin. Jay and I subscribed to the paper primarily because of the section devoted to local police reports. It contained amazing items about runaway cows and cars stuck in the sand on the Shoalwater approach. The *Gazette* printed all the police calls, so serious matters appeared occasionally, too, but the effect of the Police Blotter was soothing and statistically balanced—far more accurate than crime reporting usually is.

Annie bared her teeth in a wider smile. "I'm glad you read the Blotter, Tom. You're going to want extra copies of next week's to give to your relatives."

Tom said, "I'll save one for Bob."

Annie made an impatient noise.

I glanced at Bob. Coffee or no coffee, he had passed out on Clara's pillows. He must have been well lubricated when he arrived.

Jean Knight rose. "It was a great dinner, Lark, and we're impressed by what you're doing with the house. We have to go now, though. School tomorrow."

Jim shook hands all around and told Clara to call him if she wanted to list her house. Jay and I saw them to the door. Bob was snoring.

I thought the Knights' departure might signal the breakup of the party, but no such luck. When we returned, everyone had settled in. Bob's snores had moderated to a drone, and Clara and Annie were discussing the upcoming Show of Homes. That seemed like a safe topic. The McKay house in the Enclave was scheduled to be open.

I sat in the chair Jean had left, the better to see Annie, and Jay took my place on the couch.

As I sat, Annie gave me what I can only describe as a gracious smile. "You must see all the homes, Lark. I think you'll find ours interesting."

"How long does the show run?"

She made a moue. "Five endless days, but it's all in a good cause. Wednesday through Sunday."

"I'll try to make it."

Annie beamed. "How nice to see the Knights socially. We are so fond of Jean."

"Who's we?" Tom was gazing into his coffee cup.

Annie flushed an unbecoming red. "All of us in the Nature Conservancy, of course. By the way, Tom, that application you sent to the Historical Trust will be rejected. I wish you'd called me before you went to all that work. I could have told you your house doesn't qualify."

Tom set his wine down. "I wonder why I'm not surprised."

"What's that supposed to mean?"

Clara's rocker creaked. "It doesn't matter now, does it?"

He drew a breath. "No, I suppose not." He glanced around the group. "When I heard that Cleo was heading up the resort project, I started looking around for a defensive wall."

Annie gave a short laugh. "No wonder. *De mortuis*, Tommy, but that woman was a menace."

He looked at her. "I had the feeling Cleo was going to target my house. This spring it occurred to me that if it was listed as a historical site I could drive her lawyers crazy."

I was remembering the letter to the state historical society I had glimpsed in the stack of printouts. "Is the house historical?"

Tom shrugged. "Probably not, if you're thinking in terms of New York, or the missions in California. Anglos didn't settle this area until the 1850s. The house was built in 1901."

"The year the *Mollie McKay* sank?" Jay has a BA in history and enjoys digging into local background.

Tom nodded. "It was built of wood salvaged from the wreck. The fact that my great-grandfather was the skipper who ran the ship aground adds a degree of oddity to the story. He built the house where he'd have to look at the hulk, on what was then the shore. The beach has widened since then."

Bonnie said, "Gosh, you'd think the preservation folks would jump at the chance." She turned to Annie. "Why don't they want the house?"

Tom said, "Too many bathrooms, Annie?"

Annie snorted. "A privy would certainly be more authentic."

"But so unsound ecologically." Clara gave another small rock. A bland smile curved her lips. "Those houses in the Enclave that are listed as sites surely have modern bathrooms. What's the hitch? Not big enough?"

"We do look for distinguished structures. And also," Annie added delicately, "a level of funding I'm afraid Tom can't manage. Owners must guarantee sufficient moneys to see to the upkeep in perpetuity. We're a nonprofit organization, you know, and wholly financed by *private* funds."

"Well, hell, and there I was looking for a big tax write-off," Tom mourned.

I stared at him. "I thought you were trying to protect the house from your ex-wife."

"That, too. Killing two birds with one stone."

Annie did not smile. "You mean you can raise the endowment?"

"Annie, my little skunk cabbage, I sold the film rights to *Small Victories*."

There was a moment of explosive silence. Clara laughed.

"They're going to film it?" Annie's cup clattered in its saucer. She set it down.

Tom gave an elaborate shrug. "Who knows? Directors are always taking options they never pick up."

Clara lit a cigarette and batted the smoke away. "If the paperback sells as well as the hardcover, Tom, somebody will film it." She darted a malicious glance at Annie. "On location."

"Oh, wow." Bonnie's eyes were shining.

Annie said through her teeth, "I was going to let bygones be bygones, Tom—"

"Sure sounds like it," he interrupted.

"I read that...that travesty as soon as I found out about it, and I've been refraining, ever since, from mentioning it in print."

"I noticed."

"It's a tissue of slanders. How you could trash your own hometown, how you could do that to Nelda Pickett...."

Tom's jaw dropped. "Nelda Pickett?"

Spots of red burned on Annie's elegant cheekbones. "The Prom Queen. Poor Nelda, she was always so sweet to everybody. My dearest friend." She looked at me, eyes glittering. "Nelda was Homecoming Queen the year Tom and I graduated from high school, a brunette like Tom's stupid character, but nothing like her inside. Everybody loved Nelda. I'll never forgive you for doing that to her, Tom, and I don't care if your novel wins the Pulitzer."

Tom scowled. "What makes you think I was satirizing Nelda?" When she sniffed instead of replying, he went on, "Never mind, Annie. You have a degree in journalism so you must have taken a lit course somewhere along the line.

I write fiction. There's a difference between fact and fiction, remember?''

"Don't feed me that. *Small Victories* is a *roman à clef*. If I were Nelda I'd sue."

"By God, you did take a lit course." He leaned back in his chair and his mouth eased. "The character is a composite. Nobody who knows Nelda is going to imagine she was like that. In fact, the Prom Queen bears a strong resemblance to my ex-wife—and the dead can't sue for defamation of character."

"How convenient for you that she's dead."

There was a long pause. I thought Clara was going to say something, but she didn't.

Tom said mildly, "I can sue."

"Freedom of expression. There is such a thing as the first amendment."

"I thought it applied to everybody, even me. Are you on the library board, too?" He turned to Bonnie. "There's a town in eastern Oregon that wouldn't permit its librarians to order H. L. Davis's *Honey in the Horn*. Naturally, the ban convinced everybody Davis was writing about that town."

Bonnie laughed. "I read *Honey in the Horn* in a Literature of the West course—great satire."

"Yes, it is. It's still in print after fifty some years, too."

Jay said, "And it's probably still banned from the town's library."

Tom gave him a rueful smile.

Annie got the point. "I am not a book burner."

Tom's smile faded. "I didn't think you were, Annie, but you have to allow me my version of our wonderful high school experience."

I said, "I expect the world is divided into people who loved high school and people who hated it. Jay slept through his."

Jay said virtuously, "I was driving a pizza wagon, nights."

"I made the rally squad," Bonnie volunteered. "It seemed like the acme of my existence for at least five years afterward. College was terribly deflating."

"Hey," Freddy said from the archway. "Hey, Tom, I did it!" He was carrying a stack of paper.

Tom stood up. "You mean you got it working?"

"Piece of cake. The hard disk's sealed, of course, but I was worried about a short in the motherboard. It's okay, though." Satisfaction had ruffled Freddy's red hair.

Darla was standing beside him, glowing like a full moon. "He saved your novel, Tom!"

"Christ, don't tell me there's going to be another one," Annie said.

ELEVEN

FORTUNATELY FOR FREDDY'S self-esteem, Annie spoke half under her breath. I don't think he heard her.

Tom went over to him at once and took the printout. "You're a miracle-worker, Freddy. I'd slap you on the back but I don't think I ought to. How'd you do it?" The right response.

Jay and Bonnie clustered around Freddy and Darla, but I spared a glance at the two women before I joined the throng. Clara was rocking gently and smiling. Annie looked frozen.

I gave Freddy a light pat he probably didn't notice. He was busy laying on the technical explanations. Darla watched him with shining eyes. Hero worship. Very promising.

I went back and sat on the couch, trying to think of some way I could soothe Annie without dishonesty.

Clara gave a decisive rock. "I'm so relieved, Lark. Tom has been sweating that book. To lose it after all that work..."

Annie said, "We really should go."

I couldn't very well say don't rush off. I cleared my throat. "Would you like another cup of coffee?"

"No, I would not." She started to rise.

Clara said, "Sit down, Annie, and don't make an ass of yourself. I can see why *Small Victories* upsets you, but the last thing you ought to do is raise a ruckus."

Annie made a noise that was half gasp, half laugh, and sank back onto the couch.

"That novel is going to make a very large splash. You might as well get used to the idea. Think up a way of damning it with faint praise, if you have to, but don't let anyone see that Tom got your goat. Least of all Tom."

"But it's not accurate."

Clara sighed. "So it doesn't reflect your feelings. Why should it? Tom has already established himself as a writer of the first rank. Even if he's lying through his hat, everyone's going to praise the book for its honesty. You should be telling your subscribers how clever he is."

"Why do you care?" Tears stood in Annie's eyes.

"I care about Tom," Clara said bluntly. "I'm also fond of the peninsula, though, and I hate feuds. In spite of your silly prejudices, you do a lot of good work for the community, Annie, and you run a good newspaper. You can't derail Tom's success. He's earned it. But you can take advantage of it. Run a rave review."

Annie sniffed but she was looking thoughtful.

"Magnanimity," said Clara, whipping out a cigarette and lighting it, "is never a mistake."

"Is it a good book?"

"Well, if you haven't read it all the way through, you certainly ought to. What if it does win the Pulitzer Prize?"

Annie's eyes narrowed.

"The first one took the Western Book Award. Did you review it?"

Annie shook her head.

"Hometown boy makes good, huh?"

Annie flushed. "I didn't hear about it until it was out of print."

Clara gave an exasperated cluck. "You could have asked Tom for a copy. Last year you did a front-page story with photos on a local cookbook author. Not to mention running excerpts of Judge Claymore's boring memoirs. Very small potatoes compared to *Starvation Hill* and *Small Victories*. Do you blame Tom for feeling hostile? He has a normal writer's ego."

"You could interview him," I suggested.

Clara said, "That's the idea."

Annie made a face.

At that point, the others rejoined us, still chattering in computerese. Jay said, "Do we have any champagne, Lark?"

"No, but there's a bottle of Cointreau."

"We ought to drink a toast."

I caught Bonnie's eye and we scooted off in search of liqueur glasses.

I think Freddy enjoyed the limelight, but he had enough diffidence not to be obnoxious. All of us drank to his achievement except Bob, who slumbered on. Annie toughed it out. I had to admire her. She even took a sip when Bonnie toasted the new novel's success. I'm not sure Tom noticed. He carried the printout of his manuscript off to the guest room for safekeeping.

When Annie did announce her departure, there was the small awkwardness of rousing her sodden husband. She seemed not to know what to do. She shook his shoulder and he mumbled something, but he didn't sit up or even open his eyes. In the end, Jay and Tom had to take a hand. Between them, they got Bob upright. He stumbled along obediently until they reached the front hall. Then he turned belligerent. He took a swing at Jay and connected with the coat rack, and, when Tom extricated him, called him a Siwash bastard.

"Oh, Bob..." Annie sounded near tears.

Tom was rather tight-lipped. "All right, Colonel. Time to move out."

Annie choked. "That's not fair."

"No," Bob said. "Oh, no. Going to be sick."

I opened the front door and held the screen wide. "Get him outside, Jay."

This time Bob didn't resist. He staggered onto the porch under his own power and stood there swaying.

I stayed in the doorway and let Tom, Jay, and Annie wrestle Bob out to the gleaming Mercedes. He threw up on Matt's rosebushes.

When he was safely strapped in the car, the two men started back to the porch and Annie went around to open the driver's door. She stood in the rain for a moment, then turned and marched back to the porch.

She came straight to me. "I'm sorry we spoiled your dinner."

Tom said, "Dinner was fine."

She ignored him. "I should have left Bob at home. I knew he'd been drinking all afternoon."

I said, "It's okay," though it wasn't.

Her mouth trembled. "I won't apologize for anything I said, but Bob...he's been drinking this way since last week. I don't know what to do."

Jay said, "Maybe he should see a doctor, if he doesn't drink so much ordinarily."

Annie's face set in bleak lines. "He drinks. He doesn't have enough to do. But he's been much worse the last few days."

Tom said, "He tried to hit Jay. Has he turned violent?"

"With me?" She looked at him as if he had suggested she vote the socialist ticket. "No. Bob's a gentleman."

Jay said patiently, "What Tom's saying and what I was trying to suggest is that you're dealing with a sudden personality change. Sometimes there's a medical reason."

Her eyes widened. "A brain tumour?"

"Or a mild stroke. There are other possibilities."

Her mouth eased. "I hadn't thought of that. Maybe you're right. Thank you."

"It's worth a try. Is there someone to help you get him into the house when you reach home?"

She nodded. "Our son's still here—his school doesn't start for a week. We'll manage. Thanks. I am sorry."

We said good night and she left.

Freddy and Darla were giving Bonnie the lowdown on word processors. When we entered, Darla broke off an impassioned defense of the Macintosh and said, with the righteousness of twenty-one years, "He was really disgusting."

Freddy nodded. "Gross."

Bonnie raised her coffee cup. "I'll drink to that."

Clara rocked. "Now, children. Don't be judgmental."

Darla said with spirit, "I don't see why not. I'll bet he makes jokes about drunken Indians."

I said, "He called you a Siwash, Tom. I hesitate to ask, but what does that mean?"

Tom shrugged. "In the Chinook jargon, it was just the way the native people referred to themselves. They called the white men Bostons."

"When white men use the term, they usually say 'dirty Siwash,'" Darla added. "In English it's a pejorative."

Tom sat in the chair beside Bonnie. "Actually, he called me a Siwash bastard. My mother decided to pioneer single parenthood before it was fashionable and the McKays disapproved. You will note that I didn't clean his clock."

Jay had fetched the coffee from the dining room. "If you'd knocked him out he would have been easier to get to the car."

Tom grinned. "True. Half a cup, thanks."

Freddy refused a refill. He was looking droopy. "I guess I don't know why having the McKays to dinner was such a big deal."

Clara rolled her eyes. "They wield a lot of power, my innocent. The family practically owns Kayport. Not to mention a vast Victorian gothic in the Enclave that's listed with the Historic Trust. Annie's not a bad egg. Robert McKay is no prize, but he's usually smoother. He's a womanizer."

"No shit." Bonnie took a sip of hot coffee and set her cup down. "I put up with that kind of harassment when I worked in an office, but I'm getting less tolerant in my old age."

Me, too.

Jay said, "A womanizer. Who, Clara?"

She contrived to look embarrassed. "He was supposed to be having a flaming affair with Cleo Hagen."

That created a silence that might have been called pregnant. I wondered what Clara's game was. She hadn't planned to come to the dinner, yet here she was springing revelations on us.

Jay leaned forward.

Tom frowned. "Are you sure? Bob wasn't her usual type."

"I'm not sure. I'm relaying gossip of the lowest sort. His affairs have been notorious for years, though."

Bonnie said, "What a jerk. Why doesn't Annie divorce him?"

Clara lit a cigarette. "The McKays own the *Gazette*. I imagine she could get a decent divorce settlement if she hired a good lawyer, but she couldn't stay on as editor of the family newspaper. She'd hate to lose the paper."

Jay said, "Did *Annie* know Cleo Hagen?"

"I'm sure they met." Clara flicked an ash. "But probably not socially. Annie's very busy these days, what with the paper and her committees and causes. She doesn't hang around cocktail lounges. Bob is at loose ends, though. His brother took over management of McKay Construction last January. Bob does a little investing and sits on a couple of boards, but he's basically retired. He's at the Blue Oyster almost every night. I've seen him there with Cleo and the real estate crowd."

"Including Jim Knight?" Jay asked.

I gaped.

Clara sighed. "I was hoping you wouldn't ask that. Jim and Cleo had a thing going when she first came up here, but it didn't last long. Rumor had it that Jean was ready to leave him, but I guess they ironed out their differences. That was, oh, sometime in the fall. Cleo took up with Bob in January or February, after he retired and started staying at the house in the Enclave during the week. Before that he had an office in Olympia."

Jay set the empty coffeepot on the freshly painted hearth. "What about Donald Hagen, did you see *him* at the Blue Oyster?"

Clara shook her head. "I've never seen the man at all. In fact, I used to wonder if he existed."

I retrieved the pot. "He exists."

Tom said, "Any other juicy tidbits, Clara?"

"Ungrateful whelp." She stabbed out her cigarette. "Tom said you were thinking of looking into the murder, Jay. I decided you ought to know about Bob and Cleo, but I wasn't sure how to approach the subject credibly. Fortunately, Bob made it easy for me. I thought he might."

Jay said, "Nelson will have to know."

She nodded. "Okay. He should interview Kate Dalton. She's the bartender. And the other regulars."

"He did a round of questioning there. He got nothing."

"They're a clannish bunch and Bob is a regular."

Tom scowled. "So was Cleo."

Freddy said, "You mean that drunk did the murder?"

"Freddy!" Darla sounded genuinely alarmed. She was going to be a great lawyer. Jay was frowning at his brother, too, but Freddy had leapt to the natural conclusion.

"There's one other thing, Jay." Clara pushed herself up and the rocker thumped. "Kate said she thought Cleo had an assignation with Bob the evening before she was killed. Cleo was gabbling about it with her drinking buddies."

"No shit?" Jay had stood up, too.

Tom let out a long whistle.

I clutched the empty coffeepot lest I drop it. Bonnie's eyes gleamed behind her glasses. Freddy and Darla just looked bewildered.

Jay said, "Do you mean the evening before her body was discovered or the night before that? Cleo Hagen was murdered around ten p.m. Between eight and midnight, the m.e. said, but they think nine or ten."

It was Clara's turn to stare. "I was assuming Cleo was killed the morning Bonnie and Lark found the body." She looked rather frightened. "The date was for the evening before Cleo's body was found, the evening she was killed. If I got the story straight. You ought to ask Kate."

"I will," Jay said. "Dale Nelson will, too."

"I'd better go," Clara muttered. "Before I get myself in deeper water. I don't like cops. I beg your pardon, Jay, but I was a labor organizer in my salad days. And I taught art at San Francisco State during the sixties. I saw a lot of heads busted." She fiddled with her handbag. "It would be less inflammatory to say I don't always trust the law. But I thought somebody ought to look into Bob's activities. And Annie's. I don't know that there's anything to cover up, but the McKays have the power to squelch an investigation."

Jay said dryly, "In this case, it'll be the McKays versus Donald Hagen and company. I don't envy Dale, trying to find out the truth with witnesses stonewalling all over the place."

Clara turned to me. "It was a fine dinner, Lark, and the living room looks great with a fire going."

I shifted the coffeepot to my left hand and shook hands. Though my feelings were ambivalent, I said I was glad she had come.

By the time we saw Clara off it was almost ten. Freddy was yawning and Darla looked as if her pain pills had lost their effectiveness.

Bonnie was gathering coffee cups. She set Darla's on the tray. "You ought to be in bed, honey."

"I'm not a child."

Tom said, "I'll drive you home, brat."

Bonnie stacked Freddy's cup on Darla's. "You can use my Escort while I help Lark clean up, Tom. No need to get the pickup. Just a sec and I'll dig out my keys."

"I can drive her," Freddy protested.

"Not with that medication in you." Jay retrieved Bob's coffee cup from the floor by the fainting couch. It was half full.

"Aw, Jay."

"He's right, Freddy." Darla rose and gave him a peck on the cheek, wonder of wonders. "I'll call you in the morning."

Freddy grumbled but raised no further objections. Jay headed straight for the telephone. He left a message for Dale Nelson.

We had cleared away the worst of the debris, Jay and Bonnie were drying wineglasses, and I was transferring salmon to a storage container by the time Tom returned.

He looked beat. "Where's Freddy?"

I closed the refrigerator. "He went to bed."

"I ought to thank him decently."

"Tomorrow." Jay set the last wineglass in the cupboard. "Want a brandy?"

Tom groaned. "An Alka-Seltzer would be more my speed."

"Well, have a chair."

"I was thinking about turning in."

"Soon," Jay said ruthlessly, "but I need answers to a couple of questions first."

Tom sat on one of the kitchen chairs. "No, I was not holding out on you. I did not know about Clara's barroom gossip. I don't hang out at the Blue Oyster."

"That was one of the questions."

He leaned his head against the high chair back, eyes closed. "What else?"

"Did you see the McKay Mercedes the night of the murder?"

"Annie's car? No."

"What does Bob drive?"

"A Blazer, usually."

"I don't suppose you saw it cruising the neighborhood?"

"No, I was writing." He opened one eye. "You could ask Ruth Adams. Or those summer people across the street."

"Or Matt," I added. "Bob might have used the Shoalwater road."

"I'll talk to Matt and Ruth." Jay joined Tom in the nook. I began to set up the coffeemaker for morning. Bonnie wiped counters around me.

I said, "You called Bob 'colonel,' Tom. Out by the coat rack. What was that about?"

"Ancient history. I owed him a jab."

Bonnie went in to the nook and I followed. "I minored in ancient history," she said.

Tom looked rather flushed. "It's a long story and doesn't bear on anything important."

I took a seat. "Annie said you weren't being fair."

"I wasn't. He...Bob is four years older than I am. He was finishing up a business degree at the UW the year Annie and I graduated from high school. His grades were lousy so that meant his student deferment would run out, and he'd done ROTC. He was going to be commissioned a second lieutenant in the army."

Jay said, "Nineteen sixty-eight?"

"Sixty-seven." Tom shifted in his chair. "The half-life of second lieutenants was about a month at that point in the war, though he might've been sent to Germany or Korea. I was conscious of his little problem because I didn't have a student deferment. I started working on the boats as soon as I graduated and I wasn't planning on going to college. So I decided to see if I could get a transfer to the National Guard when I was called up. I got my draft notice at the end of August. Right about this time of year."

"What happened?" Bonnie was fiddling with the salt and pepper shakers but her eyes were on Tom.

"Well, I wrote a really heart-rending plea to the effect that here I was an orphaned child and the sole support of my aging grandparents. There was no truth in it and my grandfather hit the ceiling when he heard what I'd done. He didn't raise me to be a goddamn draft dodger, et cetera. The local draft board agreed. I went off to Fort Lewis for basic about the time the *Gazette* announced that Second Lieutenant Robert McKay had been posted to the Washington National Guard."

"That's not right!" I admit I'm naive about government.

Jay said, "String-pulling was pretty common."

"And not popular. One of Darla's uncles was killed in Nam. I had a tour of duty. I spent enough time in combat to find out that the Great Spirit did not intend me to be a warrior."

"Doesn't take long." Jay was a combat medic.

Tom grimaced. "After Tet, I did nine and a half months typing letters and requisition orders for the battalion. I typed fast. I was also converted to the idea of higher education."

I said, "What about Bob McKay?"

Tom shrugged. "He stayed with the Guard, made patriotic appearances at Fourth of July picnics. By the time the Gulf War rolled around he was a company commander. You will recall that units of the Washington National Guard were activated and shipped to Saudi Arabia. Bob got sick."

"A chicken colonel," Bonnie muttered.

Tom grinned. "Now, now. That was the kind of irresponsible talk that circulated on the docks. Myself, I think it's a damned good thing Bob stayed at home. He did have an operation."

"Elective surgery?" I asked.

Jay said, "You're right. It's not relevant, but it is entertaining. I have some other questions, Tom, but they'll keep.
Has Darla been able to come up with an ID on the driver of
that pickup?"

Tom got up, yawning. "She's a funny kid. I think she
knows something. She's talking like a lawyer, though. Alleged this and alleged that. She won't name names unless
she's sure of herself."

"Unlike Clara," Jay murmured.

"I think Clara's terrific," Bonnie said firmly. "G'night,
everybody. It was a spectacular evening, Lark."

"In spite of Bob McKay?"

She grinned. "Because of Bob McKay."

TWELVE

TUESDAY MORNING I slept in until almost eight. When I stumbled down to the kitchen, Jay was up, dressed, and on the phone. He had made coffee.

I poured a cup and sat in the nook, sipping and staring vaguely in the direction of the Cramers' mobile home. The sky was overcast but it was not raining. The wind had died. Jay was talking to Dale Nelson, that much I registered without taking in specific content, and the conversation had been going on for a while. My coffee had cooled enough for me to work up to a real swallow before Jay hung up.

"Think you'll recover?" He retrieved his academic-tweed jacket from the back of his chair, shrugged into it, and smiled at me.

I gave a dignified nod. I had drunk one and a half glasses of wine and two sips of liqueur the previous evening, but I felt hung over. "Any news?"

He hesitated. "About the murder? Nothing definite yet. They'll be getting more of the technical data in, now that the holiday's over."

Technical data. I digested that. "Do you have a meeting?"

"Nine o'clock. Bye." He gave me a peck on the cheek and bolted out the door. After another, longer swallow of coffee, I heard the engine of his Accord starting and the crunch of its tires as he backed down the driveway.

Classes at the college were not scheduled to begin for another two weeks, an odd legacy of the agricultural past, but the faculty were assembling for meetings, class preparation, and academic advising. Jay was supposed to present his law-enforcement program to them that week. The program was on the books, but there was resistance to it from the humanities and social sciences. The professors didn't mind training nurses and accountants, but they weren't eager to educate police officers. That seemed strange to me. I thought educated cops were less likely to bash heads at random than uneducated cops.

The thought of head-bashing reminded me of Clara Klein's unexpected jab at Jay. I brooded about the painter's effect on my dinner party. In addition to giving my living room a classier image than I could have contrived on my own, she had deflected Annie. I hoped I was suitably grateful, but I felt used. Clara had showed up because she wanted to retail her gossip to receptive ears. Fine. Jay had passed the word to Dale about Bob's date with Cleo. But why had Clara needed an audience? Why not just tell Jay in private? And why insult his profession?

I finished my cold coffee and went for another cup. There was a light on in Matt's kitchen. I meant to take him some of the cold salmon for dinner and a slice of tart. I yawned and sipped, and decided to catch him later.

"Morning." Tom poked his head in.

"You look like leftovers zapped in the microwave."

He groaned. "Coffee?"

I got out a mug and poured.

"Thanks. I slept like a log for two hours last night, then woke up and remembered the novel. Naturally I had to read it." Like me, he was wearing jeans and a sweatshirt, and he did look underslept. He took a sip and grimaced at the sting of hot liquid. "I feel hung over."

"Me, too. I wonder why. Bob McKay is probably frisking around like a week-old colt."

"There is no justice."

I went back to the nook and sat. "How is it?"

He followed. "The novel? Awful. Dire. Bulwer-Lytton out of Danielle Steele. With touches of James Fenimore Cooper."

"Horrors."

He gave me a wry grin over the rim of his mug. "All writers go through a stage when they think what they've written is dreck. It passes. Tomorrow I'll be a genius again. At two a.m., though, I was reading the book through Annie McKay's eyes."

"I thought this one wasn't satire."

"It's not. It's a look at the thirties and forties, my grand-parents' era. I'm having trouble with the language."

"Can't you just listen for your grandfather's voice?"

He sipped, silent. Then he said, "That's shrewd of you. I listen, but I keep hearing my mother making wisecracks. She and Grandpa used to snipe at each other." He gave an amused snort. "My mother's voice and Annie's eyes. I sound like some kind of New Age channeler."

"I imagine writing a novel or a play must be a little schizophrenic—voices in your head."

"Yeah . . . Jesus, is it nine already?"

"Five of."

He shot to his feet and made for the back door. "I'm supposed to be at the house. The construction crew is set to show up any minute now."

"See you later," I called after him.

I thought about breakfast and thought not. We had straightened up the obvious mess the night before, so I didn't need to do much to the house but vacuum. Vacuum-ing was not my favorite activity. There was laundry. Also not fun. I went upstairs and tidied the bed. Freddy was still asleep, so I couldn't bug him about the mess in the spare bedroom where he'd assembled the computer. I didn't want to bug Freddy, anyway. I felt restless, pointless, impatient with nothing to be impatient about. I didn't want to strip wallpaper, but I wanted to do something.

I stood for a while by the doors to the balcony looking out at the ocean. Bonnie's house was dark, drapes drawn. As I watched, Matt backed out of his driveway and turned his old Pontiac toward town. I wondered how Lottie was get-ting along. I could visit her. Matt had said she was out of intensive care. I could take her flowers, some of Tom's flowers. He wouldn't mind.

Feeling more cheerful, I pulled a jacket over my sweats, chose a nice vase, found a pair of shears, and went out to the Toyota. I drove down the block and pulled over onto the grassy shoulder by Ruth's mobile home.

She was standing in the doorway talking to a heavyset man in a plaid shirt and jeans. I gave her a wave and crossed to Tom's driveway, where a white van with KEMMEL CON-

STRUCTION lettered on the driver's door sat behind Tom's pickup. There were noises from the house; Tom taking his crew on an inspection tour, probably. I skirted the vegetable garden, which was edged with marigolds to discourage bugs. The asters and zinnias flared in brilliant color along the east wall of the garage. I snipped a nice variety, trickled water into the vase from Tom's hose, and started back toward my car.

Ruth's door slammed and a pickup roared to life in her short driveway. A large pickup with an electric blue bug shield. I gaped at it as it backed around into the east-bound lane and rumbled off. Mud obscured the license plate. There was a gun rack.

I watched the pickup mount the crest and disappear over the ridge. Was it the same vehicle? I couldn't be sure. My pulse beat out a tattoo. I set the flowers on the floor behind the front seat, wedged the vase in with my squidgy purse, and got into the car, meaning to give chase. Then I hesitated.

I hadn't really looked at the man in the plaid shirt. For that matter, I hadn't had a clear look at the driver of the sideswiping pickup either. I fastened my seat belt with shaking fingers. Ruth's logger son? I knew I ought to knock on her door, ask her who the man was, but I didn't want to. I didn't want the villain to be Ruth's son.

I drove to town on Highway 101, eyes peeled for pickups, nerves jangling. I did not like my thoughts.

I was too early for visiting hours, though Matt had been allowed to go on up. I stood in the lobby of the hospital, irresolute, then spotted the pay phones. I went to the first and dialed the college. Jay was still in his meeting. If I called Dale Nelson...if I didn't call Dale...if, if. I carried my vase back to the car and drove to the mall. I bought a copy of the *Oregonian* and read it over a cup of coffee at the bakery. The murder of Cleo Hagen was definitely buried in the back pages. I saw no sign of the short reporter's color story, and I couldn't focus on world news. My mind kept returning to the pickup. There was a phone outside the bakery. I tried Jay again without result and gave up. Time to visit Lottie.

She was lying, propped, in a two-bed ward and Clara Klein was sitting with her. Matt hovered by the single window. The other bed was empty.

"Hi, Lark." Clara was holding a flat box with a felt surface. "I see you've brought Lottie some of Tom's asters. Aren't they bright, Lottie?"

Lottie blinked.

I gave her a smile and said hello, but I was shocked by the change in her appearance. Though the nurses had decked her out in a pretty pink bed jacket, one side of her face was drawn in a frozen grimace, almost a snarl, and her head had been shaved for the surgery. She wore a turban of bandages. I realized I had never seen Lottie without her neat gray wig, which she wore curled in a fashion that had died somewhere around 1956. Without the wig, she looked stern, austere. She had lost her cuddliness.

Matt cleared his throat. "I enjoyed the dinner, Lark. Good company, good company."

I said, with more conviction than I felt, "It was nice that Annie McKay could come—and Clara." I did not mention Bob.

Lottie was blinking rapidly.

"Do you want to try the letters again?" Clara asked. "Okay. How about this one?" She placed a felt L on the board.

No blink. No message for Lark.

I thought the felt-board process must be maddening for the patient, it was so slow. "Are you a therapist, Clara?"

Clara kept her eyes on Lottie. "Volunteer. I've done work with stroke patients. Mother had a series of strokes . . . not M? Okay, D, then. Do you want a drink?"

Lottie stared at her stonily.

Matt had turned to look out the window.

Clara sighed. "Well, let's be methodical, begin at the beginning." She took an A from her neat pile of letters.

I went over to Matt. "Annie and Darla were discussing the injunction the Nekana Council is bringing to stop work on the resort site. It will be served this morning."

"That's good. Good," Matt said without looking at me. He didn't turn from the window. "She's a fine woman."

"Annie? She certainly cares about the environment."

Clara and Lottie were up to D again.

"A heroine, a leader." He turned to me, eyes glittering. "I'd do anything for her. Anything. To help her," he added. He must have seen that his intensity made me uneasy. "I worked for Fisheries, you know, man and boy, for thirty-five years. First the dams went in. Then the clear-cutting and building. They've killed the salmon runs, killed them."

I cleared my throat. "So I understand."

"The hatcheries did some good." He was listening to himself, off somewhere in his youth. "I helped set up eight of them, three on tribal land. Still, it wasn't the solution. We needed a leader."

"Like Annie?"

He turned to me. "Somebody like Muir. Somebody like Gifford Pinchot. Somebody with the courage to say enough. There are too many people. Too many."

It seemed ironic to me that Matt agreed with Annie. If she had her way, his mobile home would be the first to go."

"Lark, I think Lottie wants to see your husband." Clara sounded cheerful. "She likes the letter J."

I turned to the two women with some relief. Matt's passion was disturbing, though I could understand his sense of loss. "That's very possible, Clara. Jay visited Lottie before the operation, brought her flowers."

"I see. Do you think . . . ?"

"I'll leave a message for him at the college. He can drop by on his way home."

Lottie's eyes closed.

Clara stood up. "That's enough for now. She's doing very well, Matt."

He gave Clara a tired smile. "Lottie and I appreciate your efforts, Clara. Wonderful. Thank you, Lark."

I said goodbye to him and added, for Lottie's benefit, though I thought she was asleep. "And I'll call Jay right now."

She opened her eyes and blinked hard.

Clara walked down to the lobby with me. "She'd do better if Matt would stop haunting her."

"He's devoted to her."

"Of course he is, but he ought to leave her a little space. What that man needs is distraction. Make him take you clamming, Lark."

"Clamming? I thought they postponed the razor-clam season...."

"For steamers," Clara said impatiently. "And a lecture. Matt used to haul newcomers out in a rowboat on Shoalwater Bay. They'd come back with a mess of clams and a burning desire to save the estuary. He's really very knowledgeable."

"I'm not crazy about clams."

"So feed 'em to the red-headed kid, what's 'is name, Freddy."

I considered that. I really did not want to go out in a rowboat with Matt, but I could see Clara's point. "Bonnie's the newcomer. Fishing runs in her blood. He should take Bonnie." I didn't know if grubbing for steamer clams qualified as fishing.

Clara shrugged. "Great. Whatever. Matt needs an afternoon off—and so does Lottie."

"Does she really want to see Jay?"

"Maybe. A felt board's not an exact form of communication, but it's better than no communication. Imagine being locked in your own consciousness with no way to let anyone know what you were thinking." She shivered.

I felt some of my reservations about Clara melt. "I was glad you came last night, but I have the sinking feeling it wasn't my salmon that drew you."

"I'm worried about Tom." She didn't smile.

"We all are."

"Did he tell you he's been arrested three times for assault?"

I gulped.

"More to the point, did he tell your husband?"

"Jay didn't say anything...that's awful" It was awful so many ways I didn't want to think how awful it was.

Clara was saying "The charges were dropped all three times. I don't know if they're even on record, but somebody around here is bound to remember. The first two times were right after he got out of the army, once here and once in Los Angeles. The third time was at his grandparents' funeral."

"Shit."

"That's right. Lots of witnesses. One of them called the police. Quentin McKay, Bob's brother, made Tom an offer for the house. The old McKay place has associations for that side of the family, too, you know, whether Annie's little committee wants to classify it as historical or not."

"And?"

"And Tom knocked him cold. I was there."

I shivered. "You've known Tom a long time. Is he . . . ?"

"Violent? Not habitually, and he doesn't drink a lot, not anymore, not since the funeral. The sheriff owes the last election to the McKay family, though, and they persist in regarding Tom as some kind of black sheep. And never mind," she added with fierce intensity, "that he has more talent in his little finger than that lot lumped together. Annie runs a good paper but she can't write a decent paragraph."

"Her style is a little turgid." There we were standing in the lobby of the Shoalwater Hospital worrying about Annie McKay's prose style, while Tom was in imminent danger of arrest. I edged toward the door.

Clara followed me out to the parking lot. I hadn't spotted her Karman Ghia. It crouched next to Matt's Pontiac.

Clara stood by the car door, keys in her hand. A gust of wind lifted her grizzled hair from her forehead. "What I said about cops last night was damned rude."

"People react. Usually they sort of laugh and say they feel guilty around policemen."

"Well, I don't. I was rude, though. I apologize. Jay seems like a nice guy. For that matter, Dale Nelson is a nice guy, but the police always support the status quo. That's natural enough, but it can be vicious. Around here, the status quo means the Enclave, and the Enclave means Bob and Annie McKay. And Quentin. Unlike Bob, he is not a lush." She unlocked her door and wriggled behind the wheel. "See you later."

I was so preoccupied by what she had told me of Tom that I forgot to call the college until I got home. Jay was in another meeting by then, so I left a message and fixed Freddy a sandwich. He wanted to go in to Darla's office to see what had happened about the injunction. I hardened my heart and made him take the bus. I thought I might need the Toyota.

I stewed and brooded and brooded and stewed. Finally, disgusted with myself, I crossed the road and knocked on Bonnie's door. She had been reading *Starvation Hill*. The book lay facedown on the arm of her easy chair.

"Time for coffee?"

"I guess." I perched on the edge of her downscale couch while she fetched mugs from the kitchen.

"God, that's a sad book. Beautiful but sad."

I agreed, vague, my mind on the author. It was Jay's contention that all of us have the potential to be killers, if not murderers, given the triggering circumstances. I resisted the idea, partly because it was so sweeping and partly on philosophical grounds. Although I had not had a religious upbringing, my father's family were Quakers with a long history of peaceful living. I could not imagine my grandfather killing anyone, even in self-defense. My own temperament was much hotter. I suppose I idealized Grandfather Dailey because he seemed immune to the passions that made me see red.

Could Tom kill? He had been a soldier, so he was trained to. If he had taken a swing at his cousin for trying to buy the house, it was obviously a flash point. Still, his attempt to place the house under the protection of the Historic Trust—and the letter I had glimpsed addressed to the state historical society—suggested he had tried to think of rational ways to save the place. When Cleo Hagen had made her offer, he had not known his application to the Trust would be refused.

That thought cheered me.

"Don't you agree?" Bonnie had been describing the pathos of the young girl abandoned to an alien society by her own father.

I said hastily, "It's horrifying but no worse than modern cases of abuse we read about in the papers. And Greek and

Roman parents sold their children into slavery all the time, especially girls."

Bonnie sighed. "I wish Tom hadn't made it so real."

"It's a terrifying talent. I mean, it must be terrifying to have that talent."

Bonnie cocked her head. "I suppose so. What's the matter, Lark? You're awfully quiet."

I'm afraid you may be infatuated with a killer. I could have said that. Instead I described my visit to Lottie, and Clara's presence in the sickroom. I also mentioned Clara's suggestion about clamming. To my surprise Bonnie fell on the idea with enthusiasm. She wanted me to come, too.

I said I'd think about it. Bonnie was ready to hunt down waders and clam guns.

"Good heavens, we haven't even asked Matt. He probably won't want to."

"Oh, come on. I'll bet Tom has all kinds of gear stowed in the garage. Let's ask him. Then if Matt doesn't want to take us out, you and I can rent a boat and we'll be set. Tom says there's public access to some of the clam beds off Coho Island."

I felt a stir of interest. I hadn't done much exploring yet on the bay side of the peninsula. The oyster beds for which the bay was famous were privately owned, but Coho Island was supposed to be spectacularly unspoiled, with some areas open to the public. Uninhabited except for black bears and deer, the island boasted a stand of old-growth cedar that was mentioned in the guidebooks. Bald eagles nested in the area, too, and blue herons fished the shallow waters of the bay.

"We'll have to consult the tide tables...." Bonnie had finished off her coffee and was making for the door. I shoved myself up and followed her.

A big dumpster sat on the grass in front of Tom's house. His crew was going at it hot and heavy, and he was poking around in the garden. I confessed my theft of the asters, and he said he wished he'd thought to take some to Lottie. He seemed happy to supply us with whatever clamming gear we needed, though he laughed when Bonnie mentioned clam guns. It seemed the long slim shovels were used only for digging razor clams. Clam fanciers raked the steamers or used an ordinary shovel.

We helped Tom weed for a while, until I yanked out a stalk of New Zealand spinach. Tom said it was time to water.

"Hello there, neighbors." Ruth was leaning on the fence.

The sight of her jolted my memory and I gave her a confused greeting. While he moved the sprinkler, Tom filled her in on the house repairs, so I had time to sort out my thoughts. At the first lull in the exchange, I said, "I think I saw your son this morning, Ruth."

"This morning? Who?" Ruth laughed. "Benny and them left yesterday. Kids had school today. You saw somebody this morning it was Kevin Johnson."

I must have looked blank.

"Melanie's old man, remember? He's back, more's the pity, and he came over to rank me down for calling the Methodists. His family don't need no charity. My ass. I gave Kevin a piece of my mind and he went off in a huff. That boy is always going off in a huff. He was bragging about having plenty of cash, though. Must've found him a job after all."

Some job. I said, "I think his pickup was the one that almost ran me off the Ridge Road." And almost killed Freddy and Darla.

Bonnie said, "Did you call Dale Nelson?"

Tom was frowning. "Kevin? He's a blowhard, but he wouldn't..." He looked at his house. The odds were good that the sideswiper had also tossed the firebomb.

Ruth's hair stood up in indignant tufts. "Land sakes, no child of mine would do a thing like that. My Ben wouldn't hurt a fly."

She sounded so shocked I had to apologize. "I didn't think your son could have done it either, Ruth. That's why I didn't report it."

"You'd better report it," Bonnie said grimly. "Before the maniac runs Jay off the road or burns *my* house."

Tom was still brooding, his thoughts darkened his face. "I wonder who hired him?"

"I don't know. Donald Hagen?" I had been wondering the same thing since Ruth mentioned Kevin's cash. It was somehow more frightening to think of the sideswiper as a hireling than as a disgruntled citizen acting on his own out of prejudice. What else had he been hired to do?

Ruth said, "Better use my phone, honey."

"What is this, a conference?" Jay had reached the yard unnoticed. He slipped around the fence into the garden. He must have been home for a while because he had changed into jeans and a T-shirt.

"I saw what may be the pickup that ran Freddy off the road," I said. "Ruth was offering me the use of her telephone."

"When did you see it?" He skirted the marigolds.

I explained the sequence of events and he swore under his breath. "I tried to reach you," I added, defensive.

He tugged at his mustache. "Well, you'd better come home now and give Dale the whole story."

"Okay. Did you stop by the hospital?"

"The hospital?"

"I think Lottie wants to see you. I did leave that message with the secretary."

"I knew I should have checked with the office before I left campus." He did a double-take. "How do you know Lottie wanted to see me? I thought she couldn't talk."

I explained Clara and the felt board as we headed home together. Bonnie showed no disposition to leave the garden. *She* hadn't weeded out spinach. As we went off, Ruth called out, "He would never do a thing like that, not my Ben."

I gave her what I hoped was a reassuring wave. Tom started the sprinkler.

THIRTEEN

JAY GOT THROUGH to Dale Nelson, after some delay, and sat in the nook with me while I explained about the man with the pickup.

"You're not sure." Nelson sounded resigned.

"I just caught a glimpse. Ruth Adams said he was bragging about having a lot of money. He's been unemployed."

Dale sighed. "Kevin's a sorehead, but I hope it's not him. We went to school together. I'll bring him in, Mrs. Dodge. Will you be available?" When I said I would, he added, "Tell your brother-in-law we'll need him, too. I'll contact Ms. Sweet."

"Freddy's in Kayport with Darla. The injunction..."

"Yeah, it was served this morning. Been a busy day. I'll call you when I've tracked Kevin down. Thanks. Will you put Jay back on?"

Jay listened to him. I made a fresh pot of coffee and a cup of herb tea. Finally Jay muttered something and hung up. He was looking thoughtful.

"What did he say?"

"He pulled the McKays in for questioning. Annie says Bob was with her all evening the night of the murder."

I clucked my tongue. "Bonnie will be disappointed. Bob was her number-one suspect."

"Tough." He smiled.

The right frame of mind. I said, "Did Tom say anything to you about assault charges?"

He raised his cup, grimacing when the hot liquid touched his lips. "Dale told me right after the murder. Tom told me later, while we were doing the floor."

"And you didn't mention it?"

"The charges were dismissed, Lark."

"Guys. You always stick together."

"It was confidential information. I spent the morning listening to faculty members' nightmares about violation of privacy, and God knows your mother's made her feelings clear. I even agree with them, most of the time. I hear a lot I keep to myself. If Tom had wanted you to know about the . . . episodes, he would have told you."

"Wonderful. The man is living under my roof."

"Our roof." He swallowed tea and set the cup down with deliberation. "The first time was a flashback. There's less excuse for the second, the one in California. That was a drunk and disorderly charge, while he was at UCLA. How did you hear about Tom's rap sheet?"

"Clara Klein."

"She's a busy woman."

"She's worried about Tom."

"So she says. What's the deal with Lottie?"

"I don't know. Maybe you should call Clara and ask her to come to the hospital with you."

"Maybe I should." He picked up the laughably slim telephone book and started paging through it. "Klein with an *ei* . . . here it is." He reached for the phone and began poking numbers. Clara was out. He left a message.

"Lottie was expecting you this afternoon."

"I'll call her room. Matt's probably still there." He flipped to the front of the book and looked up the hospital. Matt answered almost as soon as Jay gave the switchboard the room number. He told Matt he'd try to make it in during evening visiting hours.

I was still brooding. When the phone conversation ended, I said, "Does Bob's alibi hold up?"

Jay shrugged. "Annie's staff at the *Gazette* say she only popped in for ten minutes after dinner the night of the murder. That was unusual because she tends to hang around while they're putting the paper to bed. According to Dale, Annie says Bob drank his way through dinner. She made him follow her to the *Gazette* office afterward."

"Sounds like Bob. What time?"

"About eight-thirty. He was driving the Mercedes. She had the Blazer. He parked behind the newspaper office and waited while she checked on the printing crew. When she went back to the parking lot, he seemed soberer, so she followed him home in the Blazer. They spent the evening together in their house in the Enclave and went to bed early. Nobody's contradicted Annie's version of things so far.''

"Two cars?"

He nodded. "She says she kept Bob's taillights in sight all the way home. They drove on the Ridge Road."

"There's not much traffic on that route."

He smoothed his mustache. "No. Dale's unlikely to find another driver who saw them, though the Mercedes is distinctive. Dale's looking for corroborating witnesses, of course."

"What about the staff at the Enclave?"

"There's a handyman. He's out of town at the moment."

"The son, then...."

"Rob McKay says he was out with friends until two a.m. When he got home, the Mercedes and the Blazer were in the garage and his folks had gone to bed, as far as he knew."

"I hope Dale's double-checking."

Jay looked pained. "He's a good investigator, Lark. He went to the Blue Oyster first and got confirmation of Clara's story. Then he drove to the Enclave with a warrant to search the vehicles. The m.e. thinks the body was moved, post mortem, and there were fibers on her clothes that came from a type of carpeting used in cars."

That was news to me. "What kind of car?"

"Not a Mercedes." Jay's mouth twitched at the corners. "Dale said Bob McKay was a little under the weather this morning."

"God, I hope so. What about Bob's date with Cleo?"

"When Dale started in on that, Annie called her lawyer. Bob clammed up. Hell, they both did."

"That's too bad." The word clammed reminded me of Clara's proposed expedition. I described it with less than enthusiasm, but Jay said he thought distracting Matt was a good idea and that he'd like to go over to Coho Island himself sometime. Before I could protest again that I didn't like clams, Tom came in covered with grime. He went off for a shower. Then Freddy and Darla showed up. Darla was full of the injunction saga.

The archaeologist the tribe had hired had found evidence in James Swan's pioneer diary, and in an unpublished letter at the Kayport museum, that the sight of the resort had been a major Nekana summer encampment in the 1840s. He wanted to dig.

I had once spent a summer on a dig in northern California. "Why didn't they find out about the encampment before they bulldozed the dunes? I thought the government required an archaeological survey of all big developments."

Darla's lip curled. "They sank a couple of test pits, but they didn't *want* to find anything. This is our guy. He says the test pits were in the wrong area. What's more, he can prove it."

"That's great, Darla." I was hungry. I'd skipped lunch. I began taking leftovers out of the refrigerator.

"I wish I didn't have to be in Portland this fall." Darla's eyes sparkled.

Jay took plates from the dishwasher. "Will the dig delay construction?" He began setting the table in the nook. Maybe he'd skipped lunch, too.

Darla found paper napkins and folded them neatly. "Our guy says he can keep it going until the rainy season, even if he doesn't find anything."

According to the *Oregonian*, the peninsula had received two inches of rain in the previous four days. I set the ceramic container of pilaf in the microwave. "It gets rainier?"

Darla laughed. She was in a fine mood.

Freddy had gone up to verify that Tom's computer was still working. He thudded into the room. "Hey, dinner. Where's Tom?"

"Shower." I set the time clock, started the oven, and retrieved the leftover veggies from the refrigerator. I decided we could do without salad.

Jay doled out flatware. "Lark thinks she saw the pickup that ran you off the road, Freddy."

"No lie? When? Who is it?"

I explained about Kevin Johnson through a flurry of excited speculation. Darla didn't know Kevin Johnson and wasn't sure she could identify the driver, but she'd had a good look at his passenger.

"I saw that guy Hagen in town today," Freddy said. "I'll bet he's the one who hired Johnson."

"Who hired Johnson?" Tom entered from the back hallway.

That led to another round of questions and speculations. I zapped the veg and set out the remaining dill rolls. Clara Klein didn't call during dinner, which disappeared like rain in the Mojave. We polished off the tart before I thought to save Matt a slice. Jay was uncharacteristically silent during the meal. So was Tom.

Afterward, before I started the clean-up, Freddy announced that he and Darla were taking in a film in Astoria.

"You rented a car," I deduced—not a difficult mental exercise. After all, they hadn't come home on the county bus.

Freddy made a face. "It's a Ford. Pretty boring."

"Boring is good," Jay said. "Be careful."

Freddy swore he'd keep a wary eye out for pickups. He and Darla made a perfunctory offer to do the dishes. When I told them to forget it, they dashed off in obvious high spirits.

I carried the salmon platter back to the kitchen. There was quite a lot left. It was a large salmon.

Tom joined me and started scraping plates. "Ah, youth. They probably don't even feel their bruises."

Jay was using the phone. After a wordless pause he hung up. "Clara's still out. I'm going in to the hospital, Lark. I want to see Matt anyway, and I've got a weird feeling about Lottie. You're sure I was the one she wanted to see?"

I thought of Lottie's frantic blinking. "As sure as I can be. Clara thought so, too."

"Okay. It's only six-thirty. I'll swing by Dale's office first."

I slid the boneless slab of salmon into a plastic bag and sealed it. "Take care."

He brushed a kiss on my cheek as he went out.

Tom and I loaded the dishwasher in silence. I felt constrained in his presence. Finally I asked him how the work was coming on his house.

"Okay, I guess. A little depressing. They were throwing stuff into the dumpster—clothes, bedding, curtains, mattresses, the sofa."

"Don't let them touch the Morris chair."

He poured soap into the proper slot. "I salvaged that and the sideboard. Took them to Kayport in the pickup to an outfit that does refinishing."

"Won't the chair have to be reupholstered?"

"They said they could do that, too. I was relieved. I do most of my thinking in that chair."

"I hope you aren't going to modernize the kitchen."

He smiled. "I thought I'd cover it all with yellow tile."

I looked around my too-perfect kitchen. "I overdid it, didn't I?"

"It's a nice room, Lark. It just needs to, uh, weather awhile. Your living room is exactly right."

"Thanks to Clara." I swabbed the counter and drainboard. "Cup of coffee? Oh, I forgot, with the computer up and running, you probably want to write."

He groaned. "I'm still in the revulsion stage. Do you play gin rummy?"

I laughed. "Only at gunpoint."

"Then I'll settle for coffee and conversation. I've been wanting to talk to you anyway."

I filled the coffeemaker and set out mugs. "What's on your mind?"

"Room and board."

I made a ritual protest, which he overrode. The contractor had told him he'd be back in his house in a week. Tom thought that probably meant a minimum of ten days and more likely two weeks, contractors being contractors. He was worried about his intrusion into our lives and felt uncomfortable freeloading—his words—but admitted that the arrangement was ideal for him otherwise. I said I liked all the free salads. He smiled but he looked troubled.

I was troubled, too. I poured coffee into the mugs and laced mine with creamer. "I'll set up house rules, if you like.

I did that for Freddy. If you're really bothered about not paying, I can charge your insurance company a modest per diem. And when Jay and I want the house to ourselves, I promise to kick you out for the evening."

We carried our mugs into the nook and sat down.

"You probably have writing rituals, Tom. Why don't you move your computer down to the guest room? Then you can hole up whenever you want to."

"Sounds great." He eyed me over the rim of the cup. "I'm not just any burned-out neighbor. I'm a murder suspect. That has to bother you."

It did bother me. I drew a deep breath. "Tell me about your grandparents' funeral."

I think I surprised him. His brows drew together and his hand clenched on the mug.

I went on doggedly, "I ran into Clara Klein at the hospital today."

He set the cup down but he didn't say anything.

I bit my lip. "Jay said you told him about the assault charges last week."

His cheeks had flushed. He was looking into his mug, anywhere but at me. "I guess I expected him to tell you."

"Did you? Or did you hope he'd protect the little woman from unpleasant thoughts?"

In the silence that followed I could hear my heart thudding. I took a swallow of coffee.

Tom cleared his throat. "I have a problem dealing with anger."

"So do we all." I shifted in my chair. "I'm inclined to take direct action myself, and God knows I have a hot temper. So if you're about to tell me I can't understand, don't do it. I'm reasonably intelligent and reasonably empathic, and you are a master of the English language. Tell me what happened."

He laughed. It was not a mirthful sound, but it seemed genuine. "Here I thought you were going to ask me about Cleo."

I waited. I had said more than enough.

After a moment, he sighed. "When my grandparents were killed, the state patrol called me at my apartment in San

Francisco. I'd divorced Cleo the year before and I was living alone. It was the classic, middle-of-the-night phone call.
My first reaction was straightforward disbelief. I flew north
at six-thirty the next morning, still hoping I'd wake up and
find out it was a nightmare. I rented a car in Portland and
drove to Kayport. Somewhere around Clatskanie—that's
about halfway along the highway to Astoria—I started to
believe what the officer told me."

I was watching his face. He had an inward, remembering
look, and sweat gleamed on his forehead.

"And then my emotions just shut down."

"What do you mean?"

"I mean I couldn't feel anything at all. My senses were
working overtime and my physical reactions were sharp. It
was a rainy winter day, cold and overcast, and the road was
dangerous in the mountains. Slick. I drove fast, but my
timing was excellent. Everything worked but my emotions."

I sipped and tried to visualize the drive. We had brought
a U-Haul truck along the same road.

"I behaved awfully well when I got to Kayport," Tom
continued. "Everybody said so. I made the funeral arrangements, and I said the right things to Aunt Caroline—
Grandma's sister. I came to the house here, hoping I'd thaw
out, but I just went up to my old bedroom and had a nice,
dreamless eight-hour sleep. When I got up, I walked around
the house, trying to remember, trying to force myself to feel
something, even nostalgia. I walked on the beach for a couple of hours in a driving rainstorm, and I felt cold and wet,
all right, but I didn't feel sad or happy or sick or grieved or
even angry."

"That must have been terrifying."

He looked at me. "It would have been, if I'd been able to
feel terror." He turned his mug slowly. "When they held the
funeral service three days later, I was still frozen. I put on a
decent suit and tie and got to the Reilly Funeral Chapel at
exactly the right time. There was an organist. My grandfather's lodge master delivered the eulogy. My grandparents were cremated. The funeral parlor set up a reception
after the funeral, with coffee and cookies and the Method-

ist ladies pouring. Aunt Caroline and I stood at one end of the room. People came up and shook hands. They said how awful it was and what a blessing my grandparents didn't suffer, and so on.''

"People say dumb things at funerals."

He went on as if I hadn't spoken, "A lot of people showed up. All the LaPortes, of course, and half the population of Shoalwater, even some of the summer people my grandfather had worked for as a handyman. I met Clara that day. Grandpa had installed her deck the year before. What surprised me—no, not surprise, I wasn't up to feeling surprise." He frowned, groping for words. "What was intellectually interesting was that the McKays came. My grandfather was the last of the senior branch of the family. There were all the McKays from the Enclave, from the cadet branch, paying their respects and saying polite things. I remember thinking I should have been touched."

"What happened?"

"Quentin and Bob and Annie came up together. We shook hands, and Annie said she was sorry. I said I thought her dad had done a nice job. That was tactless of me. She doesn't like to be reminded of her father's profession. However, I was so out of touch with my own feelings I was deaf to anyone else's. Then Bob said, 'Anything we can do?' And Quentin cleared his throat like a bishop. He said, 'You'll be wanting to unload the old McKay place, Tommy. I'll take it off your hands.' He's pompous the way lawyers are sometimes, so he probably phrased the offer less directly."

"What an appalling thing to say."

"Yeah, and Quentin didn't mean well, either. I stood there gaping at him. My mind raced, as if it had shifted gears, and I knew why they'd showed up. They'd come because they saw an opportunity to pick up a piece of desirable real estate cheap. And to rid themselves of a social embarrassment. Me."

"Then what?"

"I must have turned green or something, because I can remember Annie asking me what was wrong. Then I let fly. I hit Quentin smack on the point of his chin with a long,

solid right. He went down. Annie was shrieking. Then I
turned around, marched out the door of the funeral parlor,
and walked home, all the way from Kayport to Shoalwater.
By the time I got here, I was feeling everything I was supposed to feel, and the police were waiting for me.''

I took a long swallow of cold coffee. ''Maybe I'm reading what you said backward but it sounds as if Quentin
McKay did you a favor.''

''You're right. He also jolted me into moving north. It
took me the better part of a year to realize that.'' He fiddled with the mug. ''An emotional freeze wasn't a new thing
with me, though. I should have known what to expect. For
almost two years after Tet, a good year after I got out of the
army, I had no emotions except for an occasional burst of
anger. It wasn't safe to feel anything, so I suppressed my
feelings. It's a very dangerous state of mind, Lark.''

''Yes, I can see that. The feelings were there, hidden, and
they could sneak up on you.''

His mouth eased and he took a reflective sip of coffee.
''Funny thing. I've never been able to feel grateful to
Quentin for the 'favor.' I spent two nights in the county jail
before he decided to drop the charges.''

I sat for a while digesting the story. ''Were you in an
emotional deep freeze the night Cleo was killed?''

''No.'' Outside, the wind had picked up but it sounded
halfhearted. ''Was that what you wanted me to say?''

''I just wanted to hear your version. Now you can tell me
about Cleo.''

''One narrative a night. For two I charge double.'' He
spoke lightly but his jaw was set. I had been pushing him
hard.

''My mother is a writer. She says the truth of a story lies
in the way it's told.''

''She must be uncomfortable to live with.''

I stared. ''Thomas, my friend, I am not a murder suspect. I probe, you wince, not vice versa.''

''Do you think I killed Cleo?''

''You asked me that earlier. No, I don't. She didn't surprise you with her offer. The Historic Trust business proves
that. And I think you're a happy man, or you were until

somebody dumped her body on your doorstep. You're doing what you want to do where you want to do it."

"She was threatening my base of operations."

"Not very seriously, from the sound of things. Was she vindictive?"

"She could be." He brushed a wing of black hair from his forehead. Bonnie was going to have to haul him to the barber. "Cleo was a superb businesswoman. If she could dislodge me from my house with minimal effort and make a profit, she'd go for it, but she wouldn't pursue a vendetta at all costs. By the time I filed for divorce, I knew her mentality, so I gave her an edge in the property settlement. We had stocks, equity in a very expensive condo, a trendy car, some antiques. I let her have the condo and the BMW. We split the rest. She thought she'd made a score against me."

"Didn't she?"

He shrugged. "When I decided to move up here and write full time, I had enough left to set up a trust fund. It keeps the taxes and insurance paid on the house. I did all right."

"Why did you divorce her? You said you loved her."

"We had a basic disagreement about children. I wanted them and she didn't. I could have adjusted to not having kids, but she lied to me before we were married, and afterward she kept delaying. When she hit thirty-five, she finally admitted she didn't want a family, had never wanted one."

I wanted a family. I felt a stab of resentment. Cleo could have had what I wanted.

Tom said, "There were other problems, but I couldn't live with deception."

"What were the other problems? Infidelity?"

He hesitated. "I got the impression that she didn't enjoy sex. She used it to manipulate people, including me, but she wasn't promiscuous. And she hated Shoalwater. The LaPortes made her uneasy. They teased her, and she didn't have much sense of humor. I think she was also racist."

"Racist?"

"She grew up in small logging towns on the Oregon coast and probably internalized the local prejudices. Native Americans were trendy when we first married, though. She used to talk about My People at cocktail parties. At first I didn't mind. I was always proud of my Nekana relatives. But being paraded as an ethnic specimen got old."

"You weren't raised traditionally, were you?"

"No, and I was always conscious of being a mixture. My grandfather saw to it that I thought of myself as a McKay." He smiled. "Not, you understand, in the Enclave sense of the term. Grandpa collected rascally anecdotes about his forebears. He liked to tell them wherever they'd cause his cousins maximum embarrassment. At political gatherings, for example."

I eyed him. "He must have been uncomfortable to live with."

Tom grinned. "Touché. Grandpa was contrary on principle. I spent six months at the height of puberty being embarrassed by the old man, but I got over that fast. Mostly I got a kick out of him. And I respected him. He taught me a lot."

"But Cleo didn't appreciate him."

"No. Grandpa refrained from sarcasm in her presence, but I could see he didn't like her. She patronized my grandmother. Sooner or later, that would have caused a flare-up. We didn't come up here very often while the marriage lasted, but we came often enough for Cleo to scope out the real estate opportunities. When I heard that her husband's company had bought the resort site, I felt as if I'd let the enemy in the back gate."

"Who do you think killed her?"

He shook his head. "I don't know. My best guess, and it's probably prompted by wishful thinking, is Donald Hagen. He could have hired the arsonist-sideswiper, but if he killed Cleo and set Kevin Johnson off, who planted Bonnie's bag of dead seagulls?"

I thought about that. "Not Kevin. Are you saying that the carpetbag was symbolic and the other crimes weren't?"

"The carpetbag feels different. And why would Donald Hagen persecute Bonnie, if his motive was jealousy? The shooting incident doesn't make any sense at all, if Hagen had the coolness to dump Cleo's body where it would implicate me, and if he was thinking far enough ahead to hire Kevin. The shooting was impulsive."

"I think Hagen was on coke when he shot at Jay."

His eyes narrowed. "I suppose that might explain why he confused Jay with me, though I still find the stupidity incredible."

"I found the whole incident incredible." I was scratching at the edge of insight. "Maybe not incredible. Faked. There was something phony going on, as if he were playing a role and doing it sloppily, without attention to detail."

"That's interesting. He could have killed Cleo, hired Johnson to harass me and my friends, then staged the shooting to persuade everybody he was just a distraught widower out to avenge his wife's death."

"It hangs together." I felt a stir of excitement.

"But Bonnie got the carpetbag *before* Cleo was killed. I hadn't met Bonnie then, or you and Jay and Freddy. Neither had Cleo. Why would Hagen bother to harass innocent bystanders?"

I sighed. "We're going in circles. Maybe what we have are half a dozen separate crimes with as many criminals."

Tom carried our mugs to the coffeepot and refilled them. "I can buy two criminals, but I balk at six."

"We know Donald Hagen took a shot at Jay, and I'm pretty certain the pickup I saw today was the one that tried to run me off the Ridge Road. That's two criminals for sure."

He set my mug at my elbow.

"I take cream."

"Sorry." He retrieved the creamer and set it and a spoon on the table.

"Thanks." I dolloped more powdered plastic into my cup and stirred. "Suppose Hagen is just a grief-stricken widower who made a little mistake with his target. Suppose the real killer, the mastermind, is Bob McKay." I didn't believe Bob's alibi. Annie was just covering for him.

"Cousin Bob." Tom looked thoughtful. He was warming his hands on the mug of hot coffee.

"The man is a scuzz and a drunk."

"And Annie said he started drinking hard a week ago. After Cleo died or before?"

I warmed to the theme. "So he had an affair with Cleo and she told him it was all over. He killed her in a fit of jealousy, then dumped the body near your property."

"On my property," Tom corrected. "I own the accreted land."

"The what?"

"The peninsula is one of the few places on the West Coast where the shoreline isn't eroding. Silt from the Columbia washes up on the beach. When Grandpa was growing up, the *Mollie McKay* lay well offshore on a shoal."

"Aren't there times when you can walk around the wreck on firm sand?"

He nodded. "On a minus tide. The beach is technically a state highway. It extends to the mean high water mark. Every ten years or so, the state moves its property line west, and people who own beachfront get another chunk of dune. My land is two lots wide on the highway, but it extends west almost a third of a mile."

I whistled. "Valuable."

"It will be if the dunes adjoining Cleo's resort are re-zoned to allow for multiple-unit structures."

"You could build a motel west of your house."

His mouth twisted. "I won't."

"But another owner might."

"You've got it."

The phone rang as I was taking in the implications of what Tom had said. Maybe he had underestimated the deviousness of Cleo's offer. His house was probably worth only $75,000 on the local market, but the land had a much greater potential value. I picked the receiver up on the third ring to prevent the message tape from kicking in. "Hello?"

"Hi, Lark." It was Bonnie. "I just wanted you to know I have a telephone. The nice man installed it this afternoon. I bankrupted myself talking to my parents. They want me to move back to L.A. where I'll be safe."

I laughed. "If you're feeling brave enough, come over for a cup of coffee. Tom and I are sitting here b.s.ing about the murder."

"Bob McKay's the killer," she said firmly, and hung up.

A minute later the doorbell rang. I let Bonnie in. She heard our speculations with bright-eyed interest. She admitted that the random pinching of derrieres was not prima facie evidence of wider guilt, but she stuck by her conviction that the murderer was Bob McKay.

Tom said, "I think he's too inert to come up with a complicated plot. I'm surprised he had the energy for an affair. Cleo could be a demanding lady."

Bonnie scowled. "We defer to your deeper understanding. I still say she told him to kiss off, so he killed her in a fit of macho angst."

Tom winced. "If 'macho angst' is a sample of your style, I hope you stick to satire."

"What would you call it? 'The pangs of disprized love?'" Bonnie sniffed. "If a man kills a woman, he doesn't love her, whatever nonsense he may whine later."

"I wasn't objecting to the idea, just to the linguistic hash."

"English *is* linguistic hash," Bonnie said with dignity. "That is its charm."

I felt obliged to defuse the literary argument, so I told them about Bob's alibi.

Tom's eyebrows shot up.

Bonnie groaned. "I don't believe it."

I took a sip of coffee. It was cold. "Jay says they haven't found anything yet to make them doubt Annie's word."

Bonnie crossed her eyes. "She's just standing by her man."

At that point it occurred to me that I had blabbed confidential information. Jay rarely discussed cases with me. If he found out I had blurted what he told me at the first opportunity, he'd clam up for good. I explained that to Tom and Bonnie, and swore them to silence, adding "Of course, we're not being fair to Bob."

Bonnie gave another groan.

"You and I haven't seen Bob sober," I insisted. "We don't really know what he's capable of. If the McKays covet your land, Tom, that gives him a double motive, though, and it explains why Bonnie's house was a target, too." I summarized for Bonnie what Tom had told me about the accreted land.

Bonnie shook her head. "I don't own beachfront, just the lot the house stands on. The original owners kept the dunes to the west of me. I even let them hold back a strip on the south side of the house for an access road."

"So you're not a major property owner. Another theory down the drain." Tom took his cup to the sink and rinsed it out, suiting the action to the words. He leaned on the counter.

"Well, I say Annie's lying. Bob killed Cleo."

"And got shit-faced so we'd think he was too stupid to function? Come on, Bonnie." Tom was amused.

"He got drunk because he was haunted by remorse." Bonnie said the cliché with relish. She cocked her head. "Want to spy on the McKays, you guys? The Show of Homes starts tomorrow. Annie invited you, Lark."

Tom backed off, theatrically, hands up. "Count me out. I'm going fishing."

"Coward."

"Absolutely."

"Are you crewing for Henry LaPorte?" I asked.

"I owe him. He's expecting a boatload of tourists from Portland. They come down every year for the Buoy 10 season."

I'd heard of the Buoy 10 season. It involved sports fishing for salmon at the mouth of the Columbia, and it ran for a very limited period. The Kayport Jaycees gave prizes for the largest catch of the day and week. The short salmon season was almost as great a magnet for tourists as the equally limited razor-clam season along the ocean beaches.

"I thought Mr. LaPorte was a commercial fisherman."

"He is, most of the year, but he bought a small charter boat about ten years ago when the commercial runs started to decline. He does a lot of business hauling sportsmen these days."

"And you're going to bait their hooks and hold their heads when the going gets rough," Bonnie jeered.

Tom grinned. "Do you know what they call tourists out on the river?"

"Something demeaning, no doubt."

"Pukers," Tom murmured. "Water's choppy crossing the bar."

Bonnie and I exchanged looks. Bonnie said, "I think I'll avoid the river. What do you say, Lark? I'm curious about the Enclave, and I doubt that I'll get an invitation to tea there any time soon."

I had nothing scheduled for the next day and I was curious, too. Maybe seeing how they lived would help me understand the McKays. They seemed stranger to me even than Cleo and Donald Hagen. I found it difficult to envisage either Annie or Bob committing murder in the first person, yet they were obviously key players in the melodrama. "When are the houses open?"

"Ten until four."

"Let's go early then."

Tom yawned. "Speaking of early, I'm going to bed. I have to be at the dock by four-thirty a.m."

Bonnie shuddered.

I heard gravel crunching outside on the driveway. A door slammed. "That can't be Jay already. It isn't even nine." Hospital visiting hours ran from seven to nine.

It was Jay, however. I took one look at his face and my light mood dissolved. "What is it?"

He pulled a chair and sat heavily. "Lottie's dead."

My stomach lurched. "Oh, no."

He reached across the table and touched my hand. His was cold. "I'm sorry, darling."

I swallowed hard. "So am I. You liked her a lot, too, didn't you?"

He closed his eyes.

Tom came in from the kitchen and took a chair beside Jay. "How's Matt? Did you see him?"

Jay opened his eyes. "Yes, I saw Matt. He's at the hospital, under sedation." He cleared his throat. "Dale had to order an autopsy. There's a possibility Matt killed Lottie."

Silence pooled in the bright room.

Jay shook his head as if to clear it. "He's babbling confessions. Nothing Dale can use as evidence, of course."

"You mean Matt *said* he killed Lottie?" Horror tightened my throat. I barely got the words out.

Jay nodded. "And Cleo Hagen."

I was too numb to react, but Bonnie sat up, eyes wide.

Tom drew a sharp breath. "That's impossible."

Jay turned and looked at him. "Why?"

"He didn't know my... Cleo. Why would he kill her?"

Jay smoothed his mustache. "He said she deserved to be executed because she was an evil woman, because she was destroying the environment, because her resort was going to block Lottie's view of the ocean." His hand dropped. "I heard him, Tom. He hated Cleo Hagen almost as much as he admires Annie McKay. He said he wanted to do something to help Annie's cause."

"That's crazy," I objected, but the objection was mechanical.

"Matt is... disturbed." Jay sounded incredibly weary.

I scrabbled for hope. "Then he may be making it all up?"

"Maybe, maybe not. He has some of the physical details right. Either he knows things about the murder that didn't make the news, or he's a good guesser." He turned to Bonnie. "He said he dumped the dead seagulls on your porch and trashed your house. That part's likely to be true. According to Dale, the lab thinks the printing on the note is Matt's. They compared it with some form he filled out for the county." The muscle in his jaw jumped. "At my suggestion. Dale told me that before the call came from the hospital."

I was appalled. "You suspected Matt?"

"I suspected him of the carpetbag. He certainly had the opportunity. Apart from us, he's closest to Bonnie's house."

That was true. I shivered. Matt could have vandalized the place while we were off gawking at Tom's fire. He was lurking by our driveway when I walked home.

Bonnie had gone white. "That nice old man."

Tom ran his hands over his face. "Do you believe his confession?"

Jay shoved his chair back and rose. "I don't want to. If I believe him, then I have to believe he may have murdered his wife to keep her from giving me evidence of what he'd done."

I cleared my throat. "If Matt killed Lottie, which I do not believe, it was mercy killing." I said that, but it didn't fit what I knew of Matt. He'd been too determined to care for Lottie himself, too blindly optimistic about her condition.

"Maybe." Jay didn't sound convinced. "In any case, I should have gone to the hospital this afternoon." He walked out through the kitchen, touching my shoulder briefly as he passed. I heard him go upstairs.

"Shit." Tom got up, too. "Matt and I used to swap cuttings. And Lottie..." There were tears in his eyes. He shook his head. "I can't take it in. G'night."

When he had gone, I looked at Bonnie. She was wiping her glasses on a Kleenex.

I felt as if I had sunk to the bottom of a dark pit, though the kitchen was, if anything, too bright. I wanted to cry, too, but I felt more like throwing up.

FOURTEEN

WHEN I HAD SEEN Bonnie off, I went up to our bedroom and held Jay. We both cried.

After a while we talked, too. I had to make him see that Lottie's "message" for him was purely conjectural. It hadn't crossed my mind that she might want to tell Jay something incriminating about Matt. If she had wanted to see Jay, it was because she liked his attentions.

Before her second stroke and hospitalization, Lottie had enjoyed receiving company. She had been pleasant to me, but she was the kind of woman who blossomed in the presence of a personable man. Jay flirted with her in a mild way, talked to her about local events, described his work. She had drunk it up. She had probably just wanted more of the same.

And Matt? Matt was obsessed with taking care of Lottie. If he had said he killed her, it was because she died while he was with her and he wasn't able to save her. I convinced myself that she couldn't have seen anything worth reporting to a policeman. I don't think I convinced Jay, but at least I gave him another way of looking at the tragedy.

Matt couldn't confess to the shooting. That was one good thing. We knew who the villain was. According to Jay, Matt hadn't claimed he was the arsonist, either. He had confessed to Bonnie's incidents and to Cleo Hagen's murder. And to killing his wife. That was all. That was enough.

Around ten, Jay's mother called from LA. They talked briefly, mostly wordless murmurs and grunts on Jay's part. I gathered they were talking about Donald Hagen. When I asked what Nancy had told him, Jay shook his head. More confidential information.

The phone call interrupted our talk halfway through. Jay finally fell asleep around eleven. I lay beside him, staring at the ceiling and turning the meaning of Matt's confession over in my mind. Freddy drove up at midnight. When I heard the rental car roll onto the gravel, I slid out of bed. He usually raided the refrigerator before he turned in for the night.

I met him at the back door.

"What's happening?" He sounded goofy and looked blissful. Darla's good mood must have survived the film.

"Tom's asleep. He has to get up early. Go on up to your room. If you want a sandwich, I'll bring one up to you."

"Good deal." He tiptoed past me and scaled the stairs with only a few thumps. I made a salmon sandwich, poured a glass of milk, and carried the snack to his room.

When Freddy fled Stanford, his mother shipped him north. He brought his infatuation, his clothes, the Trans Am, and his personal computing station, which was very high tech. He installed the PC and accoutrements in the bedroom we gave him, in case the urge to 'pute should overcome him at, say, three in the morning. Sometimes it did.

He sat in his padded office chair and dived into the sandwich. I perched on the foot of his bed and told him about Lottie and Matt. He said the correct phrases, but he hadn't seen much of the Cramers. Their tragedy didn't impede his appetite.

When I wound down and blew my nose, he blinked at me like an owl. "It's sad, I know, but I don't think he killed Mrs. Cramer, Lark. That's just survivor guilt."

I sniffled. "Good heavens, what do you know about survivor guilt?"

"Well, see, when Dad died, Mom had gone out to lunch with a friend. She'd been with Dad all the time he was in the hospital, and the nurse said to go ahead because he was stable, so Ma went out to lunch and my father died. She felt awful."

"I didn't realize..." My voice trailed. Freddy's father, Alf, had not got along with Jay, so we hadn't visited very often. We had attended the funeral, of course, but I hadn't thought a lot about the effects of Alf's death on Nancy. Or on nineteen-year-old Freddy. Why would a bright kid flunk out of college in his senior year?

His round face was pink with earnestness. "I had to talk her through it. My psych professor explained it to me."

I said, "I hope you're right. Matt seemed so devoted to Lottie. That makes the idea of his killing Lottie twice as shocking, I suppose."

"Killing that real estate woman is something else. He could've done that, for sure." He finished the milk in one gulp.

I was silent. By then I had had several hours to digest the idea of Matt murdering Cleo Hagen. After the first fierce denial, I had begun to sift what I knew of Matt through the sieve of possibility. He had seemed strange lately, obsessive. I remembered his adulation of Annie McKay, his outrage over the resort, his moments of mental confusion, his verbal tics.

Matt had been under stress for a long time. I could visualize him going for a walk on the beach after he put Lottie to bed. I could see him stumbling across Cleo, if she was there waiting for Bob. I could imagine them exchanging words, Cleo laughing at the old guy, Matt picking up a piece of driftwood. I didn't think Matt had killed Lottie, but he could have killed Cleo Hagen in a burst of rage.

I said good night and left Freddy to his computer. I fell asleep picturing Matt, his mild face contorted with fury, his wire-rimmed glasses gleaming in the moonlight as he raised his driftwood club again and again.

I didn't hear Tom the next morning—or Jay, either. When I dragged myself out of bed at seven, Jay had gone for a long run on the beach. I found coffee and a note saying he'd be back soon. He must have had nightmares. Running was a way of coping with them. I thought about running myself, but I felt too limp to go upstairs and change out of my sweats.

When Jay came in, he went up to the shower without even poking his head in the kitchen. That was ominous, but he seemed calm when he came down. He was dressed for school.

"Another meeting?"

"Today is the day I present the program to the faculty."

"Oh, Jay, how awful. Are you okay?"

He shrugged. "I feel like the contents of a spittoon, but I have everything organized. I'll be back around four."

"I'm going with Bonnie to the Enclave."

He frowned. "I wish you wouldn't. Dale hasn't pulled Kevin Johnson in yet, and I don't like the idea of you driving around the area with Johnson still at liberty."

I thought he was being paranoid and said so, but I promised I'd keep my eyes peeled for the pickup.

Jay was at the phone. "Let me call Dale."

I fixed him a cup of tea and listened without enlightenment to the brief conversation. When Jay hung up, he looked more puzzled than anxious.

"Well?"

He took the tea with absentminded thanks. "They still haven't found Johnson, and his wife is missing, too."

"Melanie's missing?"

He nodded. "Dale said the kids are at her mother's. Kevin and Melanie dropped them off Labor Day and headed for Astoria. Melanie said they were going to a party." He sipped tea. "Kevin was flush. He gave the grandmother fifty bucks. Then he and Melanie took off in the pickup. The woman is worried because her daughter's eight months along and has been having false labor."

"If Kevin is driving around with a pregnant woman strapped in beside him, he's not likely to run Bonnie and me off the road." I meditated. "He was alone when I saw him yesterday, and I'm not sure he was the driver anyway."

Jay sighed. "If he was, he's probably long gone."

"But where's Melanie?"

"Who knows?"

The phone rang. I picked up the receiver and said hello.

It was Clara Klein and she sounded absurdly cheerful. I told her about Lottie and Matt. She was silent so long I thought she'd left the phone. I said, "Clara?"

She blew her nose with a noise like a small explosion. "My God, that's terrible. I don't believe it." I heard her gulp. "I can't...look, I need some time. Can you come over later and tell me what happened?"

"I don't know much more, Clara, and Bonnie and I are driving over to the Enclave to see the McKay house."

"Well, drop by on your way home. Bring Bonnie, too. I need human company. I need to talk."

I said we'd come and hung up. Jay was gathering himself together like a man leaving for work. I went out with him and gave him a big, morale-building hug by the Accord. When he drove off, I trotted across the road to Bonnie's. She was up, though still in her robe, and she gave me a cup of coffee. Gibson watched from the refrigerator.

She sat in her rocker and shoved her glasses up on the bridge of her nose. "I know it's an awful tragedy, and I'm sorry for Matt Cramer, but I slept better last night than I have since I moved in."

"Bonnie!"

She shot me a defiant glance over her coffee cup. "Don't you see? Now I *know* who left the seagulls and tossed my place. He's in the hospital, under observation, and I don't have to worry that he'll come back some night while I'm here alone."

I was sitting on her loveseat. I curled my legs under me and held my mug with both hands, warming them. Sometimes I am not as imaginative as I ought to be. I knew the harassment had shaken Bonnie, not to mention finding Cleo Hagen's body, but I had been preoccupied with my own reactions. I hadn't thought what it would be like to come back to that tiny house alone every night with a murderer on the loose.

She was talking about the Show of Homes, suggesting that we drive into Shoalwater first to see the two houses that were open there before we went to the Enclave. I mentioned Clara's call.

"You didn't give her a time, did you?"

"No."

"Good. The houses in Shoalwater sound as if they're worth looking at. One's Victorian, one ultra-modern. I like houses. Sometimes, when I lived in Santa Monica, I pretended I was in the market for a new place just so I could go through a house that looked interesting."

I told her about my parents' restored cobblestone house in Childers, New York. We had a nice architectural chat.

Then she shoved me out the door with strict orders to dress up.

We chugged off to Shoalwater about a quarter of ten in Bonnie's Escort, I in a flowery knit dress and Bonnie in white leggings and a hot-pink tunic that shouted California Girl. As she put the car in gear and nosed onto the highway, I remembered to tell her about Kevin Johnson.

"I bet he took off for Portland. He could lose himself there." A car pulled in front of her from someone's driveway and she geared down.

Kevin had probably headed for Portland, but why had he come back first, all the way from Astoria, to berate Ruth? I said, "I can see why you're breathing easier, with Matt under observation. If Matt killed Cleo, though, the motive for the fire and the sideswiping incidents is wide open. I'll feel happier with Kevin Johnson in custody. He may not be the villain, but Ruth said he had money. We don't know who paid the arsonist."

Bonnie nodded and passed an ancient person driving fifteen miles an hour below the limit. I clutched at my shoulder strap.

"Two separate sets of crimes," she muttered.

"Plus Donald Hagen."

We entered Shoalwater and she slowed down to thirty. "D Street and Eighteenth. There it is." It was not quite ten. She parked in the street about half a block from a Victorian fantasy in shades of cream and lilac. She turned to me. "If Donald Hagen hired Johnson, there are only two sets of crimes, two sets of criminals." She looked wistful. "I hate to let Bob McKay off the hook, alibi or no alibi."

We trotted through the two houses in short order. They were nice, but my mind kept turning to Lottie and Matt. We headed north. I sat in silence the first mile or so. Bonnie negotiated a curve, geared down to accommodate another cautious driver, gunned the engine, and passed as the road straightened. She gave me a glance. "Brooding?"

I admitted my mind was on the Cramers.

She reached down and activated her tape player. The Grateful Dead blared out loud enough to melt her stereo. The car juddered and Bonnie's acceleration developed a palpable rhythm, but the music took me out of myself. In one of the pauses, she said, "Great stuff, rock. Prevents rational thought."

The Enclave lay ten winding, wooded miles north of Shoalwater, on the bay side of the peninsula. The northernmost reach of land hooked to the east, forming a small, shallow harbor. A couple of square miles of sand and coast pines had been zoned off on the bay side. We boogied around a last, long curve and there it was, the famous wall. It was made of rather ugly native stone and topped with a course of toothed rocks that looked as if they'd tear the odd cat burglar to bits. Bonnie slowed to a crawl as we approached the entrance.

At the open gate, a uniformed rentacop took the names of drivers and the license numbers of alien vehicles. Bonnie's Escort was more alien than most. The Show of Homes was bringing out everyone on the peninsula who aspired to wealth and exclusion but hadn't yet got there. We were third in line, behind a Lincoln and one of those new Japanese luxury models, so we had leisure to look around us.

The tape wound to its end and clicked off. Bonnie gave the cop her name and slid the Escort onto the impeccable asphalt road, which was more like a long driveway than a street. The houses of the Enclave strewed the enclosed area, each cluster of buildings surrounded by an expanse of cropped lawn and flowers. I spotted a croquet game in progress. The houses were big and most of them were, or at one time had been, Victorian. Several boasted tennis courts and glass annexes that might have been greenhouses or the roofs of indoor swimming pools. Each establishment had a big detached garage.

We followed the Lincoln toward the water until another uniformed flunkey waved us to a stretch of roped-off lawn. Bonnie parked beside the Lincoln and yanked the brake on.

"This is it. Got your ticket?"

I nodded. We had been sold rather pricy passes at the first house in Shoalwater. The proceeds, we were assured, would be divided between the Historic Trust and the Nature Conservancy. The passes were tax deductible. I clutched the stub of mine as Bonnie led the way up the curving walk toward the front porch of the McKay mansion. A huge monkey-puzzle tree dominated the yard. Beyond the house I could see the ferry landing and the gray sheen of the bay. I was glad we were not the first viewers to arrive. If we had come straight out to the Enclave we might have been.

The walk arced past beds of autumn flowers, carefully color coded to complement the gray blue of the turreted house. The fandango of scalloped shingles and orna-mented moldings was muted by the lighter gray of the trim. The McKays had chosen a deep carmine as the accent color. The result was less flamboyant than the Carpenter Gothic vision in Shoalwater, and it fit into the pervading air of dis-creet wealth. Rich but by no means vulgar.

A covered porch wrapped the front of the house. Though the enamel gleamed as if it had been freshly hosed, it was quite dry. Gray wicker lawn furniture sat empty, waiting for the McKay clan to assemble. There was a porch swing. Someone had set out ceramic containers of lobelia on ei-ther side of the stately front door, the blue so intense it al-most hurt the eyes.

A young woman in a long mauve skirt and a white shirt-waist, her hair upswept under a vast mauve and white hat, glanced without interest at our ticket stubs and murmured permission to enter the foyer. It was very handsome in-deed. The woodwork and the long curved banister of the stairway gleamed a rich brown.

"Philippine mahogany," Bonnie muttered as she headed for the guest book. I signed in, too, and took in the hall. No wonder Annie had found my entryway unimpressive. Tall, tall ceilings, wide mahogany molding, period wallpaper, oval portraits of dead McKays, a gleaming refectory table with a floral set piece in cut glass. Shucks.

"Hello, there. I'm Robert McKay."

I thought the kid in tennis whites was speaking to Bonnie and me. I opened my mouth to respond but his glance passed over me to the driver of the Lincoln.

"Robert McKay the fourth, actually, if you know my dad and grandfather."

Sycophantic murmurs indicated that several of the visi-tors did know the other extant Roberts.

"Everybody calls me Rob."

I was willing to bet they called him Robbie.

"If you'll move into the small parlor, I'll come back to you in a few minutes. My mother is putting the paper to bed today, so she deputized me to guide you around."

Several women and one depressed man had come in after us, and the Lincoln and the Nissan had beat us to the guest book, so our little group filled the hall. We moved through the archway Rob indicated like sheep before an intelligent collie.

Bonnie headed for the window. Behung with what looked like nineteenth-century lace, it framed the monkey-puzzle tree. "He looks like his mom."

I nodded and took up a station beside her. Another youth in tennis whites strolled across the lawn to consult our guide. Reinforcements.

Rob McKay was a year or two younger than Freddy, blond, with Annie's definite features and slight build. He was a couple of inches shorter than his father. So far he had not pinched Bonnie. When he returned with two more customers and began his spiel, I decided he probably had his mother's brains, too.

He summarized the history of the house crisply. It had been built for the first Captain McKay in 1882, at the height of the old robber's fortunes, and it passed into the hands of the first Robert after the famous shipwreck of 1901. The elder branch of the family, he explained, had since died out.

Bonnie's elbow jabbed my ribs but she didn't say anything. We had agreed to keep in the background.

Young Rob explained that the house was available to the whole family, though only his parents lived in it year round. They had a suite on the second floor overlooking the bay. The girl at the door was Rob's cousin, Ashley, Quentin's daughter, a senior at Mills, and her brother, a freshman at the University of Washington, was also going to usher people through the house. Rob himself was a junior at Stanford and would be returning to school the next week. I wondered if Rob knew Darla or Freddy.

Rob's Uncle Quentin and family lived on Bainbridge Island near Seattle, and his Aunt Paige lived in San Fran-

cisco. Both lots apparently used the place as a summer
house. He explained that the McKay Fourth of July party
had numbered nineteen, counting guests, and that ten had
stayed through the month without crowding. Must have
been fun to clean up after.

Somebody asked about staff. There was a housekeeper
with rooms near the kitchen and a groundskeeper who lived
over the garage. The rest of the help came from the village.
I think Rob meant Shoalwater. My brother Tod married a
woman whose family had a similar place in Bar Harbor, so
the housekeeping marvels were less interesting to me than
they might have been. My mind turned to Bob and Annie
McKay. They had to have been married for at least twenty
years. Annie had probably been covering for Bob the whole
time.

I trailed through the impeccable rooms without really fo-
cussing. Had Bob wanted to bring Cleo to the big house
party? I visualized Annie facing Cleo on McKay territory
and annihilating her rival with graciousness. Too bad it
never happened.

We saw a lot of well-preserved Victoriana. People made
admiring noises whenever Rob paused in his most accurate
descriptions. Bonnie's wide eyes and pink glow suggested
she found the furnishings impressive.

I was rather impressed with young Rob. He kept up an
easy, informed patter, made a couple of jokes at his family's expense, and answered his guests' questions with good
humor. He also herded us through the rooms that were being shown—all of them on the ground floor—without
making us feel rushed.

The kitchen was strictly from Jenn-Air. No Victorian
nonsense there. I couldn't help feeling that was a shame.
The sideboard in the dining room gleamed with crystal, and
Annie had had the huge table set for ten with the old family
Spode. That was the last room on show. When we had all
duly admired it, we drifted out to the porch. Quentin
McKay's daughter was reciting the background spiel in a
bored voice for seven or eight other people. She led them
into the house as we straggled out. The other boy was
guarding the door.

Everyone seemed bent on thanking Rob for the tour, shaking hands, exchanging little stories that showed how well they knew his mother or father or uncle or grandparents. Bonnie and I hung back.

He saw the last grande dame down the steps and returned to the porch, smiling.

Bonnie beamed at him. "That was great, Mr. McKay."

He blushed. "Call me Rob."

"I'm a little disappointed, though, Rob. No horse and carriage."

He laughed. "No, and there never was a carriage. A narrow-gauge railroad used to run north as far as Shoalwater, with a private spur into the Enclave. Most people kept pony traps to haul luggage from the train, but they left their carriages in Olympia or Portland or wherever."

"I thought residents commuted by ferry," I interjected.

"We do now, but that didn't start up until after the Korean War. My grandfather got a deal on an old ferry the state was mothballing and he persuaded the other owners to chip in. They built the landing with private funds. A yearly fee takes care of maintenance and fuel and so on. After the ferry started running, people built garages and brought their cars."

"If this house is listed with the Historic Trust, didn't they object to a modern garage?"

I glanced at Bonnie. She looked earnest and eager, a real Victorian purist.

Rob's eyes narrowed. He waved an arm bayward. "We hired Jenson and Brevard in Seattle to design a garage that would fit in with the house. Most people think they did a good job."

"Can we see it?"

"It's not part of the tour, but I suppose you can walk around and have a look at it."

Bonnie gave him a ravishing smile. "Thanks. Around here?"

"Follow the walk." And stay on it, his tone said. "Pardon me, ladies, I have to go."

"Thanks for the tour," I murmured.

Bonnie was halfway to the edge of the house. I trotted after her. When we got beyond the kitchen wing, the garage hove into view, an uninteresting two-story structure about the size of a tithe barn with a little cupola on the top. It looked like a garage to me. The doors were open and three vehicles showed us their polished rear ends. There was an empty bay for a fourth. The Mercedes was gone.

"A Porsche, a Trans Am, and a Blazer," Bonnie intoned. "What do you want to bet Bob drives the Blazer?"

"He was driving the Mercedes the night of the murder," I offered. "Or so Annie claims. She followed him home in the Blazer." My gaze drifted past the cars. "I wonder who rides the bikes?" Half a dozen gleaming bicycles lined the far wall.

We were advancing gently in the direction of the Blazer when a voice came from behind us. "Satisfied?"

Chills ran up and down my spine. I said, "The cars are a little anachronistic, but I suppose you could make a case for the bicycles."

We turned and smiled at Annie. She bared her teeth and her eyes glittered. It was clearly time to head for the Escort.

"Nice cupola," Bonnie said.

As we trudged back toward the parking area, I spotted the Mercedes. Annie had driven it off onto the lawn.

"Hard on the grass," Bonnie murmured.

I agreed absently. Annie must have come home in a roaring hurry.

CLARA KLEIN FED US homemade bread and black bean soup for lunch and I told her what I knew of Matt and Lottie. Clara was still distraught. She talked a little about her mother, who had also suffered a series of strokes. She was horrified by Matt's confession and inclined to agree with Freddy's diagnosis of survivor guilt.

"Have they arrested him yet?"

"Matt? I don't think so." I buttered a third slice of the luscious bread. "Jay said the doctors sedated him and were keeping him overnight for observation. I suppose Dale Nelson will take Matt in for questioning when he's released."

"It's so sad." Clara was drinking burgundy. Bonnie and I had passed on that. If I drink wine at lunch I fall asleep.

Bonnie polished her soup bowl with a crust. She had listened to the dialogue without comment. I was grateful. I didn't think Clara would appreciate Bonnie's relief that Matt was in custody.

"Dessert?" Clara passed a bowl of fruit. Bonnie took a plum. "Lark?"

I was eating bread for dessert. "No, thanks. Do you think Lottie wanted to tell Jay something incriminating?"

Clara sighed and lit a cigarette. "I just don't know. She was trying so hard to communicate she must have had something urgent to say. But it could have been that she didn't like the color of the privacy curtain. Whatever. I'm going to miss Lottie. She was such a fighter..." Her eyes teared and she took a long pull on the cigarette. "Tell me about the Enclave. Was it your first visit, Lark? I know it must have been Bonnie's."

I said, "First time for me, too. Do you go there often?"

Clara exhaled through her nose. "A couple of times a year. One of my steady customers lives in that neo-Bauhaus box beyond the ferry slip. I've only been to the McKay house twice, though I see Annie fairly often. She's on the library board, too."

"Everything in that house matches," I blurted.

Bonnie said, "What?"

Clara stubbed out her cigarette and smiled at me as if I were a particularly bright pupil. "Go on."

"I've seen a lot of Victorian restorations near my home town. For that matter, my mother restored an old house that was built after the Erie Canal went through. Ma didn't try for a single period. She just wanted us to be comfortable, so we have stuff from the 1840s alongside modern bookcases and halogen lamps. Our house is fun. Living at the McKay place would be like living in a decorator's show home."

Bonnie said, "Hey!"

Clara nodded. "That house is too perfect. It's Annie's pride and joy, though. I've never had the heart to tell her at least three of her collector's items are modern forgeries."

I laughed.

Bonnie said, "No kidding? Which? How can you tell?"

That set Clara off. She really knew her stuff. It turned out she'd taught art history as well as painting at San Francisco State. I was glad my coverlet was authentic.

By the time the lecture ended Clara had cheered up. We told her about our abortive look at the McKay garage and she seemed to find our impressions amusing.

Bonnie said, "The Historic Trust is a fraud, isn't it?"

Clara sighed. "No, but it is political, like everything else. The McKays can get away with their tarted-up garage and space-age kitchen. Lesser folk toe the line."

"And Tom's house is going to be rejected. . . ." Bonnie took a savage bite of plum.

"It seems unfair," I ventured.

Bonnie wiped off the excess juice. "That insufferable prig. . . ."

"Who, Rob?" I interrupted. "I thought he was a nice kid."

Bonnie glowered. "He was patronizing as hell." She turned to Clara. "He gave us this antiseptic history of the house and said that the senior branch of the McKays had died out. What is Tom, chopped liver?"

Clara poured coffee for us. "I don't think the McKays go in for matrilinear succession." She tasted the delicate euphemism, adding "Tom doesn't really want a bunch of tourists trotting through his house, telling him how quaint it is, anyway. And now he won't have to worry about that."

Bonnie subsided but indignant spots of red burned on her cheeks. "I hope they make a blockbuster film of *Small Victories*. Then Gray Line can run tour buses past the Enclave so everybody can see where the Prom Queen wound up."

That was a good thought, pure Hollywood. I entertained the fantasy. "And Tom can buy a big house in the Enclave and paint it black and orange."

"And decorate it with nude statues in lifelike colors." Clara seemed taken with the idea, too.

We left after the coffee. Clara thanked us for coming and said she felt much better for our visit. She was an interesting woman but I still found her puzzling. I told her I'd keep her posted on Matt's situation, but I didn't say anything to her about Bob McKay's alibi. Whatever she might be, Clara was undeniably a gossip.

"I suppose we can't go out clamming without Matt to guide us to the public clam beds." Bonnie heaved a sigh.

Clara had come out to the car with us. A breeze lifted the errant lock of hair from her forehead. "Do you really want to go for steamers? I'll take you out."

Bonnie was digging for her keys. She paused with one hand in her small shoulder bag. "Will you? Gosh, that'll be great, Clara. When?"

Clara smiled. "Tomorrow if you like. Low tide is around three. It's best to start a couple of hours before then. You'll have to put up with my ratty old rowboat, though. I don't believe in using engines on the bay."

I said, "I like to row."

"Good. You're elected. Bring waders and buckets, and dress warmly. We can drive to the dock around noon and be home with a mess of steamers by four or five. If the weather cooperates. It's supposed to stay calm."

When we tried to thank her, she said it was okay. She needed the distraction. So did I. Bonnie just wanted clams.

At home, I discovered Darla playing with Freddy's computer and Freddy packing a duffel. They had decided to drive to Portland to survey Darla's apartment. School was set to start on Monday.

"She thinks I ought to enroll in some programming courses." Freddy looked shy and hopeful.

"That's a thought."

"I did flunk out."

I had no doubt the college would overlook Freddy's little academic peccadilloes when the finance office discovered he could pay their tuition without student aid. I assured him of that, in somewhat more tactful terms. He thought he might move in with Darla. Darla seemed amenable. She had taken off the neck brace and looked pretty and excited. I wished her luck in law school.

All that took awhile. Jay dragged in at four-thirty, spent but not miserable. He said his presentation had gone well. Matt was still in the hospital undergoing tests. At least he wasn't under arrest. As Freddy was bringing Jay up to date on the Portland expedition, Tom appeared, tired, grimy, and thirsty, with a sackful of canned smoked salmon.

I picked one of the tuna-can-size tins up and turned it over in my hands. "You went fishing for this?"

He opened a beer. "One of the old guys gave me his catch. Likes to fish, hates to eat fish—can you believe it? I figured we were oversupplied with frozen Chinook, so I traded for smoked. It comes in handy around the holidays.

I thanked him and stowed his booty in the cupboard. Freddy and Darla called Dale Nelson to notify him they were leaving town for a day or two. Then they took off. Tom said he was going to cook spaghetti for dinner, so I took a nap. I needed it, for some reason.

I woke at six, refreshed and energized. Tom was yawning over a pan of meat sauce and Jay was on the phone. Jay hung up almost at once. He looked perplexed.

I began setting the table for three. "What's up?"

He fetched salad bowls. "Dale thinks he has a lead on the other man in Johnson's pickup. I wish the kids hadn't gone off. You aren't going to disappear, are you?"

I doled out flatware. "Not until noon tomorrow. Clara's taking Bonnie and me out clamming."

Jay tugged his mustache. "I guess that's all right."

Tom was filling a big pan with water for the pasta. "I bet Clara conned you into rowing."

"Conned?"

He turned the burner up high and rummaged for spaghetti. "She likes to paint the Shoalwater dock from Coho Island. Bread-and-butter pictures for the local market. She had a boat with a greasy old outboard for years. Then last year she decided to be ecologically correct and row. It's a long haul to the island, so she usually persuades a friend to share the labor.

I said ruefully, "I volunteered."

Tom grinned. "Patsy. You and Bonnie will want waders. Help yourselves. I'll unlock the garage for you in the morning."

"Thanks."

Jay pulled a big green salad from the refrigerator and laced it with olive oil. "Is Bonnie coming over tonight?"

Tom said, "She took a rain check. Wants to spend the evening with Gibson and a book."

She was reading *Starvation Hill*. I said casually, "How's the writing coming?"

Tom began breaking pasta into the boiling water. "I got a couple of ideas while I was bobbing up and down on the river. I may move the computer down tonight. If I don't fall asleep over the spaghetti."

Tom's pasta was basic bachelor cookery. After our salmon glut it tasted good. Jay had made the salad so it was only fair that I wash dishes. Jay helped Tom move the computer, and Tom announced that he was going to sleep for twelve hours. He vanished into the guest room, and Jay and I drifted upstairs for a little connubial cuddling. The telephone interrupted our idyll. It was Dale Nelson.

When Jay hung up I said, "Give. I'm tired of listening to your half of phone conversations."

"Dale said Lottie's autopsy showed no sign of facial bruising, no fibers in the air passages. There was a lot of medication in her blood, but no more than was consistent with the meds prescribed for her. She died of a massive cerebral hemorrhage."

"Then Matt didn't kill her?"

He set the phone back on the bedside table. "The m.e. didn't rule that out entirely. Those guys like to play it safe, but Dale thinks she died of natural causes. So does the prosecutor." He began rubbing my neck with his left hand.

I wiggled closer. "That's good news."

"It sure is. Come here."

"Mmm. I am here."

We twined.

The telephone rang. Swearing, Jay fumbled the receiver off the phone and stuck it between his left ear and shoulder. "Hello. No, but you're giving substance to the term coitus interruptus. All right, I'll stop talking dirty. Your younger, purer son just took off for Portland with his girlfriend. I think they're going to cohabit."

It was, I deduced, Jay's mother. I wondered why we hadn't programmed the phone. I flopped back onto my side of the bed and listened.

"Uh-huh. Yeah. No, he's okay. Really. Healthy as a horse. Come on, Ma. You didn't call about Freddy. What's happening?"

He listened. Nancy has a nice voice in person. Over the phone she sounded like a hen squawking. Jay kept her going quite a while with skeptical noises. He scrunched up to a sitting position against the headboard and began jotting on the notepad we kept by the phone cradle. Finally he went through the farewell ritual and hung up. He was looking perplexed again. He clasped his hands behind his head and leaned back against them, staring at the ceiling. Maybe bemused was the right word.

I slid over to him again. "What is it?"

"Ah, hmmm."

"Cut that out, Jay. Am I or am I not the wife of your bosom? I promise not to tell anybody anything, but the suspense is killing me. Put me out of my misery."

"It was just more scuttlebutt on the Hagens."

"Jay!"

He rubbed the bridge of his nose. "I shouldn't say more."

"Give!" I pummeled his head until he grabbed my hands.

"Well, according to Ma's sources, Donald Hagen is gay."

I sat up. "Gay as in . . . no kidding?"

"He married Cleo because his father is one of those dolts who imagine homosexuality can be 'cured.' "

"By proximity to a good woman? That's nineteenth century!"

"You may not have noticed, darling, but there are a lot of nineteenth-century people running around out there."

"Is Nancy fantasizing?"

"My mother?" He tweaked me where I am tweakable. "She's not, but her friends may be. They say the old man threatened to boot his son from the payroll if Donald didn't start flying straight, so Donald looked around for a cooperative woman. Apparently Cleo drove a hard bargain, but Ma's informants seem to believe Donald and Cleo got along well enough. They entertained a lot, never squabbled in public, patronized the right charities. Arrangements like that are not unheard of, Lark."

"You believe the story?"

"Halfway." He nuzzled my neck. "But it shoots holes in my best scenario. I had Donald killing his wife in a fit of sexual jealousy, then trying to incriminate Tom every way he could think of. If Ma's buddies are right, Hagen wasn't jealous of Bob McKay or even of Tom, and the last thing he would have wanted was Cleo's death." He added with grudging fairness, "That would be doubly true if he and his wife were good friends. It sounds as if they were."

I said, "I don't want to feel sorry for Donald Hagen."

"Mmm. Me either. The sucker tried to shoot me." Jay was nuzzling my neck. I nuzzled back.

FIFTEEN

"KEEP YOUR EYE on the oyster cannery and you'll stay on course." Clara's Goretex rainsuit was purple. Her wide-brimmed rain hat, in a paisley print, flopped with the boat's motion. Clara weighed down the stern of her rowboat like a Wagnerian soprano.

I squinted past her and put my back into a long, smooth pull. The oars cut the water without splashing. We were about fifty yards out from the dock and our progress was not rapid.

Bonnie said, "Are we going to see whales?"

"The south reach of the bay is too shallow. Killer whales nose around once in a while, but they're not really whales. Dolphins." Clara settled her waterproof sketching kit onto the seat beside her. A large Thermos reposed between her feet.

I envisaged the boat being nudged by a playful killer whale and caught a crab. That is to say, I misstroked and drew a water-spangled arc in the air with one oar. There were crabs in the area, but crabbers caught them in pots. So I was given to understand. Clara was delivering an amiable lecture on the sea life of Shoalwater Bay. I rowed.

I had been running all summer, so my legs and lungs were in good shape, but I should have been lifting weights. My arms ached and my palms smarted through the gloves Clara had made me wear. I rather thought Clara was going to row back. Or Bonnie. Or Clara and Bonnie in tandem.

The weather was dead calm and misty. Wisps of fog blurred the receding dock and the evergreen copse behind it. I kept my eyes on the white siding of the cannery. A van load of tourists gawked at us from the pier.

"I wonder if the folks in the Enclave are watching us?" Bonnie piped from behind me. She had draped herself over the prow like a figurehead. We had loaded our pails and waders into her end. I was straddling the long handles of the two clam shovels. I felt Bonnie wriggle. "That house on the point has a widow's walk."

"They'd have to use binoculars." Clara gave a flip with her left hand. "The Enclave's way over there to the north."

My oars dug below the placid surface of the water and the boat inched onward.

Clara spent a lot of time telling us about oysters, though none of the oyster beds was open to the public. Overharvesting and disease had destroyed the tiny native oysters in the 1920s. The larger, less succulent type now harvested was a Japanese import. Tom's oyster bed lay around the point of the island on the east side. Clara lit a cigarette and waved it grandly north and east. I glanced over my shoulder but the island was still a blue blur in the distance.

Then she launched into a dark history of ghost shrimp. It seemed they were not good for oysters. Their numbers were increasing.

Once in a while Bonnie tossed in a question. Clara talked on. I think she was lecturing because she didn't want to brood about Matt and Lottie. After ten minutes of steady pulling, I lost myself in the rhythm and stopped my mental grumbling.

We were alone on the gleaming sheet of water. As the peninsula began to recede, a thin mist gave it the insubstantial beauty of a Japanese painting. Colors grew subtler. Gray shafts of sunlight touched little clearings and their undistinguished houses with mystery. The northern hook, the Enclave, was lost in mist. As I watched, the ferry slid into distant view, bound for the far shore and civilization. Coho Island lay about a third of the distance across the narrow, southern neck of the bay. The ferry headed northeast, across the widest part.

"Angle a few degrees to your right, Lark." Clara interrupted a commentary on the blue heron. "Yes, you're okay now. Almost halfway there."

Halfway? I felt as if I had been rowing for hours. I gripped the oars and pulled.

"Want me to spell you?" Bonnie wriggled. So did the boat.

"Not yet." I wasn't into lengthy utterances. After a few strokes I caught the rhythm again and rowed on smoothly. The mist was lifting. As the light shifted, the wooded ridge behind the now-distant cannery changed color. "I can see why you like to paint it, Clara."

Clara twisted and looked back. "Oh, yes, it's different every time."

"Rouen Cathedral?" I bent and pulled.

Clara smiled. "That's a subject for oils. This is pure watercolor. You have a good eye."

"Thanks." Bend, pull.

"Do you paint?"

"I'm just a looker. I tried sketching class once."

Bonnie said, "When I got tired of the singles scene in Santa Monica I started taking night classes, a different subject every semester, in order to scope out the student body. I took a life drawing class. All the students were women. Even the model was a woman."

"Pity." My back gave a definite twinge. I knew I would be bent like a crone the next day. And I still hadn't dug a clam.

"I enjoyed the class but I wasn't any good," Bonnie went on. "As an artist, I'm definitely a wordsmith. I had better luck with economics."

Clara cupped her hands around her lighter and exhaled a stream of blue smoke. "With the subject or your classmates?"

Bonnie gave a reminiscent snort. "Both. Hey, watch it!"

The boat grounded and slid sideways. I straightened and rested the oars. When I turned around I saw we were still at least twenty yards offshore.

"Shoal," Clara said, rocking to port. "They shift." The boat wallowed free. Smoke curled around her head like a wonky wreath.

I rubbed my back. "Can you do a little depth analysis there, Bonnie? I don't need a herniated disc. Sound the bottom or something."

Clara was groping in the slosh at the edge of the crude decking with her free hand. She pulled up a damp yardstick and leaned forward, passing the dripping thing over my shoulder. Clearly the situation was not unprecedented.

"Shove off a little with the left oar, Lark, and Bonnie can guide you along the rim of the sandbank. The tide's farther out than I anticipated." Clara wiped her hand on her purple pants.

"Is that a problem?"

"No. But we do want to ease in closer to the shore."

After perhaps fifteen minutes of gingerly maneuvering, we nosed around the leading edge of the shoal. Between it and the slope of beach ran a temporary channel. Clara decided I should row us aground on the island side. Bonnie would then leap overboard in her waders and pull the lightened boat farther up on the sand. I would repeat the process. I thought it likely the boat would upend, bow over stern, the moment Bonnie deprived us of her weight.

Pulling the clumsy rubber waders over our wool socks took a while. Tom had lent us a rubberized bag for our tennies, fortunately. After some awkward wobbling and rocking, Bonnie managed to slide over the edge. She landed in about a foot of water, which a sneaker wave augmented, but she hung on as she scrambled to higher sand. Then she pulled and I rowed.

We advanced about half a boat length on the next mild wave. I made my way forward, having shipped the oars, and, as the next wavelet receded, I flung one leg over the side onto hard-packed sand. The prow rose considerably with Clara's weight on the stern. Bonnie and I pulled hard with the next little surge, and the rowboat grounded.

Clara stood, with hardly a wobble, tucked her sketching gear under one arm, picked her way forward with surprising agility, and stepped down onto nearly dry sand. She was wearing calf-high purple boots the exact hue of her rain suit. She beamed at us. "There. Nothing to it!"

Bonnie and I looked at each other. It crossed my mind that Clara was putting us through some local initiation rite, like submarine races or snipe hunting. The clams were probably mythical.

While Bonnie and I lugged the boat up onto the beach and removed our pails and shovels, Clara strolled toward the salal and huckleberry bushes that rimmed the wooded island. She had taken a small folding campstool from her pack and was sitting on it, high and dry, by the time Bonnie and I joined her. She began to rummage in the pack.

"What do we do now?" Bonnie put my question into words.

Clara was rigging an ingenious easel with telescoping legs. "Oh, dear, I forgot my Thermos."

"I'll get it." I slogged back to the boat, grabbed the Thermos and the waterproof bag that held our sneakers and, Tom's suggestion, a change of socks apiece. I also tugged the boat a foot or two higher on the sand. The tide was still going out.

"Good girl." Clara gave me a big smile and took her Thermos from me. "Coffee?"

I set the bag on the sand beside her. "You brought three cups?"

"Certainly." I expected her to unscrew the lid and reveal a series of cups, each inside the other like a Gorbachev doll, but she reached into her pack and pulled out a stack of cardboard hot cups instead. "I always come well supplied."

The coffee was laced with brandy. When I had warmed my hands and my innards with Clara's brew, I began to feel my hostility leak away. "So where are the famous steamer clams?"

"That depends. Do you want softshells, cockles, littlenecks, or quahogs? You might luck out and find horse clams and geoducks today, because of the minus tide, but that's only if you don't mind a good wallow in the mud."

"Mud?" The sand beneath our boots was clean and pale gray.

Clara smiled gently. "I like this stretch of beach. The view of the dock and cannery is ideal." She took a last sip of coffee and gestured southward with the inevitable cigarette. "The best softshell clam bed lies about a quarter of a mile down there, around that grove of pines. The sand gives way to a mixture of gravel and mud. You can't miss it."

"Ew," Bonnie said. "Mud."

"Well, just beyond the mudflat, there's a gravelly sand beach that's supposed to be pretty good for cockles. I was teasing you about geoducks and horse clams. There aren't many littlenecks or quahogs around here either. They do better along the Hood Canal and in Puget Sound. God knows why, considering the pollution. This is a relatively clean estuary, so far. Your best bet is the softshell. It likes mud...." When Bonnie let out another Valley Girl "ew," Clara relented. "People have been known to find softshells in the sand and gravel area, too."

"Let it be mud," I said. I reminded myself that I did not like clams. If Bonnie got her fill of mud right off the bat, we could be home by three-thirty. "What do we look for?"

"An oblong dent in the mud, about three-fourths of an inch long. It's hard to see sometimes. When you find the sign, dig a bit to one side so you don't smash the shells."

"How deep do we have to dig?"

"Cockles are really shallow—one to three inches usually. Softshells lie deeper. Half a foot to a foot and a half. If you find a big concentration, dig a trench and pull them out as soon as you see them. They don't burrow, so you won't have to chase them the way you do geoducks."

Chasing clams sounded like a barrel of fun. "What's the limit?"

"Forty apiece of the softshells, and twenty-five cockles."

Bonnie let out a long whistle.

I was surprised, too, and not thrilled.

Oblivious to my dismay, Clara went on with the rules of the game. "You have to dig separately, and you ought to wear gloves if you go for softshells. They can cut up your hands."

Bonnie said, "I didn't bring gloves."

"Maybe you should look for cockles, then. They have a less fragile shell."

I swallowed the last of my coffee. "I brought gloves. You can dig the holes, Bonnie. I'll grope for the little devils."

Clara said, "Trade off. Be sure to take both buckets. I doubt that you'll run into a warden, but it's best to stick to

SHEILA SIMONSON   209

the letter of the law. Fines for violations can be hefty. And be sure to fill your holes. That's the number-one rule."

Bonnie shouldered her shovel and grabbed her pail. "Let's go, Lark."

Hiking in waders was no damned fun, but Bonnie said we should save our sneakers for the trek back. I carried the bag of shoes, along with my shovel and pail. We plodded on. By that time the sun had burned off the last of the fog. A tiny breeze riffled the water. We stopped to admire a blue heron.

"Just like an Audubon print."

I glanced at Bonnie. Her face had a look of purest ecstasy. Of course, she hadn't rowed across the bay.

When we rounded the shoulder of wooded land, we lost sight of Clara and the boat. One of the many ships' crews that had wrecked in Shoalwater Bay in the 1840s had wintered on Coho Island. I decided I wasn't enough of a pioneer to want to be similarly stranded. Clara had said we had plenty of time for clamming. It was not yet low tide. I imagined a freak wave floating the boat out to sea—and lapping around Clara's purple boots.

When we finally reached the stretch of mudflat and got down to the business of looking for clam sign, I began to see the utility of our rain gear. I had left my jacket unzipped while I rowed, and even so I had worked up a sweat. The waders felt like a portable sauna.

The day was cool but by no means cold. It wasn't raining. Still, one slurp with the shovel in the sticky mud persuaded me I'd need a total cover-up. I handed the digging over to Bonnie, took my gloves from the pocket of my jacket, and zipped up.

Bonnie was sure the dents she had spotted in the mud were clam airholes. She found quite a few worms but no clams. I dissuaded her from digging deeper. We strolled farther out and tried again. This time we found seven undersized softshells. At least we knew what they looked like.

We picked our way over mossy gravel strewn with dead crabs and bits of shell to another streak of mud. As we intruded on their territory, half a dozen gulls squawked and flew off.

Then we lucked out. Bonnie spotted the oddly rectangular dents almost at once and began digging. About a foot down she uncovered a cluster of fine specimens. I knelt and began to pull them out.

Perhaps we went a little mad. Bonnie dug. I scooped clams. When she saw my primitive delight, Bonnie leaned her shovel on her pail and started scooping, too. We found fifty-two keepers in ten minutes. The mud felt glorious, once I removed my right glove and began squishing with my bare hand. By the time we had picked over that colony, refilled our trench, and divided the spoils, we were hooked.

We were also covered with mud, juicy, salty, glorious mud. We made a lot of noise.

Bonnie said, "It's like messing with Play-doh."

"Nope, too dry. Mud pies."

"My mother never let me make mud pies." She adjusted her glasses and left a streak of silt on her nose.

I snickered. "You look like Paleolithic Woman."

"I want to sit in that mud," she said solemnly. "Sit and roll and make grunting noises like a hog in a wallow."

I grabbed my shovel and pail. "More!"

It took us awhile to find another concentration of clams. We dug side by side, giggling and squeaking. At one point Bonnie lay, up to her shoulder in the muddy hole, and began to grope frantically.

"God, you must have found a geoduck."

"My ring!"

"What?"

"I lost my ring." She swore and groped and kept pulling up bits of shell and rock.

"Want me to look?"

"What's to see?" She stood up and shook off about half a pound of slime. "Rats, it's lost. That was my mother's friendship ring. She's going to kill me, but it was worth it. How many do we have?"

We took inventory. Definitely forty apiece. We looked at each other.

Bonnie started scooping the heap of mud and gravel over the grave of her mother's ring. "Let's go on to the gravel bar and find those cockles."

"Okay." I filled in my hole, too.

Clara had said the bar lay just beyond the mudflat. She was right, but she hadn't mentioned that the mudflat extended a good quarter of a mile south. Here the evergreens were beginning to encroach on the shore. Something had made a crude path through the underbrush. Beyond the bushes that rimmed the beach, the trees loomed taller. I hoped the pathmaker wasn't a bear.

Cockles proved more elusive than the softshells. We probed and dug, and uncovered quite a few worms. I saw the shadows of ghost shrimp in a tide pool. Once I thought I heard Clara calling. I stood and listened. The sound came again, vague and high, but not from the north. Some bird, probably, whose call I didn't recognize. I went back to serious clam hunting.

I was starting to think about the time, though. I kept glancing at my watch. A quarter of three. We had perhaps forty-five minutes of slack water. Then the tide would creep back. According to Clara, the change wasn't dramatic in calm weather, so we were unlikely to run into trouble. Still, it would take awhile to haul the pails with their burden of clams and seawater back to the boat.

I was about to suggest that we leave when Bonnie found a clump of cockles. They were prettier than the softshells, and the sandy aggregate was much less messy than mud, but cockles were too easy. They lay a mere handspan under the sand. We had sorted our limits into the pails and filled the shallow holes by three o'clock. Plenty of time.

The distant bird call came again. I listened hard, frowning.

"What is it?"

I shrugged. "Just a noise."

"A bear?"

"More like a bird."

"Whew. I don't like the idea of bears. Let's change into our sneakers before we walk back. That bucket's heavy and I don't want to walk in waders."

We sat on a drift log with our backs to the woods and stripped the waders off. I decided to change socks, too. In my clam frenzy I had slopped seawater into the left side of my waders. My sock and jeans were damp.

Bonnie tied her Reeboks and stood up, stretching. "God, that was fun. There must be some atavistic impulse that makes women want to amass shellfish. Did you read about those Stone Age sites in Spain with all the mussel shells? I wonder if the mussels in this area are good eating."

I tied my laces. "Probably. I ordered a smoked mussel appetizer once. It was good eating."

"All right, stand up. Slow and easy now."

The man had approached so carefully down the crude pathway that I hadn't heard him. I stood. Bonnie and I turned. My first thought was that the game warden wanted to inspect our catch, so I was more annoyed than alarmed. Then I saw the rifle.

He was a heavyset, ruddy man in a plaid shirt and jeans. He raised the barrel so that the little black hole pointed right at my stomach. "Follow me."

I swallowed and exchanged a swift glance with Bonnie. She looked pale and blank. Far off and inland, the bird call sounded.

"What's the problem, Officer?" Bonnie had leapt to the wrong conclusion, too.

I cleared my throat. "He's not—"

"Shut the fuck up. I said follow me." The barrel waved in the direction of the path.

I bent to pick up my shovel.

"Leave it!"

I dropped the handle on the sand and straightened. "You must be Kevin Johnson."

The rifle swung my direction again. "Yeah, so what? Who the shit are you?"

"I'm Lark Dodge. I met your wife."

"Well, ain't that nice? Move it, lady."

"Shall I bring my clams?" Bonnie had to be out of her mind.

Apparently Johnson thought so, too, for he snarled and gestured with the rifle. Bonnie abandoned her pail and trotted to the edge of the woods. I followed with Johnson behind me. I couldn't see the rifle, but I felt it in the center of my spine as if he were prodding me with it. In reality he kept his distance, but the sensation was undeniable. We stumbled along. When we slowed, Johnson swore at us.

The path would have been difficult walking without the threat of a bullet between the shoulder blades. It looked as if an elk had crashed its way through the tangle of undergrowth in a beeline for the water. Fallen branches and blackberry tripwires made the footing treacherous.

Bonnie and I were Johnson's prisoners, hostages. At first I had no idea why he hadn't just ignored our presence on the beach. We were clamming, unlikely to turn our attention inland to his hideaway. Why hadn't he just watched us and let us leave? Then the cries of the bird began to resolve into human shrieks. Somebody was hurting. I remembered Melanie.

"Has your wife gone into labor, Kevin?"

A wordless snarl answered me, but I knew I was right. He had dragged his pregnant wife off into hiding with him. She was going to have her baby at any minute from the sound of her. Kevin had spotted a couple of women on the beach and decided we would make good midwives. What a hope.

There was nothing funny about the agony in Melanie Johnson's cries, nothing amusing in the prickle between my shoulder blades, but I had to suppress a wild urge to laugh. What I knew about childbirth would take less than a typed page to tell. Kevin was going to have to go for a doctor, or a paramedic. Whatever. I would have to persuade him.

I decided the path was not the right place.

Kevin's camp indicated that he had done some planning. There was a green umbrella tent, from which came the now-piercing screams, and a fiberglass canoe rested against one of the huge evergreens that ringed the clearing. He had set up a Coleman stove. A tarp covered a hump that was probably supplies. He must have made several trips. The site looked oddly familiar, but it took me a minute or two to make the connection. He had pitched his tent under dark, towering cedars like those that dwarfed his mobile home.

When we came to a halt, I turned and tried to ignore the rifle. "Look, Kevin, I know you want us to help your wife, but the truth is she needs a real doctor."

His mouth set in a thin line. "Tough shit. You help her."

I said, "I'd be glad to, but I don't know anything about childbirth. I've never had a baby, Kevin. I've never even spent time around babies. What can I do for her?"

Melanie shrieked.

Bonnie said, "I'll help her."

Kevin and I looked at her.

Mud streaked her face and her nylon rain jacket. Her blond hair had wilted into witchlocks. She raised her chin. "A friend of mine needed a Lamaze coach. I took the course. I can help Melanie. Come on, Lark." She jerked her head toward the tent.

"No funny business." Kevin waved the rifle.

I followed Bonnie into the tent.

Melanie Johnson was lying on an open sleeping bag. She was half naked, and blood and mucus streaked her white thighs and buttocks. She lay on her side. She was sobbing as we ducked into the dim green shelter, whimpering with pain, her eyes clenched shut. A spasm rippled her too-visible belly and she screamed. My hands went to my ears. I was as near panic as I have ever been.

Bonnie knelt at her head. "Melanie, we've come to help you."

Melanie gave another soul-rending shriek. Bonnie reached out and took her face. "Look at me. I'm Bonnie. Do you see me, Melanie?"

The eyes fluttered open. "Hurts."

"Yes, I know. You're afraid. But it's just a baby and you've already had two babies. You know what to do. I'm going to help you breathe."

The next shriek was muted.

"That's better. Come on. I know you're scared, but that just makes the pain worse. Lark is going to find something to make you warmer. Did your water break?"

Incredibly, the woman nodded. "Yeah. I went to take a pee. When it broke, I come back and got out of my jeans. Oh, ow. It hurts."

Bonnie was holding her hand. "That's right. Brace against me. The pains are pretty close together, aren't they?"

"It's coming. Help me."

"Right. Do you want to lie there on your side or would you rather squat? I'll help you up."

"Lie. Ow. I'm thirsty."

"Go get her something to drink, Lark."

I went.

SIXTEEN

I DUCKED OUT OF THE TENT into the camp. Kevin's rifle barrel came up. This time the muzzle pointed straight at my throat.

I swallowed. "She needs something to drink."

He gestured with the barrel at the tarp-covered pile of supplies. "Over there. We got beer and Coke."

Beer! Hadn't the man heard of fetal alcohol syndrome? "I want water."

"Stuff in the pan's okay." He waved the rifle again. He was standing in the brush at the edge of the trail to the beach. His flat stare didn't waver from me.

Melanie gave a muffled scream. I could hear Bonnie's voice, low and calm, reassuring her. I could hear my own heartbeat.

I skirted the edge of the clearing, keeping maximum distance between me and the rifle, until I reached the Coleman stove. A rusty sediment had settled in the bottom of the pan. "It looks dirty."

"She boiled it this morning, lady. It's safe."

"Where's a cup? Never mind, I see it." A chipped mug sat on the stump behind the stove, along with two empty plastic buckets. I dipped a cupful of water from the pan, careful not to roil the silt. My hands shook. "Is there a creek? We'll need warm water soon." All I knew about primitive birthings came from old western movies. Surely the midwife boiled water.

"Spring," he said. "Over there." The rifle barrel pointed beyond me into the woods.

"Well, look, I'm going to take this in to Melanie. Can you get a bucket of water while I'm inside and put some on to heat?"

"Fetch it your own self. I'm not going nowhere."

I didn't argue the point. Melanie gave another muted shriek. Her throat had to be sore.

In spite of my trembling hands, I carried most of the water into the tent without spilling it. I knelt beside Bonnie. She had flopped the sleeping bag over Melanie's exposed body and was sitting, cross-legged, on the canvas by the woman's head, holding her hands. "Yes, that's right—puff, puff, puff, hold. That's the way. You can do it, Mel."

Between the two of us, we managed to get about half a cup of water into Melanie. The rest spilled—on us and on the tent floor. Melanie moaned rhythmically. Bonnie kept talking to her.

I was crowding them. I poked around the edges of the tent and found another sleeping bag, rolled up and tied, and a duffel bag. Melanie moaned. Bonnie chanted.

I grabbed the duffel. "I'm going to heat water. What else do you need?"

"Puff, puff, puff, hold. Good girl. Soap and warm water. We can clean her up, but I'm not going to move her into the other sleeping bag until the baby comes. That'll be the only clean warm place available." Bonnie had done some exploring, too. "Right, Melanie, concentrate...what is it?"

"Back!" Melanie moaned.

"She's having back pains," Bonnie muttered. "See if you can improvise a hot-water bottle, Lark. We need to get her warm and ease the muscle cramps."

"How soon...?"

"Hours, probably."

Melanie gave a real shriek and Bonnie bent to take up her incantation. I fled with the duffel bag.

The rifle barrel swung my way again.

I did my best to ignore it. I made for the stump, sat on it, and pawed through the clothes in the bag. A flannel nightgown, jeans and sweatshirts, underwear of both sexes, socks. The clothes were clean. The Johnsons hadn't been on the island long.

A zippered makeup kit held lipstick, eyeshadow, mascara, blusher, a toothbrush and toothpaste, handsoap in a plastic box, fingernail scissors, and a bottle of aspirin. There were no baby things at all, not so much as a disposable di-

aper, nor were there any sanitary napkins. At least there was
soap.

After a paralyzed pause, I picked up a bucket. "How far
is the spring?"

"Hundred yards. Follow the path." The barrel of the rifle glinted. "Just get the water and come right back. Don't
try no funny stuff. There's bears in them woods."

That was a confidence builder. I left the open duffel on
the stump and took the path Kevin had indicated. It led into
dense brush. Within ten yards I was out of sight of the camp
and the bushes closed around me.

It may be that I had cherished hopes of running off to
find help. If so, I abandoned them. The underbrush was so
thick I could see no more than a few yards in any direction,
and the bushes looked thorny. Huge cedars towered over-
head, blocking the watery sunlight. Condensation from the
sword ferns that lined the path soaked my jeans and sneakers. I was glad of the rain jacket.

I was far too frightened to cry. I trudged along the narrow path, crushing ferns underfoot, until I came to a reedy
bog. Kevin or someone had laid lopped cedar branches to
the heart of the swamp. I followed the branches, squishing.
I thought of the peat bogs of my home area of upstate New
York. They went down hundreds of feet. People had
drowned in them.

The water that burbled up in the middle of the reeds
flowed off to the south in a stream that was clear but tinged
with brown, like very weak tea. I filled the bucket to the
brim and squished my way back to the trail. I took the path
slowly and I began to think.

It was almost four o'clock. Clara had to have noticed our
absence. What would she do? Given the purple boots, she
probably wouldn't venture onto the mudflat. Could she see
our abandoned gear from the point? I didn't think so. The
gravel bar where we had harvested cockles lay beyond the
next headland.

I wished Bonnie and I had not pulled the rowboat so high
onto the sand. The tide was coming in, but it would take
Clara awhile to float the boat and row across the bay. That

was what I hoped she'd do. Row across the bay and call Jay or Tom.

Kevin didn't know about Clara, did he?

He knew we hadn't parachuted onto the island, and he had to know someone would wonder where we were. Soon.

Someone. Clara. What did I know about Clara? She had brought us to the island, directed us to dig clams near Kevin's hideaway. Maybe Clara was the mastermind, the murderer. No. Surely not. Hadn't she been out of town when Cleo Hagen was killed? That could be verified. My heartbeat slowed. Of course, Clara could still have hired Kevin....

I tripped on a clump of fern and a pint of water sloshed on my sneakers. Gritting my teeth, I steadied the bucket and walked on, eyes on the trail. I was carefully not thinking about bears.

By the time I returned to the camp, several scenarios, all of them appalling, had flashed through my head. The mildest featured an innocent Clara trotting along the shore in her purple boots and up the path to find us. Then Kevin would have three hostages. The worst scenario involved a SWAT team, helicopters, and a general massacre.

Jay would guess Kevin was involved in our disappearance because Kevin was on Jay's mind, but how would Jay respond? He was an experienced policeman, but he was also an affectionate husband. Sometimes his affections skewed his judgment. I hoped he wouldn't call out the National Guard.

When I emerged from the brush, Kevin's rifle targeted me instantly. At least it didn't have a hair trigger.

Though I was not skillful around Coleman stoves, I lit the balky device after much pumping and swearing. Melanie still yelled at brief intervals, but I had begun to be able to block the sound out. I set a fresh pan of water on the stove and placed the half-empty bucket on the stump.

The next hour and a half passed with excruciating slowness. Bonnie and I swabbed Melanie clean. She seemed to like that. I dumped Coke from a two-liter jug and filled the jug with almost boiling water. That made a fair hot-water bottle. I listened to Bonnie's mantra and rubbed Melanie's back. Bonnie said the baby was crowning, meaning that the crown of its head showed.

I cajoled a fishing knife from Kevin to cut up sweatshirts. The knife was only marginally a weapon. He had the rifle. He got out his tackle box and gave me the knife, grumbling.

I ripped away. The soft inner fabric of the sweatshirts would make reasonably warm blankets for the baby. I also tore up all of Kevin's undershirts and constructed something like a diaper. That gave me satisfaction. I was saving Melanie's flannel nightgown for Melanie.

Kevin kept silent. I didn't say anything either. I brooded about the situation, rejecting lines of argument. I had great difficulty putting myself in Kevin's head. I didn't know him and what I did know I didn't like. There was no use appealing to his concern for Melanie. After all, he had dragged her to the island. That he had captured us to take care of her probably just meant he didn't want to deal with her himself. What he intended to do with Bonnie and me after the baby came didn't bear thinking about. At least he wasn't drunk. Yet.

When I finished ripping cloth and improvising the layette, I took the duffel back to the tent. Melanie's Coke bottle had cooled off. I carried it out, heated more water, refilled it. Bonnie thanked me and approved the "baby clothes." When I ducked back out of the tent, I went over to where Kevin was standing, his rifle still at the ready.

"The baby could come any minute."

He grunted. His eyes shifted.

"Bonnie will need something to cut the cord with. I'm going to boil the fishing knife...."

"No way!"

"Use your head, Kevin. The knife has to be sterile, doesn't it? We don't want the baby to get an infection. Also I need some fishing line or leader." I didn't see Bonnie tying the umbilical cord in a granny knot. It was bound to be slippery. Hence the line. "I'll have to sterilize that, too, and I'm going to need more water. Is there another pan?"

"Frying pan."

"Wonderful." I had given up expecting him to help, so I went back to the stove and restarted it, found the frying pan under the supply tarp, and poured the last of the water into it. I set the grimy knife in the skillet. Then I picked up both plastic pails and went for more water. When I returned Kevin was standing near the stove. He handed me a coil of fishing line.

"Thanks."

Grunt.

I popped the line in the boiling water, trusting it wouldn't melt, filled the saucepan, and set it on the other burner. I wondered how long the knife would have to boil before it would be safe to use.

Bonnie was easing Melanie back onto the sleeping bag when I poked my head in the tent to report. Melanie gave a full-throated scream.

"When?"

Bonnie said grimly, "Soon." She knelt again and took Melanie's hand. Melanie screamed.

I explained about the fishing knife and line through the litany of puffs and groans. Bonnie nodded. "Good. Take it easy, Mel. Almost done...what's that?"

Outside the tent a man had shouted. Male voices rumbled.

Bonnie and I looked at each other. Rescue? We waited. I think Melanie was listening, too. She missed a scream. When no rifle shot came, I eased back out of the tent and straightened.

Tom Lindquist stood by the path from the beach, his hands clasped behind his neck. Kevin was holding the rifle on him. Behind me, Melanie gave a muffled shriek.

I took two cautious steps in the direction of the stove. The rifle barrel swung my way, wavered, and swung back toward Tom.

Tom said, "Are you all right, Lark?" He was wearing short boots, jeans, and a sweatshirt under a gaping nylon rain jacket. He looked as if he'd been fishing—or inspecting his oyster bed, more likely. I tried to remember if he'd said anything about coming to Coho Island that afternoon. No. Not a word. He had intended to write.

I drew a breath. "I'm fine. Bonnie's fine. Melanie is about to have a baby." I took two more cat steps toward the stove. The frying pan would boil dry if I didn't take it off the burner soon.

The barrel of the rifle wavered between Tom and me.

I said in conversational tones, "I am going to take the knife and fishing line in to Bonnie, Kevin." I turned the burner off. The water in the saucepan was boiling, too, so I turned that burner down.

I rummaged for the sweatshirt sleeve I had been using as a hotpad. I wasn't sterile, of course, so I was going to contaminate the knife. I hoped not horribly. The knife hasp protruded from the water. I picked the knife out, dropped it on the fabric, and blew on my scalded fingertips. When the sting faded, I plucked out the line and dropped it on top of the knife. Without looking at the two men again, I turned and went back to the tent.

"Who is it?"

"Tom. He's not armed."

"Tom? But why...that's it, Mel. It's coming." Bonnie was hunched over the writhing woman. "Here's the head."

Melanie pushed hard and gave a yell that was half pain, half triumph.

"Great. Now the shoulders."

I could see very little. I knelt by Bonnie and peered over her shoulder just as she pulled the bloody child from its mother's body and laid it on Melanie's stomach.

"Give me a cloth."

A cloth. Jesus. I dropped the knife and fishing line on the canvas floor of the tent and handed Bonnie the damp rag I had carried them in.

Bonnie swabbed the baby's face and cleared its air passages. It let out a mewling yowl.

"Oh, God, he's alive!" Melanie burst into tears.

"Get me something to wrap him in," Bonnie ordered.

I blinked back sympathy tears and scuttled for the duffel. By the time I found the improvised receiving blankets and the undershirt diaper, Bonnie had tied off the cord. As I watched she severed the umbilical. The baby howled and Melanie wept.

Bonnie was smeared with blood. So was Melanie and so was the baby. Bonnie looked at me. The bloody knife was still in her hand. "Soap and warm water?"

"Coming up."

"You'll have to dispose of the afterbirth, Lark."

I gulped and nodded.

Bonnie wasn't interested in my sensibilities. She had turned back to her charges. "More work, Mel. Keep pushing."

I fled in disorder. Once outside I ignored the two men and bent over, hands on my thighs, sucking in oxygen. When my head cleared I walked to the stove. Water simmered in the saucepan. I turned the burner off and added a couple of cups of cold water to the pan. The handle was hot. I rummaged for more scraps of sweatshirt to use as a hotpad.

Kevin cleared his throat. "What's happening?"

I ignored him. It was none of his damned business.

Tom said, "Lark?"

"The baby's alive. I have to take this in and then I have to bury the afterbirth. Is there a shovel, Kevin?"

He cleared his throat again. "Under the tarp."

I found a short-handled shovel, Forest Service surplus, and emptied one of the water buckets. Then I carted the shovel, the empty bucket, and the pan of warm water into the tent. Bonnie was wrestling the baby into its makeshift diaper. It was still mewling. It was incredibly tiny and manifestly male. Melanie watched, her face smeared with tears. Another contraction hit her and her face clenched.

When Bonnie had wrapped the child in the sweatshirt-blanket, she acknowledged my return. "Is that all the water?"

"All that's hot. Shall I get the soap?"

"Yeah."

I laid the bucket and shovel on the floor and scrabbled in the duffel for Melanie's makeup kit. Bonnie handed me the baby. Then she took the soap, scrubbed her hands, and moistened the scrap of fabric she had used to clean the baby's face. "Clean rags."

"Uh, yes." The baby wriggled and let out another howl. Its eyes were closed and its thin hair was plastered to its tiny skull with blood and mucus. I once picked up a garter snake. It felt just like insulated wire until it wiggled. Then it felt like nothing else on earth. It was pure luck that I didn't drop the baby the way I had dropped the snake.

I transferred the child, gingerly, to the crook of my left arm and began rummaging for rags.

Bonnie said, "Right, Mel, give it a push."

Melanie moaned. Bonnie gripped her hand. I was past nausea. I craned over Bonnie's shoulder. The baby wriggled in my arms. With a gush of blood and amniotic fluid, the afterbirth spewed onto the slimy surface of the sleeping bag.

Melanie gave a huge sigh. Bonnie patted her hand and said in an absent voice, "Nice work, Mel. It's over."

I wondered if I was going to faint. The baby wiggled.

"Lark?"

"Um, yes. Here." I handed Bonnie a wad of mutilated undershirt.

She began swabbing Melanie's face. "You'll have to bury that deep or the bears will be after it."

"That" lay glistening on the plaid flannel lining of the sleeping bag. "Then you'd better take the baby."

"Undo the other sleeping bag and lay him on it. I'm going to clean Mel up and put her into the nightgown. Where is it?"

"In the duffel." I scooted over to the other sleeping bag and undid it, one-handed. The baby struggled against my grip and mewed like a kitten.

When I had laid the little creature, still swaddled, inside the clean sleeping bag, I took up the shovel. I slid the quivering mass of the afterbirth, part person, part thing, into the empty bucket, and blundered out of the tent.

Both men were staring at me. The rifle barrel sagged.

I stared back.

Kevin said, "Mel . . ."

Fury welled in me. "What the hell do you care? That woman needs a doctor now. So does your son. . . ."

"Lark!" Tom's voice was sharp, cautionary.

I bit back the scalding words. The men stared. I shifted my grip on the pail and headed toward the path to the beach.

"Where d'you think you're going?"

"I have to bury this and I am not going to dig through tree roots to do it. I'll find a patch of sand...."

Kevin was scowling. He jerked the barrel of the rifle at Tom. "Help her and be quick about it. I'll keep both of you in my sights."

Tom and I trudged back to the point at which the vegetation gave way to gravelly beach. The mist had thickened and I couldn't see very far out on the water. Nothing moved.

I wondered where Jay was and how Tom had got to the island. There was no sign of a boat, Tom's or anyone else's. No Shoalwater Fire District rescue launch. Our waders and pails lay where we had left them.

Tom took the shovel from me, found an open patch of dirt and gravel beside the trail, and began to dig. He dug fast, not speaking. There was no point in our trying to talk because Kevin was standing in the brush at the edge of the woods. He was out of sight of anyone approaching from the bay, but he was well within earshot. I emptied the mass of tissue into the gaping hole and carried the bucket toward the beach.

"Where are you going?"

"To rinse the bucket." I didn't look at Kevin, just kept going. The tide was definitely coming in. I sloshed seawater in the pail until it looked clean, glancing around me, hoping to spot something that would clue me in. How had Tom found the camp? I refused to believe in coincidence. He had come to find us, but how? Why wasn't he armed? If he had been armed...if he had been armed we would have been birthing that child in the middle of a fusillade. My respect for Tom's judgment went up a notch.

"That's enough." There was an edge of something like panic in Kevin's voice.

I emptied the bucket of water and trudged back up the path. Tom had filled in the hole. Kevin herded us toward the camp. I had seen no sign of anyone—not Jay, not Clara, no posse, no rescue helicopters, no National Guard. I had heard nothing.

When we reached the clearing, Kevin motioned us toward the stove and the wide cedar stump. He made Tom sit on the stump and he sent me into the tent for the fishing knife Bonnie had used to cut the umbilical cord. Bonnie gave it up under protest, but she was busy with Melanie and the baby. I went back out into the clearing. Kevin made me put the knife back in his tackle box.

He wanted me to stay outside. Under his eye.

I refused. "Your wife and son need help. So does Bonnie, and my help is better than none. I'm going back into the tent. Why don't the two of you talk the situation over and decide what to do? You can't keep us here forever, Kevin."

A stupid thing to say. I picked my way across the scuffed ferns to the tent. Kevin didn't try to stop me but I could feel the heat of his frustration. The man was cornered. He'd probably decide to kill us all, then shoot himself. That was what cornered men did in this part of the country. It was a clear sociological pattern among loggers and fishermen. Jay had told me grim tales. Others I had read in the newspaper or heard of on the TV news. Tom's presence, unarmed, was a wild card.

I entered the tent and stopped. Bonnie was sitting in the middle of the floor, cross-legged, shoulders slumped, head bent. She looked up at me. "Now you can tell me what's going on."

"I don't know." I took in the rest of the tent.

Melanie lay in the clean sleeping bag with the baby snuffled against her. She was resting—or unconscious. Bonnie had rolled the other filthy bag up and shoved it against the opposite side of the tent. She had given her own face and hands a rough cleaning, too, but she looked grimy and exhausted in the greenish light, and no wonder.

I scrunched down beside her. "You were terrific, Bonnie. Are you all right?"

"We have to get Melanie to a doctor."

"Is she bleeding?"

Bonnie nodded. "Not badly. I think women do bleed after a birth. I rigged a pad for her. Still, everything in the tent was dirty. She needs antibiotics and so does the baby."

"What about milk?"

"For the baby?" She frowned. "I don't think that's a big deal the first day or so, and she was going to breast-feed anyway. But she's weak and the baby's small."

I rested my chin on my knees. "Should I fix something for her—soup maybe?"

Bonnie sighed. "It might be a good idea, but she'll sleep for a while. I wish I could sleep. I'm beat."

"No wonder."

"What did Tom say?"

"Not a lot."

Her shoulders sagged. "He must have come looking for us."

"Yes. It's too much of a coincidence otherwise, but I don't know where his boat is or who else knows where he was searching. Clara must have called him."

"Would she?"

"She doesn't like cops."

"True." Bonnie heaved a sigh. "Well, see about soup. I'm hungry even if Melanie isn't. Kevin's probably missed a meal or two himself."

"I don't somehow think the way to his heart is through his stomach."

She gave a small mournful smile. "Pity."

I creaked to my feet. I was getting stiff in the shoulders already. By tomorrow, if I lived that long, my whole body would probably seize up.

"Try to talk some sense into the man," Bonnie said softly as I left the tent.

SEVENTEEN

"AND I DECIDED to take a look at the oyster bed," Tom was saying in a ludicrously peaceful voice. "I knew Bonnie and Lark meant to go clamming, so I hiked around the point to see how they were doing. I saw the waders and buckets, and followed your trail. That's all there was to it, Kevin."

"You're shittin' me."

"No. Nobody knows where you are—yet. Why don't you haul the canoe down to the shore and take off? Search and Rescue will come looking for Bonnie and Lark sooner or later, and when they do we can see that Melanie gets medical help."

Kevin had his back to me. I considered jumping him and decided not to. A sideways flick of his head suggested he'd heard me. His hands tightened on the rifle.

I inspected the pile of supplies. I found a box of biscuit mix, salmon jerky, bacon, Rice-A-Roni, packets of dried soup. Chicken noodle soup. Tom was droning on about the oyster bed. He was still droning when the water boiled, talking about anything but the current situation. I turned the burner way down and let the soup simmer.

Tom was reminiscing about some fishing boat he and Kevin had worked on. I tuned him out and tried to think.

Kevin could use the canoe to reach the mainland, but it was still daylight and he probably feared discovery. Did he intend to take Melanie and the baby with him? Where would they go? I supposed he had hidden the pickup somewhere in the brush on the relatively unsettled eastern shore opposite Coho Island. He could retrieve the pickup as soon as it turned dark and head for Portland, but he ought to leave Melanie and the baby with us. Us. He was probably going to shoot us.

"He fired me." Kevin's voice, aggrieved. "He won't take me out no more. I was counting on that job."

Tom said, "Henry will take you out."

"I don't like that old Siwash. Besides, fishing's a dead end. I need a steady job. Maybe construction."

"There's a lot of building."

"Goddamn Californians."

"Well, it's work."

"I got money. I was going south, down around Alsea. I got friends down there with a gyppo outfit. They'd hire me. I got money." He repeated the phrase as if he were reciting a magical formula. "We was going to find us a motel in Alsea and hole up."

So he had meant to take Melanie. "What about the baby?"

Kevin spat. "Goddamn woman. She *made* me bring her along. Wouldn't stay with her ma. I had me this camp. I was going to hide out here until things calmed down. I could've, too, easy, but Mel made me bring her. Dumb cunt swore she had two more weeks to go."

Tom said, "I guess she was wrong."

Kevin growled. "Women and kids drag a man down."

Tom ignored that. "Why Alsea? I thought you wanted to stay here. You told me you weren't going to leave the peninsula no matter what."

"I got money." Kevin sounded less sure of himself.

"I suppose it's what they paid you to burn down my grandfather's house."

"Hey!"

"Well?"

I glanced at Kevin's face. It was even redder than it had been. His lips worked. "We just gave you a scorching."

"Why?"

Kevin's hands clenched on the rifle stock.

"What did I ever do to you?" Tom was pushing him. I thought that might be unwise, but I didn't understand the dynamics of the relationship so I kept still.

Kevin cleared his throat and spat.

"That's no kind of answer."

"Don't screw around with my head, Tom. I'm warning you."

"I just wanted to understand." Tom's tone was almost plaintive. When Kevin didn't answer him he shrugged. "That the gun your dad gave you?"

"Yeah."

"I remember you telling me about it. Thirty ought six. Single action?"

"Yeah. So?" Kevin worked the bolt. "I always get me an elk first day of the season. It's my good-luck piece, see?"

"Your old man used to take you hunting when you were in junior high, showed you what to look for in the bush."

"Yeah. So what?"

"You have a son now, Kevin. Are you going to take him elk hunting?"

Kevin gave a snorting laugh and didn't answer the question.

I wondered if I should dash into the tent, grab the baby, and show him to his obdurate father. It worked in old melodramas.

"I was goin' to cut out." Kevin jerked his head in the direction of the tent and his voice took on a self-pitying whine. "Mel and the kids is better off without me."

I liked that idea.

The soup was ready. I scooped out a mugful and wiped the cup with a scrap of sweatshirt. When I had retrieved a spoon and a handful of crackers from the supplies, I took the soup to Bonnie. She woke Melanie and fed her about half of the salty mixture. I held the baby. He looked around a little, waved a fist, and crossed his eyes. Then he fell asleep again. So did his mother. I tucked the baby in beside her. Bonnie finished the soup herself.

"Thanks." She handed me the mug. "What are they doing?"

"Talking in circles, mostly. Do you want me to bring more soup?"

She removed her glasses and cleaned the lenses on her T-shirt. "I ought to get more nourishment into Melanie. She's weak. What else is there?"

I described the stockpile.

"Bring salmon jerky and soup. And make some biscuits."

"There's no oven!"

"In the frying pan, Lark."

I was dubious but I thought I might as well try. "Back in a quarter of an hour."

"Okay."

I lifted the tent flap and emerged, mug first, into the clearing.

Kevin was peeing in the bushes. When he heard me he whirled, spraying, and the rifle discharged.

I smacked the ground, head down, scrabbling in the mat of needles. The air quivered from the report. I could hear Kevin swear over the ringing in my ears. I took a deep breath to yell.

Bonnie erupted from the tent. She ran right over me, hurling herself at Kevin. He was struggling with his un-zipped jeans with his left hand and the bolt of the rifle with his right, and she staggered him. I levered myself up, but my reactions were slower than Tom's.

He launched himself from a low crouch and butted Kevin in the belly with his head. The rifle flew and Kevin dropped to his knees. As I scrambled up I saw Tom grab Kevin's right arm and twist. Bonnie, screeching, had her claws into Kev-in's face. Both men roared. I went for the rifle.

I disentangled it from the blackberry vines it had landed in and carried it, arms stiff, out of range of the wrestling match.

Kevin lay prone with his right arm twisted behind his back. He was gasping for air, and he had two outraged people on top of him, pummeling his head, but he was still heaving his shoulders and trying to flip them off. Since he outweighed Tom by a good twenty pounds and Bonnie by fifty, his defeat was not inevitable.

The bolt of the rifle had not shot home. I laid the gun behind the cedar stump. Then I looked around me for a weapon. Even if I had known how to fire the rifle, even if I had been willing to, I would not have had a clear shot at Kevin. I grabbed the bucket that still contained water. As I reached the melee, Kevin heaved to one knee, slewing Tom sideways and relieving the pressure on the twisted arm. Bonnie was pulling Kevin's head back by the hair with both hands and he was yelling, mouth wide. I sloshed the water straight at his open mouth.

He must have inhaled half a bucketful. He collapsed, choking, and Tom shoved him flat. Tom and Bonnie sat on him.

"Give me your belt, Lark."

"What?"

Tom had both of Kevin's arms pinned behind him. "Your belt," he panted as Kevin gave a choking heave.

I undid the ornamental buckle and handed Tom my belt. When he had lashed Kevin's arms together at the wrist, he rolled Kevin over and yanked the man's jeans, still unzipped, down around his knees. Then he tied Kevin's boot laces together. Kevin's face squinched red, like a baby getting set to cry. His plaid shirt was soaked. He coughed.

"Okay, that'll do." Tom staggered to his feet and pulled Bonnie up. She had lost her glasses and one cheekbone showed red, as if she had been struck a glancing blow. She was panting, too. Tom held her by both shoulders, staring into her face. "Are you all right?"

"N-no."

Tom kissed her on the mouth.

Kevin choked and coughed. In the tent the baby wailed. I was holding onto my jeans.

I said, "What do we do now?"

Tom drew a long, shuddering breath and released Bonnie's shoulders. "We wait for your husband. I left him a note. Where's the rifle?"

I showed him and he picked it up and slid the bolt home. At the sight of the rifle, Kevin lay very still. Bonnie was hunting for her glasses.

I said, "Where was Jay, still at the college?"

Tom kept his eyes and the gun on Kevin. "I don't know, Lark. I left a message for him with the secretary. And a note on the kitchen table."

"Clara must have called you from the dock."

"Yes, she said you and Bonnie had vanished. She thought you must have wandered into the woods and got lost, so she rowed for help. I put two and two together. Kevin was still on the loose. I knew he was more likely to run to ground in a wilderness area like Coho Island than in Astoria or Portland. He hates cities.''

"Did you call Dale Nelson?''

He hesitated, eyes and rifle fixed on Kevin. "I was afraid to. Kevin was likely to shoot everything in sight if he felt cornered. He knows me. I thought maybe I could talk some sense into him. He's a jerk and a blowhard, but he's not a killer. It didn't occur to me that he'd bring Mel to the island. I thought he'd just taken the two of you as hostages.''

Bonnie said, "We were hostages, all right, and I hate to contradict you, Tom, but he is a killer. That slime mold came close to killing his wife and child. He put that woman through torture.'' She gave Kevin a kick in the ribs with the toe of her sneaker. "Can you hear me, Kevin?''

He snarled, coughing. When he quieted, Bonnie said, "I want you to know something, Kevin. I am going to do everything I can to see that you never ever come near your son. I don't know how I'm going to do that yet, but I'm going to.''

After a still moment, in which the only sound was the baby's thin wail, Tom said, "Better check on your patients, Bonnie.''

She blinked at him and nodded. She had found her glasses but the frames were bent and they hung crooked. She held them in place with her forefinger and ducked into the tent. We could hear her voice calming Melanie. The baby's wails subsided.

I am not very good at waiting. Also I was suffering the aftermath of terror. I needed to pee. I took the water buckets and headed for the spring. On the way I went potty in the woods like a bear.

When I got back Tom was talking to Kevin and Kevin was sniveling. "You're looking at five, maybe ten years in the slammer, Kev.''

Kevin moaned.

I poured a skillet full of water on general principles and set it heating. I couldn't remember what Bonnie had asked me to do. I shivered, too, more from reaction than from cold.

"Arson," Tom was saying. "Attempted murder, reckless endangerment. You're headed straight for Walla Walla, Kev."

The state penitentiary was in Walla Walla. Kevin's voice rose an octave. "I'll get AIDS!"

"Probably. What you need to do is strike a bargain with the prosecutor."

Kevin groaned a little hiccuping groan. I shouldn't have felt sorry for him, but I did.

"Plea bargain," Tom murmured. "That's the idea. You're lucky Dale Nelson is in charge of the investigation. You went to high school with him, didn't you?"

"Yeah. Him and me played basketball. Big deal." Kevin sniffed. He was probably cold. My water had soaked his shirt.

"You had a partner," Tom was saying in the same musing tones, as if he were working out a plot line. "If it was Wally Baldock, he'll spill everything the minute they pick him up."

"How'd you know? Fuck!"

"Good old Wally," Tom mused. "I should have thought of him when Lark described the baseball cap. Dale probably did. Wally will sing like a canary. And he'll lay everything on you, won't he, Kev?"

Kevin's mouth trembled. "Wally won't squeal. Him and me is partners. He was the one found the job. He roped me in on account of the pickup."

"That so? I don't see old Wally as the brains of the outfit somehow. He's dumber than a quahog."

"We was just following orders," Kevin said sullenly, as if the inability to think independent thoughts were a virtue.

"Whose orders?" I interposed.

Tom shot me a sidelong look that was hard to interpret.

I stared back. "I want to know."

He shrugged and turned to his prisoner. "Who's your boss, Kevin?"

Kevin's lips tightened. He didn't reply.

Tom sighed. "Did you kill Cleo?"

"That real estate broad? Naw, but she was no loss."

"She was my wife." Tom described a small circle with the barrel of the rifle. "You can tell me one thing. Did Cleo pay you to burn me out?"

I gaped. I hadn't thought of that possibility.

"Her? No, it was . . ." He stopped.

"Who, Kevin? Who?" Tom sounded like a spotted owl. When Kevin didn't respond, he said, "Why are you protecting a murderer? That's aiding and abetting. Another couple of years in stir."

"You ain't the law."

"I'm not. Dale is. He probably doesn't like you any better than I do, but he's a sentimental guy and he remembers those high school basketball games. You ought to hire yourself a lawyer with all that blood money you've been bragging about and cut a deal."

"Isn't the money evidence?" I thought Darla was going to find the legal situation interesting.

Tom wiggled the barrel of the rifle. "Good question. Man, you really need a lawyer. You should go see old Haakenson—he's always making deals for his clients."

Kevin groaned.

"That's good advice," said a pleasant baritone voice from the path to the beach.

I let out a whoop. "Jay!"

He hove into sight, .38 in his right hand, radio in his left. He was wearing his college professor disguise and a pair of mungy rain boots. He said something into the radio, listened as it crackled back, and shoved it in his coat pocket. Then he gave me a smile. "Are you all right?"

"I'm fine, darling, but I'm glad to see you." I trotted over and gave him a hug, gun and all. "How did you find us so fast?"

He squeezed my shoulders with his unarmed hand. "Tom left a map. I also called Clara. In fact, I made her come with us."

"Us?"

"I called out the troops." He glanced at Tom. "I see you have everything under control. I owe you, buddy."

Tom opened his mouth.

I said, "You owe Bonnie."

"I don't see Bonnie—is she okay?"

"She's in the tent with Melanie Johnson." I disengaged and took a step in that direction, pointing. "Bonnie just delivered Melanie's baby without benefit of anesthetic under highly unsanitary conditions. You'd better call for the Life Flight helicopter."

"She what…holy shit." Jay holstered the gun and pulled out the radio again. After that things started moving fast.

The helicopter hovered over our cockle bed while the Fire Department paramedics moved Melanie and son out to it on a stretcher. As the chopper lifted off, Bonnie burst into tears. She buried her head in Clara's purple bosom and wailed. I felt like crying myself, more in relief than sorrow.

The Law, in temporary alliance with the Shoalwater Fire Department rescue team, had roared up in a speedboat. The volunteer firemen had wanted to try out their new powered surfboard, too, dandy for rescuing floundering swimmers, but the fat deputy said not. I wondered where Dale Nelson was.

Rather to my surprise, Jay had spent some time after he summoned the paramedics making Kevin more comfortable. Under Tom's surveillance—and ready rifle—Jay helped Kevin into a dry shirt and cuffed him with his hands in front of his body. The jeans were hoisted, the boot laces unknotted. I retrieved my belt. When they arrived, Jay also saw to it that the paramedics checked Kevin's more obvious bruises.

I suppose all that solicitude was just good procedure, but it had interesting consequences. When Jay handed the prisoner over, Kevin begged Jay to come along and promised to talk to him. Naturally, Jay went.

Bonnie and Tom provided the Fire Department paramedics with a chance to show their stuff. The two of them had collected half a dozen bruises and cuts apiece in the course of subduing Kevin. The bruises were duly treated and one of the medics even mended Bonnie's glasses. My own more modest role in the melee had left me injury free. While the medics worked on my friends, and the evidence team, the fat deputy in the lead, headed inland to look over Kevin's camp, I rescued our clam buckets.

Clara joined me. "I see you got your limit."

I handed her Bonnie's shovel and bucket. "Yes, and it was glorious fun until Kevin showed up with his stupid rifle. Thanks for calling Tom."

She looked away. Red blotched her cheeks and forehead. "I came far enough to see your waders and buckets, and I waited fifteen minutes or so, thinking you'd gone into the woods after berries or something. Then I started worrying about my boat. The tide was coming in. I'd set my painting gear in the boat and I didn't want to lose it."

"Of course not."

She looked down and sloshed the water around, stirring up the clams. "The truth is I got impatient and left."

"Clara!"

She met my eyes. "Halfway across the bay I started thinking. That's a long way to row."

"You're telling me."

She gave a shamefaced grin. "When I called Tom I still wasn't convinced that anything was wrong. I knew he had a boat for the oysters, so I told him where to look for you. Then I went home. Jay rousted me out and made me come along."

"It turned out all right. Where did Tom leave his boat?"

"I moored it at the oyster beds and hiked on around the island." Tom had joined us in midquestion. A modest Band-Aid decorated his brow where his head had connected with Kevin's belt buckle. "I didn't want to spook Kevin in case he was watching the beach. I think he bought my story about checking out the oyster beds. Damned good thing, too. He was suspicious as hell. I was watching his hands and he came within an ace of squeezing that trigger."

Clara said, "You're really okay?"

Tom smiled. "I feel great. By God, Clara, I hung onto my temper all the way. Even when I was fighting Kevin."

She set the bucket down and gave him a big hug. "Then I'm glad I called you and not the police. I've been suffering all kinds of guilt...."

"Clara thought we were picking huckleberries," I explained. "Is Bonnie going to be all right, Tom?"

We turned. As we watched, one of the medics set Bonnie's glasses on her nose. Then he shook her hand. Bonnie looked around, spotted us, and headed our way. The medics had given her face and hands a scrub, so she looked almost normal as she came up to us. She was going to have a bruise on that cheek, though.

She inspected her bucket like a hen checking her eggs. "Oh, good, you saved the clams."

"You saved our bacon," Tom said. "And Melanie's. You're some kind of woman, Bonnie."

Bonnie blushed. "The thing was, the shot came as soon as Lark stuck her head out of the tent." She turned to me. "And you fell down. I thought Kevin had shot you. I'd made up my mind not to sit there passively if he was going to kill us, so I charged him."

"He didn't have a chance," Tom said to Clara. "A tornado tore into him." He also turned to me. "I was relieved that you didn't try to shoot him, Lark. You could have hit Bonnie or me."

"Or the baby, or the Coleman stove."

Tom stayed serious. "The bucket of water was pure inspiration."

I explained that I didn't like guns, and that I, too, had been afraid of hitting the wrong target. We were all feeling very good about each other, Clara, too, I think, now that she had decided she'd done the right thing. Tom and I filled her in on the rest of the action, including our burial of the afterbirth. Finally I turned to Bonnie and said what I had wanted to say for hours. "If you hadn't had that Lamaze course we would have been dead meat."

Bonnie blushed and hung her head.

"I didn't have the faintest idea of what to do," I persisted. "You were wonderful."

Bonnie dug the toe of her sneaker into the sand. "Gosh, Lark, couldn't you tell. I was faking it."

EIGHTEEN

"YOU WHAT!" I gaped at her.

Tom and Clara drew closer.

Bonnie shoved her glasses up. "I've never taken a La-maze class."

"Then what was all that puff puff puff business?"

"I saw a couple of films on TV, and the married women in the office used to talk about their childbirth experiences all the time. I tuned them out, but some of it stuck."

"Are you telling me you don't know any more than I do about birthing babies?"

She flushed. "I do now."

Clara covered her mouth with her hand. Tom gave a snort that might have been laughter.

I was not amused.

Neither was Bonnie. She frowned as if she had a bad headache. "I just thought, women have been having babies since the dawn of time and Melanie had already had two. She was scared because of the circumstances, but she probably knew what to do. With luck, all she would need was a little confidence."

"But..."

"But what if something had gone wrong?" Her chin went up. "Melanie wouldn't have been worse off, with me there to hold her hand, than if she'd been alone with that...that dominant baboon."

I remembered my own dithering, my own fright. "At least you were capable of thinking."

Bonnie's frown eased. "There *you* were, Lark, Miss Honesty, explaining to a man with a gun that you couldn't do what he was ordering you to do. If somebody points a gun at me and tells me I'm President of Mexico, I start talking Spanish fast. I thought if we were useless to Kevin he wouldn't have any reason to let us live. So I lied."

The cheerful shouts of the paramedics packing their gear punctuated our silence.

I said, "You had me convinced you were midwife of the year."

Tom smiled. "Me, too."

Clara said, "You deserve a medal."

Bonnie shook her head. "Melanie deserves a medal. And I meant what I said to Kevin. He is not going to get hold of that little boy and turn him into a monster. I won't let it happen."

Tom's eyebrows rose. "Won't Melanie have something to say about that?"

Clara lit a cigarette. "Some women are damned fools."

I said, "I think she'll listen to Bonnie."

"You folks ready to leave?" The senior Fire Department medic strode up.

Tom picked up the waders. "I'll help you haul this gear to the raft, Myron." They were using a rubber dinghy to ferry things to the launch. "The ladies can ride with you. I'm going to retrieve my boat from the oyster bed."

"We can buzz you around the point," the man offered.

Tom shook his head. "I want to walk."

"Okey-dokey. Tide's almost in, though. What's that?"

"Clams," Bonnie said. "We're taking them with us."

"Put them in clean water overnight with a little corn-meal." Clara was ready to tell us how to clean them, too, but that was more than I wanted to know about clams.

I drove Bonnie and the clams home from the dock. Clara had driven her own car.

Bonnie said she wanted a shower and a nap. That was about all she said. I had turned inward, too. I pulled into our driveway and popped the trunk.

"Call me if Jay finds out anything interesting." Bonnie took her bucket of clams and trudged across the street.

Anything about the murder, she meant. I gave an assenting wave and hauled my own bucket out of the trunk. I left it in the garage.

I stood in the steaming water of the shower until I turned bright pink, and I barely had the energy to towel dry. I yanked on a long T-shirt over my damp hair and fell into bed. I slept without dreaming for almost two hours.

"Lark..."

I came awake with my heart hammering.

"Sweetheart, you have got to come down and take charge of the kitchen."

"You're back." I opened one eye. "I refuse to cook."

Jay sat on the bed and gave me a bear hug. "Believe me, that's not the problem."

The problem was that the local radio station had broken the story. Our neighbors, most of whom Jay had never met, were bringing food. That was their response, once their sympathies had been engaged, to death, sickness, unemployment, flood, hurricane, earthquake, and apparently, to amateur midwifery while being held hostage on an uninhabited island. They couldn't reach Melanie, so they were showering Bonnie and me with home cooking.

I got up, groaning because my shoulders had begun to stiffen, and dressed.

Bonnie had taken refuge in the breakfast nook. Her tiny house was under siege. She swore she had two tuna casseroles, a salmon loaf, a Jell-O salad with grated carrots and raisins, and a peach pie sitting in her refrigerator. She had showered and slept a mere half hour before the doorbell started ringing.

I said soothing words and tried to sort out the pie tins and casserole dishes on my counter. One nine-by-five dish contained something brown topped with very orange cheese, possibly Velveeta. I wished Freddy was home to test it.

Bonnie was worrying over the problem of Melanie and the baby. Something had to be done. I agreed. The back door banged and Tom came in, still in his boots and rain jacket. He'd lost the Band-Aid and the cut had scabbed. He was carrying a pie. He thrust it at me.

"Ruth Adams gave me this as I was walking up from the house. She says it's for Bonnie. Oh, hi, Bonnie. I didn't see you."

"Hi."

"Huckleberry?" I asked.

He grinned. "Looks like it."

Jay said, "I'm sorry, Bonnie, you can't have that pie."

She smiled absently. "Why do they do it? All that energy. They should be feeding starving children in Africa. Do you have any idea how long it will take me to eat a whole tuna casserole?"

Jay laughed. "Feed it to Gibson."

"I will." Bonnie's eyes narrowed behind the mended glasses. The bruise stood out in bold relief on her cheek. "All that energy...hey, you guys, why don't I take up a collection?"

"For Melanie?" Tom had returned from his bedroom sans jacket. He sat on the stool by the door and yanked off his boots, tossing them into the back hall. He was wearing gray wool socks. He padded to the counter and poured himself a cup of coffee. "I expect the Fire Department has already set up a fund. Let's hope it doesn't all go for Kevin's defense."

Bonnie was fumbling for the telephone pad. "I want to collect enough to send her to Arizona."

Jay handed her a pencil. "Why Arizona?"

"My parents live there. Melanie should take the children as far away from Kevin as she can. Mom could help her find an apartment, maybe even a job." She began scribbling. "New clothes for job hunting, clothes for the kids, a decent car, and a deposit for the apartment...."

"Day care," I chimed in.

"A divorce," Tom said dryly.

Bonnie looked at him. "That's number one. All of that will take money. I'm going to hit up all these nice people...."

"Be sure to return the pie tins when you do." Tom sipped his coffee.

"The pie tins are my passport. I'll take them back and make my pitch face to face." Bonnie beamed. "I feel much better. Now all I have to do is persuade Melanie that her future lies in sunny Arizona."

The doorbell rang.

Jay answered it this time and returned after a few minutes with Clara and a covered stoneware casserole. Clara was carrying a loaf of her bread.

"Dinner!" she announced. "I came to rescue you from the tuna brigade. Tom, poke it in the microwave. That is my special emergency dinner. Cassoulet of lamb, every morsel a gourmet triumph. I am going to feed you, and Jay is going to tell us all about Kevin's confession."

We looked at Jay.

He tugged at his mustache. "I suppose the sheriff made an announcement."

"'An arrest is imminent...'" Clara quoted.

Jay said, "Nelson had already arrested a guy named Wally Baldock before Johnson started talking."

Tom sipped his coffee. "There goes the plea bargain."

"Johnson will do time," Jay agreed.

I scrunched forward on the couch. "Both men confessed? Tell us what they said."

"Yeah, well, let me call Dale first."

Clara gave him a push in the direction of the telephone. "So call. Lark, Bonnie, we need plates and flatware. Tom, a salad. Dinner in fifteen minutes."

It took Jay that long to get through to the sheriff's office. The doorbell rang once—something with marshmallows. We organized a buffet while Jay talked, and Clara made Tom start a fire in the living room. She also unearthed a bottle of chardonnay that had survived Labor Day.

We brought our steaming bowls of the stew in by the fire.

"Right." Clara took a gulp of wine. Jay sidled in with his bowl looking wary. "Tell us who hired Kevin Johnson."

"Bob McKay." Bonnie tore off a hunk of bread and dipped it in the cassoulet, which was worthy of the bread.

Jay propped his shoulders against the mantel and tested the stew. The doorbell rang.

"No," I heard him say as I jumped up. "It was Annie."

I raced to the door and yanked it open.

Bob McKay and his son stood on the porch.

I blinked at them. "What...?"

Bob cleared his throat. "May I speak to your husband? It's fairly urgent."

I hesitated. "We have company."

"Please."

I flashed on Donald Hagen. "You're not armed, are you?" The evidence of Hagen's foray still decorated the hall ceiling.

Bob turned redder and Rob said, "Gosh, no. We just need to talk to Mr. Dodge. It's about Mom."

I stood back and they entered.

I realized I could well be ushering a murderer into my living room. Was Bob going to confess to Jay? I wasn't afraid of Bob, not with his son beside him, but the situation was, oddly enough, embarrassing.

As we reached the archway into the living room, everyone looked at us. Jay set his bowl on the mantel and took a step backward.

Bob said, "You've got to help me. She's going to say I killed Cleo and I didn't. I swear it."

Clara pulled her feet out of the way hastily as Jay skirted the coffee table. Her eyes were bright with curiosity. I felt a little curious myself.

Jay said, "You shouldn't be talking in front of witnesses, Colonel McKay. You need a lawyer."

"Goddamn." Bob's voice broke. "I don't want a lawyer. And I *want* witnesses." He seemed to take in the others' presence. "Clara. Tom. Ms. Er."

"Bell," Bonnie supplied. She goggled at him through the mended glasses.

"You've got to tell us what to do." Rob McKay's voice rose. "Please, tell me what to do."

Tell me who to believe? I think that was what he meant, yet there he stood beside his father.

"I did not kill Cleo," Bob repeated. "I loved Cleo." He began to weep. "God, I'm so confused."

When a woman cries she can forgive herself. When a man weeps, by golly, people go into emergency mode. We had Bob sitting on the couch with a cup of hot coffee and a box of Kleenex from the kitchen before you could say Arnold Schwarzenegger.

Clara, Tom and Bonnie stayed behind in the kitchen, to give Bob privacy, I suppose. I had no such delicate scruples. I took him the coffee and the Kleenex and planted myself on Granny's rocker.

Rob was sitting beside his father, patting Bob's shoulder and saying there there.

I avoided Jay's eyes. I thought he'd want me to leave and I had no intention of leaving.

Bob blew his nose. "I'm sorry. It's been a hellish two weeks. You have to tell me what to do, Dodge. Dale Nelson arrested Annie for hiring those thugs to burn Tom's house. I called our lawyers right away, of course, but Nelson took her in anyway and booked her. Then I got to thinking."

"About your alibi?" Jay asked. He sat on the edge of the coffee table. Fortunately, it was solid teak and bore up under his weight. He was looking Bob right in the face.

I leaned forward and the chair creaked.

Bob mopped his eyes. "I left them on the beach, you know."

"Cleo and Annie?" Jay sounded cautious.

Bob nodded. "I remember that much. I walked back to the construction site and drove the Mercedes home. Then I started to drink. I don't remember anything more until the next morning. Annie'd already left for the *Gazette* office by the time I got up. When I heard about Cleo's death on the radio that afternoon, I called Annie. She wouldn't talk over the telephone. I was having a hard time taking it in. Cleo's death, I mean."

Jay said, with care, "You were in love with Cleo Hagen?"

"I was going to propose to her. That was why we went down to the beach. We were walking along and I was explaining that I'd ask Annie for a divorce."

Rob McKay drew a sharp breath.

Bob looked at him. "Try to understand. Your mother and I, we have...had an agreement. We wouldn't interfere with each other."

"She wouldn't interfere with you, you mean." Rob's voice was cold and his face stony. *He* wasn't going to break down. And he hadn't decided whose side he was on yet, either.

Bob's eyes dropped. He twisted the damp Kleenex. "Annie isn't very interested in sex. I don't think she enjoys it much, never did after Rob was born. So I took my satisfaction elsewhere. She didn't want a divorce and neither did I—then. Too complicated."

I stared at the man. Between the McKays and the Hagens, I was getting an education about the institution of marriage.

Bob drew a breath. "But Cleo was different. She was so beautiful, so much fun. I felt alive when I was with her. Her marriage was just an arrangement. I knew that. She needed a real marriage to a real man."

Real man. As far as I was concerned, Donald Hagen was a little too real.

Jay said, "When did you tell her all that, the night of the murder?"

Bob nodded. "The night she died." He blew his nose again. "She was laughing, teasing me, and we walked along the beach, almost to the *Mollie McKay*. We were holding hands. I felt about sixteen and I wanted her so bad I hurt. I remember that. I had a real hard-on." He glanced at me and, I swear it, blushed. "That was when Annie drove up in the Blazer."

Jay frowned as if he were trying to visualize the scene. "Didn't you see her lights?"

Bob shook his head. "No lights. She drove, with the lights off, right up beside us. She jumped out. You have to understand, Annie and I had an agreement."

"Not to interfere with each other's affairs. I see. So you were surprised."

"It knocked me for a loop," Bob said simply. "I didn't know what to say."

"What happened then?"

He took a distracted sip of the coffee and set the cup back on the end table. His hands trembled. "They started talking. Cleo thought it was funny. Annie said terrible things, how she'd never give me a divorce, and so on, but she never raised her voice. Not once. Cleo got bored, I guess. Maybe she was cold. It was a cool evening. She said something like what's the big deal, it's just an affair. That got to me. I said I was serious. I wanted a divorce, wanted to marry her. Cleo, I mean. Then she looked at me and laughed. She said she was already married and intended to stay married."

I said, "What did you do?"

He flushed. "I got mad. I wanted to hit Cleo, hit Annie. I wanted to kill them both."

I moved and the chair creaked again.

He looked at me, pleading. "Just for a moment. I didn't, though. You've got to believe me. I wasn't brought up that way, to raise my hand to a woman. So I walked off. I was pretty steamed. That's why I drank so much when I got home."

Jay stood up and went to the fireplace. He poked the log and it flared into brightness. "I think you ought to be telling this to your lawyer, McKay." He restored the poker to its place.

I said slowly, "The problem is that his lawyer is Annie's lawyer."

Bob heaved a huge sigh. "That's it. You got it. I'm going to need a lawyer, but right now I want to talk this out with somebody neutral."

Rob said, "Maybe Mr. Dodge is right, Dad. I know this guy in the public defender's office. He could suggest a criminal lawyer."

"I called Quentin," Bob snapped. "He'll find somebody. Right now I need to talk. I trust you, Dodge."

Jay rubbed one shoulder on the mantel. "I'm not taking sides, Mr. McKay, and anything you tell me goes straight to Dale Nelson."

"Good, that's what I want." Bob slammed his left hand on the arm of the couch. The coffee cup rattled. "I'll stand by Annie. She's my wife. She'll have the best lawyer money can buy, but I'm not going to let her shove the blame onto me."

"For Cleo Hagen's death?" Jay ruffled his mustache with one finger.

"For Cleo's death. I loved Cleo," Bob repeated, face red and earnest.

"Are you saying your alibi won't hold water?"

"My alibi is Annie's alibi."

Jay nodded.

We were both nodding like Buddhas, looking wise. In fact, it hadn't occurred to me to turn the alibi around. I didn't particularly like Annie, but she had substance and respectability. Bob didn't. I had assumed she was covering for him.

Bob leaned forward, hands on his knees. "See, it was like this. Annie said I'd better have an alibi, in case somebody talked about the...the date I had with Cleo. Annie said it was just like Cleo to get herself killed on a night everybody knew I was going to be with her."

"'Everybody' didn't know," Jay said dryly.

"It came out." Bob ducked his head. "Just the way Annie said it would. She told me she'd say we spent the evening together at home, so we were ready when Nelson questioned us. We stuck to the story, even when he found one of Cleo's hairs in the Blazer. That started me wondering, though. I usually drive the Blazer, but Cleo didn't like it, hadn't ridden in it for months."

"Still, she had ridden in it."

"Yeah, but our handyman vacuums the cars every week."

"Even so..." Jay kept his eyes on Bob and his tone skeptical.

"I started worrying," Bob said doggedly. "When I left Cleo and Annie together, Annie was mad, but I didn't want to believe she'd killed Cleo. I thought Tom had killed Cleo. I was sure of it." He sounded aggrieved, as if Tom should have cooperated and confessed to the murder. "Annie said the police thought so, too. She has her sources at the courthouse. The alibi would keep us out of the investigation. She said she didn't want a scandal. Neither did I, and my brother Quentin sure as hell didn't."

"So you wanted to believe Tom killed Cleo, but you'd begun to have doubts."

"Yeah. And I kept racking my brain, trying to remember what time Annie came home that night. I asked Robbie."

Rob cleared his throat. "Both cars were in the garage by the time I got in."

"Davis—that's the handyman—he may know when she came in," Bob said, "but Annie sent him away."

Jay walked over and sat on the occasional chair. "You interest me. Where?"

"He's in Hawaii for another week. I told the police."

"Then Nelson will call Honolulu. He's thorough."

"Davis is on Molokai. Camping."

"Even so."

I shivered. I *hoped* the handyman was in Hawaii.

Jay said, "When did you and Annie decide to alibi each other?"

"Right away. I heard the news story, that Cleo was dead. I called Annie. She wouldn't talk then, but she drove straight home. She said not to tell anybody, not even our lawyers, that I'd seen Cleo that night. She said she'd back me up. She did, too. I kept reminding myself she was being generous."

Jay sighed. "Tell me something, McKay. What would you have done if they'd arrested your cousin?"

Bob blinked. "Tom?"

"He is your cousin, isn't he?"

He shifted. "Distant cousin."

"Well?"

He held out a hand, as if in supplication. "I thought he was guilty. I thought he'd done it."

"What made you change your mind?"

Bob leaned back. He looked baffled. "It was more like creeping doubts. I kept drinking. I drank a lot but I drank at home, and I couldn't stop thinking about the hair they found in the Blazer. That and the fact that Annie didn't raise her voice when she called Cleo all those names. Annie always goes real quiet when she's angry."

Jay said mildly, "That's no kind of proof, Bob."

"I know it." He drew a long breath. "I think Annie killed Cleo on the beach. How I don't know, but Annie could have done it. Maybe she used the jack handle, something like that."

Jay had said earlier that Cleo was killed with a piece of driftwood. I opened my mouth to speak and closed it.

Bob went on. "She and Cleo were pretty much the same size, and Annie's strong. She plays killer tennis. She could have murdered Cleo and driven the body up onto the dunes near Tom's house. The tide would have washed some of the tread marks away, and Annie could have brushed away the rest. The Blazer's a four-wheeler, you know...."

"I used to own one," Jay interrupted. "Then what?"

"Then she could have driven home and cleaned the Blazer. And phoned that jerk, Johnson. I'd passed out before midnight and I don't remember much after I got home."

"Well, all of this is interesting speculation," Jay murmured, his eyes still on Bob's face. "Let's say Annie could have killed Cleo Hagen. That doesn't mean she did."

"I keep telling him that," Rob said eagerly.

Bob was shaking his head. "She's going to confess to the arson charge and offer to testify against me if they'll do a deal. I can see it coming."

A silence followed. I was trying to imagine Annie killing Cleo. It had been easier to visualize Bob smashing heads, but his earnestness was impressive in the flesh. And the fact that young Rob was sitting there beside him, even if Rob didn't believe his mother was a murderer, said something about the father's character. And maybe about Annie's.

I looked at the kid. He was pale and taut faced. "What do you think, Rob?"

"She didn't do it," he said. "I mean I don't think she did it, but Dad deserves a fair hearing. I think everybody should be fair." He sounded plaintive, almost childish.

Jay stood up. "There is a witness."

This was news to me. I stared at him.

"Unfortunately he's in a confused mental state right now."

Matt! My lips formed the name.

Jay shot me a warning glance.

I bit the word back.

He went on. "I don't think he saw the killing itself, though he may have. I think he did witness the disposal of the body."

Bob leaned back and let out a long breath. "God, that's a relief. Who did you say it was?"

"I didn't say." Jay shot me another glance. "And I'm not going to. I need to call Dale Nelson."

Bob rose. "Will you tell him I'll be at home? I'll wait up until he contacts me."

Rob and I stood up, too. Bob held his hand out and Jay shook it. The McKays left almost at once.

The door had barely closed on them when Clara burst from the kitchen, followed by Bonnie and Tom.

"What happened?" Clara demanded. "Did he confess?"

Jay held up a restraining hand. "Not to the murder. I have to call Dale Nelson. I'm going upstairs, Lark. I suppose you may as well fill them in."

They carried me off to the kitchen and plied me with microwaved stew while I recounted Bob's story. Clara and Tom were incited to believe Bob, but Bonnie held out. It was, she suggested darkly, an obvious attempt to cover his ass.

He was trying to do that, all right. I wasn't sure what to believe.

Clara was being reasonable, though her eyes glinted with excitement. "I say Annie did it."

Tom had kept silent as I talked. He rubbed his forehead. "If Bob killed Cleo, it was a simple crime of passion. What's Annie's motive?"

"Bumping off the competition?" Bonnie swung her coffee mug. "Naw, it was Bob."

Clara said, "I told you folks on Labor Day that Annie needs the prestige she gets as editor of the *Gazette*." She looked at Bonnie and me. "And you saw the house in the Enclave. If Bob was serious about Cleo, if he wanted a divorce, Annie would lose the paper *and* the house."

Bonnie gave a skeptical snort. "What are divorce lawyers for?"

"Bob would give Annie a settlement. Of course he would. But the house doesn't belong to Bob and neither does the paper. They're McKay family property. Annie would lose both. I think she did it."

I cocked my head, listening. Jay was coming down the stairs.

When he entered, he gave a general smile and rubbed his hands. "How about a nice piece of pie?"

I said, "You're insane," but I got up and cut into Ruth Adams's pie. That took awhile, with the others tossing off questions and Jay eluding them in his bland, infuriating way.

I served everyone else, then held the last piece of pie out of his reach. "Talk or it goes into the garbage grinder."

Jay grinned. "Okay, okay. Give me the pie."

I handed him the plate. "Did they arrest Annie?"

"For hiring Johnson and Baldock to commit arson? Yes. Naturally, she clammed up and called in the lawyers. Dale tells me she's trying a plea bargain. If they drop the arson charge, or grant her immunity, she'll testify against her husband in the murder of Cleo Hagen."

A silence followed. Tom cut a judicious bite of huckleberry pie. "So Bob was telling the truth?"

"I think so." Jay waved his fork. "But I'm damned glad I'm not on the investigating team. Annie is saying she was just trying to create a diversion. She admits she picked on you, Tom, because you'd been married to Cleo and because of the book. She says she tried to call attention to you, and that she wanted to protect Bob with a false alibi. Bob was unfaithful to her, but he was her man and she was going to stand by him.''

Bonnie groaned.

"Dale," Jay said, cutting a neat bite of pie, "is waffling. He wants to believe Annie. I shook him up. He agreed to go out to the Enclave and interrogate Bob.''

Another long pause. I said, "What about Matt?''

Jay said, "He's coming along. I think he's going to admit he saw Annie place the body in the dunes near Tom's house, and that he lied to protect Annie because he hated what Cleo represented. Matt isn't crazy. He's just a little muddled.''

Tom said abruptly, "So Cleo made me an honest offer for the house? I don't know why that makes me feel better, but it does.''

"Maybe you should console Donald Hagen with your reinterpretation of Cleo's character." Bonnie spooned huckleberry syrup from her plate.

I stood up and headed for the coffeepot. "Donald Hagen—what will happen to him?''

"A suspended sentence." Jay didn't look blissful at the thought. "Hagen has good lawyers.''

I started to say I was really wondering whether Hagen's father would force him into another marriage, but the others hadn't heard Nancy's gossip. If Jay could be discreet, so could I. I poured another round of coffee by way of distraction.

Eventually Clara and Bonnie left and Tom headed for his room. We heard the computer making its warm-up noises. Tom was going to be all right. I wasn't so sure about Bonnie. She wanted Bob guilty. He could certainly be obnoxious, but I thought he was innocent of murder. The corollary of that was Annie's guilt.

Jay and I stayed in the living room, comfortably entwined and staring at the dying fire.

I rubbed up against him. "What happens now?''

He smoothed my hair. "Now it's up to the lawyers.''

"Wonderful. I suppose Darla will follow the case syllable by syllable.''

"It'll be an education for her.''

I ran a hand over his chin. Only slightly raspy. "It bothers me, not to know for sure who's guilty.''

He said, "Annie McKay is guilty. But it'll be interesting to see what her lawyers plead. If she hadn't hired Johnson, she could make a case for manslaughter—or second-degree homicide. She got a little too clever." He nibbled my ear-lobe. "I hope Melanie's experience didn't put you off maternity."

"It was pretty gory and she suffered a lot, but I thought the baby was interesting. He was tiny but opinionated." I snuggled closer. "Actually, the situation just put me off guns."

Jay is not the kind of cop who keeps caressing his .38. He knew my opinion of firearms. "More than ever, huh?"

An ember flared and crumbled.

"Definitely. What if he'd had one of those assault rifles instead of an old-fashioned thirty ought six?" I shuddered.

"Cold?"

"Just thinking."

"I did some thinking, too. You may or may not need a baby, Lark, but you definitely need a bookstore."

I sat up. "What? Here?"

"Wherever. Why not here?"

I stared at him. He smiled in the sneaky way he has that always disarms logic. "Why a bookstore?"

"If you were running a bookstore, I'd know where you were and what you were doing eight to twelve hours a day while it was open. You scared me again, lady. I had a couple of very bad hours imagining horrors. Besides, you miss Larkspur Books."

"I don't create disasters...."

He pulled me closer and gave me a disarming kiss. "So you say. A bookstore in Kayport, right near the History Museum."

"Why not at the mall? There's a great location next to the bakery.... Jay, you fiend, I want to get pregnant!"

"Go ahead. You still need a bookstore."

"Hmm."

"Bonnie would enjoy helping you set it up...."

"And Tom could do a signing." I felt a rush of pure exuberance. A bookstore and a baby. Why not?

DEATH by DEGREES
Eric Wright

First Time in Paperback

An Inspector Charlie Salter Mystery

LITERALLY—AND FIGURATIVELY—DEAD

The politics and infighting to elect a new dean at Toronto's Bathurst College turns to murder when the winner is discovered dead.

Though the case appears open-and-shut—an interrupted burglary and a suspect neatly arrested—Inspector Charlie Salter believes otherwise when he begins investigating anonymous notes warning that the killer lurks in the groves of academe.

Scandal, blackmail and layers of deception line the corridors at the college...all the way to the dark truth surrounding the killer's identity.

"Excellent series...humor and insight."
—*New York Times Book Review*

Available in June at your favorite retail stores.

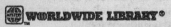 **WORLDWIDE LIBRARY®**

DEGREES

THE HANGED MAN
Walter Satterthwait

A Joshua Croft Mystery

BAD KARMA

At a dinner party for Santa Fe's leading New Age healers, Quentin Bouvier, a magician and possibly a reincarnated Egyptian pharoah, is murdered. The cops have a good case against Giacomo Bernardi, a tarot card reader believed to have killed for a valuable fifteenth-century card.

And while private investigator Joshua Croft doesn't think any of these folks are playing with a full deck, he's been hired to get Bernardi off the hook.

Croft quickly discovers some very down-to-earth motives, but the price may be his own trip to the great beyond.

"Mr. Satterthwait writes in a bright, satirical style..."
—*New York Times*

Available in August at your favorite retail stores.

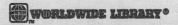 **WORLDWIDE LIBRARY®**   HANGED

This June , for the first time in paperback

NEW YORK TIMES BESTSELLING AUTHORS:

First
Time In
Paperback

SUE GRAFTON
TONY HILLERMAN

and many more...

Bring you

2ND CULPRIT

Newcomers, international names and old favorites
offer up a varied itinerary for the adventurous traveler
in crime! Join *New York Times* bestselling authors
TONY HILLERMAN and SUE GRAFTON, plus
an additional cast of 24 of the mystery genre's most
popular authors, for 2ND CULPRIT, a choice
collection of short stories.

Available in June wherever
Worldwide Mystery books are sold.

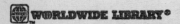